Privateer's Princess

by

Gail MacMillan

This is a work of fiction. Names, characters, places, and incidents are either the product of the author's imagination or are used fictitiously, and any resemblance to actual persons living or dead, business establishments, events, or locales, is entirely coincidental.

Privateer's Princess

Cover Art by *Debbie Taylor*

The Wild Rose Press, Inc.
PO Box 708
Adams Basin, NY 14410-0708
Visit us at www.thewildrosepress.com

Publishing History
First Tea Rose Edition, 2016
Print ISBN 978-1-5092-0653-7
Digital ISBN 978-1-5092-0654-4

Published in the United States of America

"Bloody hell, Cal! You're telling me we've kidnapped a princess?" Duncan MacDougal leaped to his feet and stood glaring down at his friend. "God in heaven, man, can you imagine the penalty? Hanging will be the best we can expect."

The captain, settled in the chair behind his desk in his cabin, looked up at the irate Scotsman looming over him. The *Jenny Jones* was far out to sea, blown before the gale that had been rising as they fled the manor house. He'd deliberately waited until they were well away to reveal the true identities of their passengers.

"If I'd told you one of them was royalty, would you have gone along with the plan?" He narrowed his eyes as he looked up at his first mate.

"Of course not! I have a fondness for my neck just as it is." Duncan ran a hand through his tangled, sandy-colored curls. "Guid God, we've kidnapped a princess!"

"Not kidnapped…shanghaied." Captain Cameron stood and went to a sideboard that held several flasks and tankards. "There will be no ransom demands. They'll work their passage as any victims of press gangs would. Once we reach New Brunswick, we'll deposit the pair of them in a convent. I've no desire to keep those creatures in my possession any longer than necessary. Then we'll head for Saint John, New Brunswick, to outfit this vessel for wartime duty."

He rolled his shoulders in an effort to relax their stiffness and felt a catch where the one he'd carried had twisted his flesh. "Whisky?" He held up the flask.

Praise for Gail MacMillan

Gail's book *HEATHER FOR A HIGHLANDER* had its heroine, Heather, chosen as Best Heroine by the Canadian Maple Leaf Romance Writers Association. The hero, Dr. William MacTavish, placed as second favorite hero.

~*~

"Be prepared to be hooked on the first word of the first page and go on to the next with anticipation. Her stories will live in your heart long after the last page is read."

~Rebecca Melvin, Publisher, Double Edge Press

~*~

"Gail MacMillan's stories delight the senses and brighten the dark days of winter like a candle glowing on a windowsill. Best enjoyed while curled up in your favorite chair…with some hot cocoa and a faithful canine companion."

~Sue Owens Wright, author, newspaper columnist, and two-time Maxwell Medal recipient

~*~

"Gail MacMillan's stories place you in a well-worn comforting chair. She writes of deep-rooted rural customs and traditions, of her love of dogs and horses. She shows glimpses of truth in revelatory detail."

~Heather White, Editor, Saltscapes Magazine

Dedication

To my dog-walking friends,
Earle, Dora, and Barb,
who know how to brighten any day.

Chapter One

"You realize this will be a hanging offense if I'm caught?" Captain Caleb Cameron narrowed keen blue eyes as he looked across the table through the smoky haze of the London waterfront tavern at the dandified man sitting opposite him.

"I'm not asking you to do murder." His Grace, William Millbank, Duke of Haverbrook, drew himself up indignantly. "Simply take her off my hands and deposit her at any convent in British North America. She was raised in such a facility. She'll be right at home in another. Dear God, I can't imagine what the Prime Minister and the Prince Regent could have been thinking when they decided I should be the one to espouse that horse-faced, ill-natured bitch. Be sure you take her blasted lady's maid, as well. She's a brazen wench. My household will do well without her."

"This woman you're asking me to abduct *is* a princess." Caleb leaned back in his chair and fingered the handle of his tankard. "You don't think all the king's horses and all the king's men, not to mention most of his ships, will be sent out to find her?"

"I have confidence in your ability to elude any pursuers. Tales of your blockade-running have become legend. At any rate, I doubt the king has any vessels or men to spare for such a pursuit, with our country at war with more countries than I can count. 1812 has been a hellish year for England, and now with the blasted Americans threatening to attack our colonies to their north…"

"Your father knew what he was about when he sent me up to Cambridge with you." The captain slanted him a derisive smirk. "I rescued you from more than one scrape. Ten years later you're still running to me when you find yourself in an untenable situation." He took a long drink.

"You were only the son of our head groom." His Grace's round face reddened. "You received an education such as no other in your position would ever receive. Now back to the situation at hand. The Prime Minister and the Prince Regent may have set up this marriage contract for diplomatic reasons, but by God there'll be nothing they can do about it once I'm legally married to Elizabeth Harrison. I plan to head to London to accomplish my desire as soon as you rid me of this encumbrance."

"Elizabeth Harrison…not *the* Lizzie Harrison, an inmate at the Vienna Music Academy?" Caleb choked on his ale. "Damn it, Willie, that place is a brothel. Granted, it provides recreation for some of England's richest and most powerful men, but it's still just a glorified whorehouse. And while Lizzie Harrison might be the most beautiful and sought after of all its exquisite ladies, she's nevertheless a doxy. You can't be serious about making her the next Duchess of Haverbrook."

"She's a lady who fell on unfortunate circumstances and was forced to make her way as best…"

"So she gave you that old line, did she?" Caleb was all-out grinning as he drew a hand across his mouth.

"Bloody hell, Willie, the woman was born in Whitechapel. She fought her way out of its squalor by being sly as a vixen and twice as predatory. Otherwise, good looks be damned, she'd have ended up just another street-corner whore."

"Shut your lying mouth!" His Grace was on his feet, glaring down at his companion. "Her mother was a celebrated Paris opera singer…"

"Of course." Seeing there was no arguing with a man as besotted as His Grace, Caleb gave off trying to warn him. *Let the silly sod find out for himself.* "There is a less costly solution than hiring me, you realize. You could show some backbone and refuse to be coerced into espousing a foul-tempered witch."

The duke shuddered. "I might stand up to Prime Minister Perceval and the Prince of Wales, but never my mother! You know the dowager duchess."

"Ah, yes, she is one formidable lady."

"Just so. Now, are we agreed? You'll do the task?"

"Very well, Willie." Captain Caleb Cameron quirked a corner of his mouth into a mocking grin as he looked up at the man. "For the sum agreed upon and no less, mind you. It is a hazardous undertaking. She is royalty, even if her country somewhere at the far end of the Mediterranean is nothing larger than one of our more illustrious English estates."

"But a strategic location in the eyes of our military experts, given the present hostilities. Nevertheless, I'm not about to forfeit my lifelong happiness to secure an alliance with some hole-in-the-wall nation."

"Carnal satisfaction must come before King and Country." Shaking his head, the captain chuckled. "Lizzie Harrison, the Duchess of Haverbrook. I recognized that she was a clever wench the first time I met her, but snaring a duke, even if he is you, Willie—quite an accomplishment for a high-class whore."

"Mind your tongue!"

"She'll give you one hell of a good time on your wedding night, Willie…if she hasn't already." He canted his companion a sly glance. "Believe me, I know. Now…" He continued as he saw the duke's hands knotting into fists. He'd taunted His Grace far enough. He wasn't about to let teasing cost him a highly lucrative venture. "To business. I assume you've brought payment."

"An ungodly sum." Muttering, the duke pulled a plump drawstring purse from inside his waistcoat and plunked it on the table in front of his companion.

"Aha! Enough to outfit the *Jenny Jones* as a privateer." Captain Caleb Cameron reached out and drew it toward him. "1812 will go down in history as the year that began a war that made men such as myself rich." He hefted the pouch. "Seems a fair measure. And you know better than to cheat me, Willie. You tried that once when we were at university together, and you'll recall how that ended." He narrowed his eyes as he looked over at the Duke of Haverbrook.

"Yes, yes, of course." The duke adjusted his silk neckcloth and picked up his hat. "Now I'm off to London. Elizabeth is waiting."

"Tread carefully, my friend. Lizzie Harrison is one clever piece of baggage." He favored his companion with a sly wink as he thrust the purse into an inside pocket of his coat.

"By God, sir, if you weren't my friend, if…" His Grace bristled.

"More to the point, if I weren't in a position to do you a service that will allow you to go to your beloved Elizabeth, you'd what? Call me out? Willie, don't talk like a fool. You know you wouldn't stand a chance. Calm down and go in peace, secure in the knowledge that the impediment to your future romantic endeavors will be removed this night." He thrust the pouch inside his coat, a self-satisfied smile curling his lips.

"Understand me, Cal. I don't want any harm to come to her." His Grace drew out a snowy handkerchief to mop his perspiring forehead. "It's not her fault her father arranged this ridiculous marriage. It's not her fault she's a horse-faced nag who can't speak a word of English, or that I'm in love with someone else." He paused, his expression becoming pensive. "Or that she does have only one redeeming feature. Her hair is a glorious tangle of golden curls…the color of a field of ripe wheat…"

"Perhaps those pretty tresses should be enough to satisfy you." Caleb couldn't resist the taunt. "She is a prime candidate for producing the next Duke of Haverbrook. Think of it. Your progeny with a princess as a mother. Now, Lizzie Harrison…I doubt she'll go spoiling her lovely figure with a pregnancy. Her profession dictates she's had to become adept at avoiding such a consequence."

"Damn you, Caleb Cameron." His Grace drew himself up angrily. "I know exactly what I'm doing. Now get on with it. And, I repeat, make blessed certain you take her lady's maid also. I can't abide that sly bit of baggage. Thinks she's too clever by half." The duke paused before continuing. "Now, take note of this. The princess's apartments are on the second floor on the right side of the manor. I've put a chalk mark on the ledge outside the window I'll leave unlatched for your entry."

Shoving his handkerchief back into his pocket, he turned and strode out of the tavern.

For all his bravado in front of His Grace, Captain Caleb Cameron was left with not only his purse of gold but an unsettled feeling in his gut that he had just thrust himself into the shadow of the noose. He heaved a deep breath.

"Cal!" Duncan MacDougal, first mate on Caleb's vessel the *Jenny Jones*, strode into the tavern and across the room to drop into a chair opposite him. "This is where you got to. The ship is loaded. We're ready to sail on the midnight tide. I'm surprised to find you here and not pacing the deck, impatient to be off."

"I've been making a business deal." Caleb signaled to the tavern girl to bring ale. "One of which you should be apprised."

"Oh, aye? And that would be?"

"Let us wait until we've ale in our hands with which to toast my clever dealings."

"I'm not sure I like the sound of this. Is it perhaps that I'll need a good quaff to swallow with whatever infamy you're planning this time?"

"Such skepticism. When have I ever led you astray?"

"Well, let me count." Duncan held up one hand. "No, no." He lowered it. "That won't do. I'd have to take off my boots and use my toes to come anywhere near the correct number."

"Ah, Molly!" Caleb ignored his mate's sarcasm and cast one of his captivating smiles up at the scowling barmaid as she plunked two tankards before them. "Thank you, my love." He reached into a pocket of his vest, drew out a coin, dusted it against his chest, and tossed it to her. "For your excellent service."

As she caught the coin and examined it, her bellicose expression vanished.

"Thank ye, Captain." Stuffing the largess down the front of her low-cut gown, she bobbed him a curtsy. "If you're needin' anything else, sir..." The smile was sly, coquettish.

"I'm flattered, lass, but not just now. I've business to transact with Mr. MacDougal."

"As you wish." Again the bobbed curtsy before she turned and swaggered back to her place behind the bar.

"Bloody hell, Cal, that was generous." Duncan stared at him. "And for nothing more than a couple of mugs of ale. Unless you're planning something for later, a quick moment with Miss Molly upstairs before we sail?" He quirked his mouth at one corner into something between a grin and a smirk.

"No, no." Caleb leaned back in his chair to stretch long legs out in front of him. "I've just brought us into some money—quite a lot of money, as a matter of fact—in payment for a venture we're about to undertake."

"Oh, aye." His mate lowered his tankard after taking a swallow. Suspicion tinged his tone. "What is it this time? Running another blockade? We near got blown out of the water that last time."

"Nothing nearly so hazardous. Willie has asked us to take a couple of ladies along on our voyage, that's all."

"Willie? Your old friend the Duke of Haverbook

wants us to take a couple of ladies to New Brunswick?" The wariness in the other man's tone deepened. "Why?"

"Let me say that at the moment they stand in the way of Willie and his desires."

"And they'll come along willingly? On a merchantman full of sailors, with no accommodations for females—or any passengers, for that matter?" Duncan narrowed his eyes as he stared over at his friend and captain.

"Not exactly."

"Good God, Cal, you're not telling me we're to kidnap them?" The mate dropped his tankard on the table with a thump, his features tightening into a mask of incredulous shock as he leaned across the table toward his captain and hissed out the words. "That's a hanging offense! What could finesse you into such a mad scheme?"

"This." Glancing around to make certain no one else was watching, Caleb drew the heavy purse from inside his coat. "Gold. More than enough to outfit the *Jenny Jones* as a privateer. More than enough to set us well on the road to becoming wealthy men."

"Sweet Jesus!" Duncan snatched the bag away from his captain and hefted it. "There must be a king's ransom in here. Who are these women, Cal? Why is it so important to His Grace that they are disposed of?"

"Disposed makes it sound like murder." He reached out, retrieved the purse, and thrust it back inside his coat. "Nothing nearly so cruel or drastic. We're simply to take them to a convent on the New Brunswick coast and leave them in the care of nuns."

"Oh, aye? And why do I have a sinking feeling in

my gut? Why is it so almighty important to His Grace that these ladies be removed to a place thousands of miles away? Never tell me they're both with child from him."

"No." Caleb returned his attention to his tankard and took a long drink.

"Don't go avoiding my questions, man! If I'm to be drawn into this venture, I'll be needing the truth."

"Very well. Willie wants his way free and clear to marry Elizabeth Harrison. These ladies might…act as impediments to that desire."

"Marry Elizabeth…Lizzie Harrison?" Duncan belted out the words.

"Keep your voice down, man." Caleb hissed. "Aye, Lizzie Harrison."

"But why does His Grace…Willie…have to get rid of these two women before he can espouse London's most notorious whore?"

"It seems no one at the manor knows of Lizzie's past except these two serving girls who came from the London streets." Caleb avoided his friend's penetrating stare as he perpetrated the lie. "They've threatened to expose her for what she is if he doesn't pay them a sum even bigger than that in the purse I've shown you."

"But surely he can't keep his lady's past a secret forever. Any number of the male visitors to the duke's manor might recognize her."

"Aye, but by then she'll be the Duchess of Haverbrook. No one will dare rake up her colorful past. Willie is, after all, a royal duke, and like the old fable in which no one dares acknowledge that the king is naked, none of the men will have the nerve to mention Her Grace has a notorious past. As for the ladies, they won't know her history, and Lizzie can act the aristocrat so well they'll never guess what she once was. I've seen her do it."

"So we're to cart off two poor little serving lasses for no better reason than the knowledge they possess?" Caleb didn't like the suspicion in his friend's eyes.

"We're hardly selling them into slavery, Dunc." He was finding it difficult to continue the lie in the face of the other man's expression of disbelief. "In fact, we're giving them a chance at a better life. They may find husbands in New Brunswick, or they might decide to take the veil. At any rate, they'll be better off than slaving in those great dungeons that pass as kitchens in Willie's manor. I've seen them. I know."

"And where are we to house this pair? We can't put them in the crew's quarters, or let them sleep on deck while we're crossing the North Atlantic."

"Your cabin will have to suffice."

"My cabin? Where do you expect me to sleep?"

"With the crew…just for this crossing." Caleb hastened to add the qualifier. "You and I both slung our hammocks under the bow for a number of years before we became officers."

"Good God, man! Don't you recall the smells, the snores, the breaking wind…?"

"You should be willing to put up with a bit of discomfort for the rewarding future it portends."

"All right, all right." Duncan lowered his head, shaking it. "I can see nothing will deter you from this madness. Furthermore, you hold double the shares I do in the *Jenny Jones*, so I can't veto your decision."

"Think, Dunc!" Caleb indicated the pocket into which he'd deposited the gold. "With this we can outfit our vessel as a first-class fighting ship. As privateers in the war between the Americans and British, we can make ourselves wealthy men."

"A war that has yet to be declared. Differences may be patched up. Then what?"

"Incoming vessels have brought news that convinces me war will be declared no later than the middle of next month. President Madison, aside from being fed up with British ships harassing American vessels, sees the British colonies to the north as easy conquests. He and his cabinet are spoiling to annex them. Those colonies, with no navy and the English fleet involved in conflicts scattered around the globe, have neither ships nor men to protect them. Privateers willing to fight for British interests will be welcomed with open arms."

"Being captain of a prosperous merchant ship isn't enough for you?" Duncan leaned across the table toward his friend. "We're doing well, Cal. We don't need to risk life and limb in a war that doesn't concern us."

"Well isn't good enough." The captain drew himself up and squared his shoulders. "I spent too many years bowing and scraping to Willie and his like. I plan to be rich—rich enough to retire to a manor house with a lady wife by my side. I'd expected you to have similar goals."

"Have you thought what might happen when we return to this country?" The mate's Highland accent broke through as it did whenever he felt forced into a situation not to his liking. "Do you not think that weasel of a duke will have turned on us and have the law waiting, just to get us and what we've done for him out of his way once and forever?"

"We won't be returning." Caleb narrowed his eyes. "We'll be fighting in the war off the coast of America. When it's over, we'll be wealthy men and we'll build manor houses over there. We'll be the aristocracy of the New World. Men in the province of New Brunswick, lumber barons, have made fortunes in the timber trade. What we'll make privateering during the war will far outstrip even them."

"Never come back? Never is a long time." Duncan stared at him.

"What have either of us to return to? I sure as hell don't want my father's job on Willie's estate, managing his stable and getting my neck broke like he did trying to settle a half-mad stallion for the hunting field. And you? Would you be wanting to return to the Highlands, with your family dead and your lands confiscated for sheep?"

"No, no, there's nothing for me there." The big Highlander lowered his head and shook it sadly. "But hell and damnation, Cal!" He pulled himself back to the moment. "You'd better have a right excellent plan to carry out this operation. I'm not ready to die, not just yet."

"I do." He stood. "Now, we've got work ahead of us. We have to sign on the best fighting crew this town has to offer. We want to be ready for battle the moment the *Jenny Jones* is outfitted with cannon and boarding pikes."

Chapter Two

"Ginny!" The name was a hiss as lady's maid Annie Pudden eased open the kitchen door and let herself into the huge, cavernous room lighted only by the embers of the fire dying on the hearth.

From where she'd been dozing in a chair in front of the massive stone fireplace, the young woman in a shabby gray garment jerked upright.

"I've not let the fire die, Mrs. Pots." She scrambled to her feet, all but falling in her haste. "It'll be going something fierce if her ladyship requires tea on her return." Tripping and staggering, she made a lunge for the woodbox.

"Ginny, it's me, Annie." In the shadowy scullery, the new arrival caught at the other young woman's arm. "There's nothing to fear."

"Bloody hell, Annie." Coming fully awake, Ginny Tart turned to face her friend, who was garbed in the neat black dress of a lady's maid. "You fair scared the daylights out of me."

"What are you doing here anyway?" Annie looked about at the dingy kitchen. "When I crept to the servants' quarters to find you, that nasty piece of work named Ruby sneered and said you'd taken over from her in the scullery. Why are you dressed in that shabby rag? Where is your parlor maid's uniform?"

"Mrs. Pots has me doing penance because of a

dropped dish at dinner." The words came out in a weary sigh. "She's warned me that one more mistake will see me permanently taking Ruby's place scrubbing pots. Two blunders will send me packing."

"And would that be so bad…getting out of here?" Annie waved her arm at their surroundings, the kitchen with its stone floor and walls, gray with smoke and cooking grease, its windows so high over their heads they let in only the barest bit of light during the day and at night were dark, brooding holes.

"You don't know what I've come from." The young woman hung her head.

"Which was?"

"From my uncle's tavern." She wet her lips and kept her eyes downcast. "My parents, what with eleven others to feed, were only too glad to give me to my uncle to work in his tavern when I was ten years old. Made me into a right drudge, he did. And when I got a little older, I had to learn to battle like a fighting cock to keep off his miserable customers."

"Ginny, I didn't know. I'm so sorry."

"Annie, I can't go back to that!" She looked up at her friend, desperation glowing from her brown eyes.

"Of course you can't." She put a consoling hand on the rough wool of Ginny's dress. "I'm sorry I startled you, but I have news."

"What? Never tell me you've been called back to serve at Closers Hall. I don't think I could bear your leaving, Annie Pudden. You're the best friend I've ever had, the only bright spot in my days."

"No, no, nothing like that…although I must say I wish there was some way we could both escape servitude in any house." Annie heaved a sigh and ran her hands down the front of her black wool dress. "No." She brightened. "We're about to attend a soiree."

"A soiree? Have you taken leave of your senses? No one in their right mind would invite a pair like us—even if you are lady's maid to a princess—to such a fine-sounding event."

"I'm inviting you. Come along. The bigwigs are all gone to Rannoch Manor for the evening, and the servants have retired to their rest. Just be quiet, quieter than that mouse lurking in the corner by the woodbox."

"Annie Pudden, if I get dismissed for shirking my duties…"

"You won't. Bank the fire, and follow me. We're about to have a well-deserved frolic."

****

"In here," Annie hissed as she opened the door of the princess's apartments.

"Oh, God in heaven, Annie, we'll not only be dismissed if we're caught. We'll be transported." Ginny tried to hesitate, but her friend caught her by a hand and pulled her inside.

Annie shut the door softly after them and slid the bolt into place. The room, lighted only by two tall tapers on the mantel and the low-burning fire on the hearth, lay bathed in more shadows than light.

"Good God, the woman is a pig," Ginny breathed, looking at the gowns, stockings, undergarments, and shoes thrown helter-skelter about the room. "You've got a right job ahead of you, sorting out this lot."

"Given short notice by the invitation, Her Highness couldn't decide what to wear. I'll get to it later. Right now we're going to indulge in some well-deserved pleasure. Look." She pointed to a table near the bed, where an ice bucket held a wine bottle. Beside it was a small bowl containing a dark blob, and a saucer filled with wafers. "Just for us."

"Annie, no! If we're caught…"

"Don't be a goose. The princess will never miss it. At dinner she ordered these treats, but they weren't delivered until after she'd gone out. Since she's always flinging out commands, she'll have forgotten these delights by the time she returns. Furthermore, at the moment we're safely locked in, and no one is due home until well after midnight. Even if they do arrive early, we'll have ample time to clear things away before they get out of the carriages and are ready to come upstairs. They may even call for tea…"

"Oh, God, tea. And I won't be on duty to see to it. We're doomed!"

"Stop it! Stop it right now." Annie stepped close in front of her friend, seized her by the upper arms, and shook her. "We're going to have a lovely evening. Nothing bad is going to happen. Stop cringing like a frightened dog. I know you'll enjoy the champagne."

"Champagne?" Ginny looked at the bottle resting in ice. "Bloody hell, that's the biggest wine bottle I've ever seen."

"It's called a magnum." She grinned at Ginny's astounded expression. "The princess orders nothing but the largest and best. The small bowl beside it contains caviar. You spread it on those wafers. It does go down nicely with bubbly wine. It would be sinful to let it go to waste."

"Oh, very well." Ginny heaved a sigh and crossed the room to join her. "What's life without a bit of adventure…I guess. I may as well go out with a bang as a whimper."

"Excellent. Hold the thought."

"I've little choice, now that you've dragged me into this madness." Ginny heaved a resigned sigh as she looked down at the table. "Very well, milady. Let us get on with it."

"Tonight is an unexpected treat." Annie headed for the ice bucket. "That last-minute invitation from Lord and Lady Barclay for the princess and the dowager duchess to dine at Rannoch Manor was a blessed reprieve." She drew the bottle out of its bucket with a rattling of ice. "Small wonder her royal nastiness's own lady's maid died on the voyage to England. Probably worked to death. What a horrible creature to have to serve."

"Maybe the poor soul has been lucky." Ginny Tart's lips twitched into a sardonic grin. "She's probably in heaven now. Lord knows she's earned a place there, after taking care of that spoiled bitch. But maybe the good God didn't stop there." She chuckled. "The high and mighty princess got a handful when they replaced the dead girl with you. You're a bold one, Annie Pudden, and that's for sure. Her Royal Highness has met her match in you, my fine lady."

"I don't doubt that she has." Annie Pudden ran her hand over the bottle's cold surface and smiled slyly.

"I'd never have planned anything like this on my own." Ginny rolled her eyes to look around the luxurious room. "I *must* trust you, Annie Pudden. Otherwise why would I be letting myself get involved in this daft venture?"

"And I trust you, Ginny Tart." Annie returned her attention to the wine. "Otherwise I wouldn't have thought it safe to include you in this evening of illicit enjoyment."

She inserted a screw into the cork and began to turn it. The stopper released with such vehemence that Ginny Tart flinched.

"Bloody hell, Annie! You'll be waking those in the family crypt!"

Wine welled up and began to overflow. Annie Pudden brought the bottle to her mouth and gulped down the excess. When she finally lowered it, she choked, and grinned at her companion.

"An excellent vintage." She coughed, then sneezed. "Mustn't waste a single ounce. Wonderful bubbles. I do enjoy the way champagne tickles my nose."

"Gad, Annie, how can you quaff that stuff? I'd be upchucking, and no mistake."

"Years of experience at taking my treats where I can find them, fast and without hesitation. Now"—she filled their glasses—"let's get on with enjoying this prohibited evening before our supposed betters return."

"Yes, oh, yes." Ginny seized her drink and plunked her bottom down on the satin-covered bed. A wistful expression in her brown eyes, she ran her free hand over it. "Just imagine, Annie, being able to wear fancy clothes and eat and drink only the best…and sleep in a bed such as this."

"Someday we will. Furthermore, we'll have rich, handsome men with whom to share our lives, and they'll make all our dreams come true." She gulped down her wine, refilled her glass, and held the bottle out to replenish her friend's.

"Ah, Annie, how you do run on." Ginny Tart paused only long enough to swill down a mouthful. "No rich, handsome men are going to take up with the likes of us."

"I prefer to keep an open mind on the subject." Annie set her drink aside and bent to pick up an emerald-green gown that had been left crumpled on the floor. She held it to her breast and swirled about. "In preparation for our glowing future as the wives of those remarkable men, we'd best accustom ourselves to wearing appropriate clothing." She swung an arm to indicate the litter of fine clothing spread over the room. "Choose something. I think the pale peach suits your dark hair and eyes. I'll try on this green one."

"Annie, no!" Ginny's protest was a gasp. "We daren't…"

"Oh, for heaven's sake! We can't have a decent evening soiree without dressing appropriately. Fortunately, the Princess Cassandra isn't fat. We ought to fit quite nicely into her outfits. And she does have hair very nearly the shade of mine. The color of her gowns suits me perfectly."

Annie freed her golden tresses from beneath her maid's cap and tossed her head to send them cascading about her shoulders and down her back.

"Well…" Ginny fingered the luxurious peach gown trimmed with deep fringes of creamy lace.

"Oh, go on. I've seen you brazen off stable lads more times than I care to count, even slap them into place when the situation demanded. Putting on a nasty bitch's finery is small cheese by comparison."

"Well…" Ginny continued to fondle the elegant cloth. "I would like to feel silk or satin against my skin at least once before I die."

"Put it on." Annie began shedding her maid's

uniform. "But rest assured, Ginny Tart, if you throw your lot in with me, it won't be the only time. I'm bound for better things in life than bowing and scraping to a nasty foreign piece. I'll take you along with me…if you've the courage." When the black woolen dress fell about her feet, she kicked it aside to stand in front of her friend in her chemise.

"Oh, Annie, you are a brazen hussy. But I'll not put on that gown. Unlike you, whose lady has gone out for the evening, I'm a parlor maid. I could be called back into service at any moment."

"Suit yourself. If you're not about to join me, the least you can do is fasten me into this elegant garment, like a good little lady's maid." She stepped into the gown and pulled it up around her body. Swinging her back to her friend, she glanced coyly over her shoulder and fluttered her eyelashes.

"I swear, if you weren't wearing the princess's finery, I'd plant my foot up your backside." Ginny chuckled as she stood to set to work. "Oh, look," she continued, glancing over her friend's shoulder. "The window has been left open."

"Don't close it. Her royal nastiness ordered a fire lighted before she left. The place is stifling. There's a fair breeze rising. It will help to dissipate the heat and the stench of that awful scent the woman insists on using."

"As you wish, your ladyship." Chuckling, Ginny returned to her task of fastening her friend into the gown.

"Ginny, do you ever dream of the kind of man you'd enjoy having in your life?" As her friend finished her task, Annie turned on her, green eyes sparkling, and picked up the glass. "A fine, tall, strong man with broad shoulders and curling hair black as midnight and eyes as blue as a summer sky? A brave man with just enough swagger to him to make him a cut above the crowd, a man whose smile can light up your day, whose touch can make your entire body tingle?" She took a drink and suppressed a hiccup.

"I'd be content with one who washed himself once in a while and didn't paw at me like a dog seeking a bone." Ginny drained her glass, replenished both it and that of her friend, and sank down on the bed.

"Really, Miss Virginia, how mundane." Annie stuck her nose in the air and flitted about the room like a dancer. "For once, let your imagination run free. You want more than that, and you know it. Tell me your wildest dream." Annie stopped her dance to sit down beside her, champagne in hand.

"Very well." Ginny drew a deep breath. "I'd like a man much like yours in appearance, only with sandy curls and a mischievous twinkle in his eyes. A man bold and brave but with a tender side, a man who could be the most gallant of gentlemen when circumstances required such."

"You *have* thought about it." Annie grinned over at her friend as she paused to take a sip of the bubbling wine.

"We all have our daydreams, Annie Pudden." She avoided her friend's teasing, picked up a wafer, dipped it into the caviar, and took a bite. "It's what gets us through these days of drudgery. What is this stuff anyway?" She popped it into her mouth. "Tastes right fine."

"Fish eggs." Annie chuckled.

Ginny choked.

"Good God! What muck! And you say the bigwigs love the stuff? Blimey. Give me another swallow of wine. Maybe it will take my mind off what I've just shoved into my mouth. Bloody hell, helping myself to a princess's treats has to be one of the boldest things I've done in my life—right up there with our swimming naked in the sea that hot night last week. I'd never have done such a mad thing on my own. You tempt me into taking daft risks, you do, Annie Pudden."

"When you told me you'd grown up near the ocean as I had and loved to swim as much as I did, I felt we couldn't waste the opportunity. We were back before anyone came looking for us. In fact, no one even missed us."

"We took a bloody great risk, but I'll wager it wasn't the first time you pulled such a stunt. Tell me how such as yourself ended up as drudge to a foreign twit. You never did explain."

Annie paused. A mellowing sensation had settled over her. She knew it was because of the wine, but on reflection, she decided it was also because she was comfortable with her companion and felt she could trust her. Ginny Tart had been the one bright spot in her forced servitude to the princess, the one person in the manor with whom she could share her moments, good and bad.

"Have you ever heard of Lady Sophia Mannering?" she asked.

"I'd have to be deaf, dumb, and blind not to have." Ginny sucked up more wine before continuing. "She was the mistress of Closers Hall. It's been whispered, since her death, that she was the masked bandit who relieved many a rich man of his purse while riding the northern highways, she and a companion equally small in stature to herself."

"And on what do people base these assumptions?" Annie looked over at her with narrowed eyes.

"After her death, a highwayman's outfit was found in the stables at her residence of Closers Hall," Ginny said, "and a horse resembling the great black the bandit rode was found in the pasture lands nearby. Furthermore, since she died in that terrible carriage accident, no more robberies have occurred."

"And I take it her companion in crime hasn't been found?" Annie's lips turned up at the corners.

"Not hide nor hair. Seems to have disappeared without…" Ginny was staring at Annie, her eyes widening as her words faded. "Good God, Annie, you were sent here from Closers Hall. You were lady's maid to Lady Sophia. You were…? You are…?"

"Lord Mannering dispatched me to this place on the day of his wife's funeral." After another swallow of wine, she began her story. "He didn't want the authorities questioning me. He threatened that if I spoke to anyone about my mistress, he'd see me transported a good deal further away than to this place."

"Did he know of his wife's exploits?" Ginny's eyes continued rounded like those of a shocked owl.

"He never revealed that he did, but I don't think he was entirely ignorant. How could he be?" Annie drew a deep breath. "To admit his wife was robbing the rich and giving to the poor would have ruined him."

"Why didn't he stop her himself?"

"You didn't know Lady Sophia." Annie chuckled and paused to take more champagne. "Lord Mannering is a thin stick of a man. I believe he was afraid of her. At any rate, he much preferred to spend his time about London, gaming and in certain establishments for gentlemen who have a preference for those of their own sex. I believe he feared her revealing his weaknesses. As a result, he allowed her to do as she chose. In a way, they held each other hostage."

"But why in the name of all that's holy did she marry such a creature?"

"It was an arranged marriage, arranged almost from the time of her birth. It united two great estates. It had been her father's lifelong dream to join those two holdings into one. Lady Sophia loved and admired the man. I believe she went along with it for his sake."

"Even though her husband had no interest in the bed of a woman." Ginny guffawed. "How did you come to end up in her ladyship's service?"

"Much as you ended up at your uncle's tavern." Annie heaved a sigh that caught the hiccup rising in her throat. She coughed and continued, "Too many youngsters to feed. When I was thirteen, my parents sent me into service as a scullery maid."

"That's a long way from being lady's maid to the mistress of the house." Ginny looked over at her narrowed eyes. "How'd you manage to rise up?"

"When Lord Mannering married Lady Sophia, she was but fifteen. Even then she had a wild, adventurous streak. One day she caught me riding her favorite horse out of the woods behind the manor. I thought I was doomed, to be either dismissed or maybe even sent to a workhouse. Instead, she complimented me on my ability to ride without a saddle, and we began to talk. With a disinterested husband nearly two decades her senior, she was lonely in that house of strangers and longed for a youthful companion. Things progressed from there. Shortly, I became her lady's maid."

"Quite a tale, my fine lady, but didn't her lord and master find it strange, his lady wife taking up with a kitchen maid?"

"As I've said, he didn't much care what his wife did as long as she stayed out of his way and allowed him to continue with his preferred lifestyle."

"Bastard!" Ginny hiccupped. "Just like all the rest of them what calls themselves our betters! Do as they please, and we're supposed to turn a blind eye. But when we fall short, even in the least, there's bloody hell to pay."

"I don't have your eloquence with words, my friend." Annie let a corner of her mouth curl in a sardonic grin. "But I heartily agree."

"Tell me the rest of your tale, Annie Pudden. I'm sure there's more."

"The morning after Lady Sophia's death, he called me to his study." Annie turned a bit too quickly and had to step sharply to right herself. *Maybe no more champagne.* "He said he'd found a position that suited me perfectly. Lady Sophia had taught me to speak French so that we might communicate confidentially when necessary. Lord Mannering, a friend of the Duke of Haverbrook, had learned of his need for a lady's maid for his intended...his intended who needed someone who could speak French. So off I was sent, with the threat hot in my ear that if I ever so much as hinted at any adventures his wife and I may have shared, I'd disappear off the face of the earth in a most unpleasant manner."

"Great pile of horse manure!" Ginny's small hands knotted into fists. Then, her ire cooling somewhat, she continued less vehemently, "But aren't you taking an awful risk telling me?"

"I've been here over a month, Ginny." She looked over at her friend. "I've come to know who I can trust, and you're at the top of my list."

"What brought you to that decision, pray tell? I hope this isn't simply the wine loosening your tongue."

"Perhaps a bit, but it doesn't take a person long to understand that every word you utter is the honest truth, at least as you see it, even if sometimes there are a goodly number of salty ones in the mix. Duplicity or betrayal isn't in your character, Ginny Tart. I've seen you take the blame for that miserable Ruby more times than enough and never utter a word as to the incident being her fault. You're brave and loyal—all that a friend should be."

"Huh! Well, I guess that's all good...but a tad salty?"

"Ginny, you know you can curse anyone who crosses you, and with words that would curdle milk."

"Maybe. How about a bit more of that bubbly stuff?"

"Ginny," Annie continued slowly as she added more wine to her companion's glass. "If the opportunity arose for us to escape this place, to make lives of our own, would you cast your lot in with me?"

"Get out of this hell hole and become a notorious woman with you, Annie Pudden?" Ginny grinned a bit crookedly and held up her glass. "Of course I would. A toast! To two wild and wonderful women in the making!"

Chapter Three

Caleb Cameron inched along the stone ledge outside the second floor of the manor house, a black silhouette among the moving night shadows cast by the lofty oaks tossing in the wind.

This is insanity.

The thought raced across his mind, not for the first time. Yet here he was, with no turning back. He eased forward until he found the chalk mark Willie had made on the wall.

In spite of the stiff breeze making the velvet draperies undulate, the window was not only unlatched as Willie had promised but open. Wide open. Better than anticipated. Now there'd be no danger of squeaking or grating of the casement when he attempted to enter.

Moving with a stealth that would have become a prowling cat, he positioned himself to be able to peer inside. Two ladies, backs to him, sat on the edge of the bed, a table holding a wine bottle to their right. One wore emerald silk, golden curls spilling over her shoulders, and the other a shabby gray dress, the ties of an apron visible at her back.

Good God, is that how this princess dresses her lady's maid? The woman looks no better attired than a scullery maid.

He sucked in a deep breath. This was no time for

speculation. He'd accepted, if not the king's shilling, the duke's gold. He'd been paid to do a job, and by God he'd do it. He half turned to the dark figure crouching behind him to give a thumbs-up gesture. The outline acknowledged with a curt nod.

Caleb pulled a mask over his face, grasped the sack he carried into a white-knuckled grip, and eased through the window. The rising gale masked any slight sound he and his companion made.

Before either woman was aware of the encroaching danger, they were enveloped in burlap sacks. A hissed command ordered them to silence or death.

Within a minute, they'd been securely trussed and were being carried to the window over the shoulders of the invaders. Again ordered to be quiet or meet a swift end, the pair allowed themselves to be thrust outside.

From the ledge, Caleb tossed his bundle into a length of sailcloth held hammock-fashion off the ground by two men below. The pair caught it, cast it aside, and resumed their stance to catch the following one thrown by his accomplice. As they deposited it beside the first, Caleb swung to the ground on the vines he and his companion had used in their ascent. All three waited until his partner had joined them.

"Time to get the hell out of here." With a grunt Caleb hefted the first bundle over his left shoulder. "Dunc…" He jerked his head toward the second. "She's all yours. Doucet, Munro, follow me."

The four men scuttled into the trees, the two kidnappers burdened by their human booty in the lead. The howling wind muffled their retreat and disguised their forms in the roiling shadows of the great oaks. A wave of relief washed over Caleb. The first and most dangerous part of his assignment lay behind him.

Through the sack, fingers grasped the flesh of his back, pinched and twisted. He winced and whacked the backside on his shoulder.

"Stop it!" he growled. "Princess though you may be, I'm not above dropping your pantalettes and giving you a sound spanking."

The resistance ceased.

"Good, very good," he breathed, huffing under his burden. "We understand each other, Your Highness."

****

"You can release our passengers now, Mr. MacDougal." An hour later, with the *Jenny Jones* well out to sea, Caleb stood over the two bundles on his deck and addressed his mate.

The Scotsman glanced at his captain, then drew a knife from his belt and knelt on one knee to cut the bindings on the sack nearest to him. The moment its prisoner was freed, she thrashed the burlap over her head and scrambled to her feet. Eyes blazing red-hot anger, she staggered a few steps as she fought to get her footing in the starlight on the rising and falling deck.

"Bastards!" she screamed. Dark curls tumbled free about her face and shoulders. "What in hell do you think you're doing?" She glanced out at the rolling waves that surrounded them before refocusing her fury on the two men. "You take us back to shore right this bloody minute and release us!"

"I'll do nothing of the kind." Caleb faced her squarely. "You've been shanghaied. Shortly, you'll begin working your passage."

"Work? For the likes of you? There will be snowballs rolling around in hell before I do a lick of labor for a black-hearted cur that abducts decent ladies!"

"Now, now, lassie, is that any way to talk to the master and first mate of the *Jenny Jones*, one of the finest merchant ships afloat?" Duncan MacDougal came to confront her, affable grin in place. "I promise that spewing insults will get you nowhere. Captain Cameron and myself have been cursed out by a good many in our time. Such insults have rolled off our backs like water from a duck. I'll wager you won't be able to come up with anything new or disturbing."

"You think not, you great pile of horse manure? Well, you haven't heard anything like my best…"

The moon slid out from behind a cloud, revealing the countenances of all three for the first time. The woman's tirade skidded to an abrupt stop as she stared up at the mate.

Caleb glanced from one to the other.

What in bloody hell just happened? Dunc is a man few women seem able to deny is a fine specimen, but now this vixen from hell is looking up at him as if she's just witnessed a blessed miracle.

"Mr. MacDougal, you'll be getting on with your task." Duncan MacDougal was returning the woman's gaze with the charming grin he'd been known to use to seduce women on more than one occasion.

"Oh…aye, aye, Captain." The words stumbled out as he turned back to the second bundle.

When he'd finished cutting the cords and pulled the sack over the head of its contents, the second woman stumbled to her feet to stand beside her companion. Caleb caught his breath. Not only did she have the remarkable hair Willie had described but, sweet Jesus, the woman was beautiful—a heart-shaped face with a complexion that looked as soft as cream, long dark eyelashes, and a mouth that appeared sculptured to be kissed. As she drew herself up regally to confront him, an urge to take her hand and drop to one knee to kiss it all but overwhelmed him. She had the bearing of a princess of the first water, and no mistaking. Lizzie Harrison's charms must have blinded the duke.

"Take them below to your cabin, Mr. MacDougal." With a supreme effort, he wrenched himself out of his thoughts to snap back into command of the situation. The woman's unexpected beauty and proud stance had sent shock waves rushing through his mind and body, rendering him for a moment mute. To make it worse, she was gazing at him in much the same manner the first of his captives had looked at his mate.

What in bloody hell is going on here? Has this turned into a bewitching night? Damn that full moon!

"Verrae well." As it always did when he was annoyed, Duncan MacDougal's Highland accent surfaced. "This way, ladies. I'll chust be removing a few of my personal items…"

"Already done." Caleb indicated a bag on the deck behind the mainmast. "I had the place readied for the ladies before we set out this evening."

"How convenient," the mate muttered, in a manner in which few ship's officers would dare to address their captain. As Caleb Cameron's best friend, he permitted himself the retort.

"Yes, it is." Caleb's tone indicated Duncan had gone far enough in front of the ship's crew. "Off you go."

"Where are you taking us?" The maidservant whirled on Caleb. "And I don't mean to some hell hole of a cabin. I mean, where is this floating tub headed?"

"To a convent in America, and not a league farther."

"America? Are you mad? We'll not be thrust into some dirty sailor's badger hole for the weeks or months such a voyage will require and then thrown into a nunnery." The dark-haired one shrugged the mate's hand from her arm. Whatever charm Duncan MacDougal might have cast over the creature had apparently worn off. "You'll take us back to shore this instant and…"

"I will give you but two choices. Returning you to England is not either." Caleb towered over her. "You can either go peacefully with Mr. MacDougal to a warm, comfortable cabin, or you can stay here on deck for the remainder of the voyage. I warn you, the night winds blow bitter off the North Atlantic, and neither of you is dressed for such elements."

Glowering, she faced him, arms wrapped around her body, the cold already having set her shaking. Turning to her companion, she raised her eyebrows. A shrug was her reply.

"Very well. We'll go, but if you or any member of your crew dare come near us…"

"Trust me, young woman. None of my men have the courage or desire to venture near such a creature as yourself…or your mistress."

"This way, ladies." Duncan MacDougal swept out an arm to indicate the direction as he bent into a courtier's bow.

The dark-haired one hesitated, then drew herself up

proudly and nodded to her companion. The princess cast Caleb a demeaning glance before acquiescing to the mate's directions.

Arms crossed on his chest, he stood on the rolling deck and watched the pair follow Duncan MacDougal toward a door beneath the quarterdeck. The princess, shoulders squared, held her nose in the air, as if he and his entire ship stank, as she walked away from him. Her maid sashayed along behind her, hips swaying, head high as she cast disapproving glances left and right. No wonder Willie had been adamant that they take the creature along with her mistress.

Good God, what a pair. I have a feeling I'll be earning every ounce of Willie's gold.

"Get back to your stations!" He swung on a few of his crew members who'd paused to watch the drama unfolding. "We've taken on a couple of passengers, nothing more."

Aware of Captain Caleb Cameron's reputation, they headed off to obey. Caleb prided himself on being a good master, firm and fair, but not to be trifled with nor defied. Furthermore, the spoils he'd promised this rugged band of men if they obeyed him and worked hard was another incentive not to defy him.

Chapter Four

"Bloody hell, Cal! You're telling me we've kidnapped a princess?" Duncan MacDougal leaped to his feet and stood glaring down at his friend. "God in heaven, man, can you imagine the penalty? Hanging will be the best we can expect."

The captain, settled in the chair behind his desk in his cabin, looked up at the irate Scotsman looming over him. The *Jenny Jones* was far out to sea, blown before the gale that had been rising as they fled the manor house. He'd deliberately waited until they were well away to reveal the true identities of their passengers.

"If I'd told you one of them was royalty, would you have gone along with the plan?" He narrowed his eyes as he looked up at his first mate.

"Of course not! I have a fondness for my neck just as it is." Duncan ran a hand through his tangled, sandy-colored curls. "Guid God, we've kidnapped a princess!"

"Not kidnapped...shanghaied." Captain Cameron stood and went to a sideboard that held several flasks and tankards. "There will be no ransom demands. They'll work their passage as any victims of press gangs would. Once we reach New Brunswick, we'll deposit the pair of them in a convent. I've no desire to keep those creatures in my possession any longer than necessary. Then we'll head for Saint John, New Brunswick, to outfit this vessel for wartime duty."

He rolled his shoulders in an effort to relax their stiffness and felt a catch where the one he'd carried had twisted his flesh. "Whisky?" He held up the flask.

"After what you've told me, I doubt you've enough spirits on this vessel to calm my nerves, but yes. I'll be taking a fair guid dram." Duncan MacDougall sank into a chair.

"Who did you think we'd be bringing unwillingly on this voyage?" Caleb poured a hefty measure into a mug and handed it to his mate. "I told you my friend the Duke of Haverbrook wanted rid of a couple of women who knew too much about his intended."

"Aye, well, knowing the intelligence of his Grace and his proclivity for buxom women, I thought they were a couple of wenches he'd gotten in a family way and wanted placed in the care of nuns rather than have them thrown out into the streets to fend for themselves. That story you told me about a pair of lassies who knew too much about his intended didn't hold water. I've come to get pretty fair at recognizing when you're lying, Captain Cameron."

"Two of them in a family way? Willie's a horny little toad, but that's expecting a lot even of him. Sound sensible, man."

"Perhaps he and a friend could have gotten the two of them with buns in the oven? I don't know, Cal." He took a swallow of whisky and bared his teeth. "I never thought you'd do anything as daft as kidnapping a princess."

"I repeat, shanghaied."

"Shanghaied implies persons abducted to work their passage, then released. You received payment for this venture, a sizeable payment if it's to be enough to outfit this ship as a privateer. It may not have been an actual ransom, but…"

"Dunc, listen to me. No one gets hurt. We deliver the women to a convent, where they'll be well cared for by the good sisters. Once the nuns learn the princess's identity, they'll no doubt try to contact people back in England. By that time, Willie will be well and truly married to that trollop Lizzie."

"Well, then, I guess there's nothing to be done but to get on with it." Duncan MacDougal heaved a great sigh and swirled his drink in his mug. "There's no going back now."

"That's the spirit." Caleb slapped his friend on the back. "You'll be glad we undertook the venture once the *Jenny Jones* is outfitted for taking prizes and we're on the way to becoming rich and famous…or infamous."

"I have to admit, princess or no, the woman's got spirit." Duncan leaned back in his chair as his captain lowered the bottle to his friend's mug to replenish it. "Did you see the way she looked at us…as if we reeked to high heaven?" Good humor returning, he chuckled. "I'm guessing, since she didn't say a word, that her royal highness doesn't speak English. Therefore she won't be annoying us with a lot of regal demands. But her maid, now, there's a lass with a wicked tongue. When I shut her in my cabin with her precious princess, she called me names that would make a drunken sailor blush."

"There, now." Caleb grinned. "All it took was a bit of good Scotch whisky to put you back in humor."

"Aye, well, maybe something good may come out of this madness." Duncan took a swallow of whisky.

"Perhaps the maid can cook. God knows she couldn't do worse than Higgins. Why you hired that man to work the galley, I can't fathom."

"I hired him as a fighting man," Caleb replied. "But you know how it works aboard ship. Any man with a disability automatically becomes cook when there's not an actual one available. Higgins lost an eye and took a splinter in the leg fighting with Nelson. Half blind and limping, he's the obvious choice. That's not to say he can't do his share in a battle. You've seen him. He's a bear of a man with the courage of a lion. He can crack a man's skull with a single blow and fracture a jaw with one punch."

"Oh, aye." The Scotsman slanted him a sarcastic glance. "Not to mention cripple a man with a pot of swill he calls stew or set guts roiling with his coffee. I'll be praying to the good Lord that the foul-mouthed little creature can do better."

Chapter Five

"I still can't believe it!" In the light of a swaying lantern, Ginny Tart faced her companion in the cramped cabin into which they'd been thrust. "You let those great louts abduct us, truss us up, and throw us into this cubbyhole without a single word! You left me to do all the cursing, all the wishing them to scorch in Hell!"

"Hush, Ginny." Annie put fingers over her friend's mouth and spoke in a whisper. "I had an excellent reason. As my lout was carrying me from the manor, he referred to me as 'princess' and 'your highness.' Don't you see? He believes he's kidnapped Princess Cassandra!"

"God in heaven, do you really think that's what happened?"

"I do."

"But why take me as well? If it's ransom they're seeking, I'm not worth a farthing."

"He had no choice but to abduct us both. He couldn't risk leaving you behind to raise the alarm. Quite possibly, because of your attire, he may think you're my lady's maid."

"He…they couldn't be so daft." Ginny's eyes rounded.

"Think about it. We were in the princess's room. I'm wearing one of her gowns, I have the same color hair, and they saw only our backs. We both know the duke had no desire to marry her royal highness. I'm guessing he hired these picaroons to abduct her."

"Bloody hell! I didn't think the blighter had the guts to do such a thing."

"It's the only explanation I can fathom."

"That makes sense, but why do I have to pass myself off as a blinkin' servant? Blimey, if you're to pretend to be a blasted princess…"

"Firstly, because of the way you're dressed. Secondly, you have to be my English-speaking servant, the only person who can communicate with her mistress, through signs and signals." She grinned. "You do have a way with language…especially when you're annoyed."

"Reckon as how I do." Ginny relaxed into a sly smile. "Being able to keep my own way of saying things will come in right handy when I tell that big son of a bitch what threw me over his shoulder exactly what I think of him."

"I thought you already had." Annie smothered a chuckle.

"You did, did you?" She placed her hands on her hips. "I was only getting started. Be prepared to hear a whole lot better next time I see the bugger, your royal highness."

She paused and looked around the cabin. "Clean enough, but little more than a hole in the wall. Bed looks wide enough for both of us, though. And just look at these." She gave the two belaying pins hanging on hooks on the wall above the bunk a contemptuous push. "Imagine that great brute of a mate grinning when he said he was leaving them here to make us feel safe from any crew member who might attempt to invade our sanctuary. Some sanctuary! The arrogance! What made him think we might not use them against him?"

"Because he's assuming we're reasonably sensible women," Annie replied. "Knocking him or the captain senseless when we're miles at sea would be like signing our own death warrants, since they're probably the only two aboard who can navigate."

"I suppose." Ginny turned to the mate's sea chest, which took up most of the room aside from the bed, and tried to lift its lid. "Locked." She screwed up her face. "As if he'd have anything we'd want to steal. What do you think they plan to do with us?"

"Since our abductor thinks he captured a princess, I'd say ransom describes his intent."

"Bloody hell." Ginny plunked her bottom on the chest. "So we haven't got a snowball's chance in July. Once they find who we really are, they'll know we're not worth a farthing to anyone and chuck us overboard like so much garbage."

"That's why it's so important to maintain the fiction that I'm Princess Cassandra…at least until we get to a port where we can escape. We have to make them believe they've got the correct victims. Otherwise, we may become, as you suggest, fish food…or worse."

"I'd like to see any of these sea tramps try the 'or worse' part with me." Ginny clenched her hands into fists in her lap. "I'd…"

"Ginny, be rational. There's a full crew aboard. We'd be overpowered in seconds. Now, tell me you'll go along with the farce I've proposed. Believe me, it's our only hope."

Her companion drew a deep breath, glanced around

the rolling cubicle, and finally sighed.

"Very well...your highness."

"Good, very good. Now we'd best settle in as comfortably as possible. Since we're bound for America, this will be our home for some time."

"I suppose." With a sigh, Ginny began to straighten the rumpled bedding. "But, Annie, did you look at the one the captain called Mr. MacDougal? Tall, sandy curls, a grin that could make a curmudgeon smile..." She turned back to her friend in the shadowy illumination of two lanterns fastened to the wall. "And that devil-may-care twinkle in his eyes..."

"The embodiment of your perfect man? The one you've just termed a great lout?"

"Oh, don't tell me I didn't catch you ready to devour the captain, with more than a bit of interest," she snapped, returning to her task. "Quite a fine-looking specimen, isn't he?"

"Perhaps...if you care for the overbearing, arrogant type. Help me out of this ridiculous gown. I'm exhausted. We both need our rest if we're to be bright and strong enough to handle those two brutes for the remainder of the voyage. My head is beginning to ache from too much champagne."

"Your highness." Ginny started to favor her companion with a mock curtsy but the ship dipped and heaved. Tossed backwards onto the bed, she bumped her head on a beam near its head.

"Miserable, bloody tub!" She rubbed the sore spot. "I can't get off it soon enough!"

Later, as they lay in the bunk in their chemises, wrapped in woolen blankets, Annie pulled herself up on an elbow to look down at her friend in the swaying lantern light.

"You know, Ginny, this adventure might not be all bad." Her words were slow and calculating. "We'll be free in America, a land full of opportunity. We can make our own way, become wives to rich and powerful men. I've heard there's a dearth of marriageable women in the colonies, and we're not exactly ugly."

"But that beast of a captain said they're taking us to a nunnery!"

"Convents aren't prisons…at least not for a shrewd couple of ladies such as us. We'll be out of there and looking for likely mates in no time." Grinning, she punched her friend lightly on the shoulder. "Come on, Virginia Tart. It's time we took our own fate in our hands. Let's show the world it's not only men who can be scallywags."

Ginny hesitated, then heaved a sigh. "Very well, Ann Pudden. In for a penny, in for a pound. Good God, but I've got a pounding in my head as would make a rock moan. All that bubbly wine and then being tossed about like so much baggage…"

"Nothing a good night's sleep won't remedy. We've got a busy time ahead. We'll start first thing tomorrow morning. We'll liven up this voyage no end."

"Annie, what are you plotting, you evil wench?"

Chapter Six

"Her highness requires a change of clothing." In morning sunlight, the maidservant faced Captain Caleb Cameron and his mate on the deck, hands on her hips, head tilted saucily to the left. Caleb took a nasty little pleasure when she staggered. The *Jenny Jones* was running before a good breeze, rising and falling rhythmically over the swell under clear blue, early morning skies, but this foul-mouthed creature, for all her bluster, hadn't yet gotten her sea legs.

"What are you on about, woman?" He met her demand with equal disdain.

"Princess Cassandra cannot be expected to remain a moment longer in the same rumpled gown in which she was abducted." She slanted a defiant glance at Duncan MacDougal. "Nor can I."

"Not hardly. You're both probably accustomed to much better." The mate met her brazen words and stance with a sardonic grin that crinkled his countenance to the corners of his eyes.

"I remind you that you and your precious princess have been shanghaied." Caleb shot his officer a withering look before returning his attention to the woman confronting him. "Neither of you is in any position to be making demands.

"In fact," he continued setting his feet his shoulder's breadth apart, crossing his arms on his chest, and trying to ignore the fact that she was shivering in her worn gray gown in the stiff wind, "it's time you both started to earn your passage. Mr. MacDougal?" He turned to his mate. "See that these ladies are fittingly attired to begin their duties. Swabbing down the deck might be a good place to start."

"Aye, aye, sir." Duncan MacDougal reached out to take the woman by an arm, but she shrugged away.

"Don't go touching me!" she snapped. "I'll return to our cabin. You may deliver the change of clothing there, you miserable brute." She swung away from him and marched back down the deck.

"Blasted saucy wench!" Caleb watched her go, her hips swaying, head held high. "Get back to work, you bunch of layabouts!" He bellowed at sailors who'd paused to gaze after her.

Smirking repressed grins, they obeyed.

****

"Annie, you've no talent with a needle and thread." Ginny Tart shook her head ruefully as she watched her friend struggling to alter one of the men's garments with which they'd been provided. "You're making a right mess. I wonder why Lady Sophia kept you on when you can't manage a straight seam."

"One can hardly be expected to do a decent job with these crude needles and coarse thread you bullied that sailor into providing." Annie grimaced as she stabbed her finger, not for the first time. "Furthermore, it's difficult to see what I'm doing in this dark hole of a cabin with only the light provided by two swaying lanterns. At any rate, I have other talents that suited my lady right down to the ground." She winked at her friend. "Lady Sophia was willing to employ a seamstress to free me for other tasks."

"I can only imagine what those tasks might have been." Ginny heaved a sigh. "I hope they'll prove useful in our present predicament. Now our bucket needs emptying." She jerked her head in the direction of the covered pail shoved under their bed. "Why don't you see to it? I'll take over from you."

"How would that look, a princess emptying waste overboard?"

"Put one of the blankets from the bed about your head and shoulders. It's been hours since that grinning bugger of a sailor brought what was supposed to pass as our supper. It will be dark by now, I reckon. No one will notice which of us it is. Just don't speak."

"Very well." Annie laid aside her sewing to stand and pick up the bucket. "It will be good to get a breath of fresh air."

"That's one of the few good things about being at sea." Ginny stabbed her needle through the cloth with more than necessary vehemence. "Those bloody bastards let us roam free. Now go! By the by, you could have waited until you were out in the fresh air to remove the cover."

Clutching the bucket in one hand, the ladder's rail in the other, Annie made her way to the deck, improvised shawl about her head and shoulders. Once outside, she scuttled to the bulwarks and threw the waste overboard. She was getting her sea legs, she decided as she walked back over the rolling surface to the door that led to their quarters.

At the door to the cabin she shared with Ginny she heard men's voices issuing from the captain's quarters next to theirs. Curious, she eased forward and put her ear to the closed panel.

"I tell you, Dunc, with the money we got for shanghaiing that precious pair, we'll be able to outfit the *Jenny Jones* as a first rate privateer." The captain's words were full of enthusiasm. "We'll be rich men within months."

"*If* we get those letters of marque and reprisal from the governor," she heard the mate reply, apprehension filling his tone.

"Not to worry. After we've deposited that pair of annoyances at a convent, it will be clear sailing. The British North American colonies have no navy of their own. They'll be only too glad to get all the support they can from independent entrepreneurs like ourselves."

"Entrepreneurs?" A chuckle accompanied the word. "Isn't that a bit of a fine term for a couple of rogues like us?"

"Not at all. As soon as this war ends, we'll set up businesses…lumbering or something of the sort…and sit back in our fine mansions to become rich and fat."

"Caleb…"

"Well, what say? Are you with me or not?"

There was a pause. Then: "Aw, what the hell. We're already candidates for the noose."

"That's the spirit. Here, drink to our success."

A sly grin curling her lips, Annie Pudden eased away. Bucket in hand, she slipped back into the cabin she shared with her friend, the inspiration the two men's conversation had ignited bursting into full flame.

****

"It's madness! Us become privateers with that pair?" Ginny faced her companion, eyes wide.

"Think, Ginny, think!" Annie grasped her friend's

shoulders and shook her. "It's the only way you and I will ever get enough money to be independent, to be able to do what we want, when we want to do it! We can buy a mansion in one of those big towns in the New World. No one will suspect we're not ladies of the highest order. We can live like queens. No more serving fat, bossy women, no more getting our bums pinched by drunken, slobbering bastards of husbands, sons of the family, and intendeds. Silver and china. Silk and lace. Champagne and strawberries. That's what it will be for us." She swirled about in the small space and banged into the edge of the bunk.

"Damn!" She stopped and rubbed her knee. "This is a rabbit burrow."

"Now there you have it, my girl." Ginny sat on Duncan MacDougal's sea chest and gave her a wise nod. "A sign if ever there was one. Your plan is too big for the likes of us. We'll bump more than our knees if we get involved in such a daft scheme."

"Ginny, don't be a superstitious goose. My plan is simple. We'll keep up the pretense that I'm a foreign princess who can't speak their language. You're my English maid. Once we get to America, we tell them who we really are. If they don't agree to take us on, we'll threaten to go to the authorities with the story of their kidnapping us."

"And what's to keep them from murdering us to shut our mouths? I tell you, Annie Pudden, it's a daft idea if ever there was one."

"No, it isn't. It's an opportunity such as we're not likely to have ever again, a chance to be rich and free. Furthermore, your concerns about their killing us are groundless. From what I've seen of Captain Caleb

Cameron and his mate, they've at least a small degree of chivalry coursing through their veins…enough that precludes them from murdering defenseless women."

"Gallant pirates? Don't talk crazy, Annie."

"Not pirates, privateers. There is a difference, Ginny. Pirates are ruthless outlaws. Privateers act on behalf of their country under legal letters of marque and reprisal. The legality of any prize they seize has to be ruled upon by a Court of Vice Admiralty."

"Now you're sounding like a bloody advocate, and all because you spent a few years as lady's maid to Lady Sophia Mannering."

"Lady Sophia was clever and modern."

"There's some as would say her ladyship was a brazen bitch, a bold adventuress."

"If so, they'd be people who felt intimidated by a woman who dared challenge their antiquated ideas. Now, back to our plans. And," she continued looking down at the heap of clothing on the bed. "You'd best get back to the task of making those garments fit for us to wear. Elegant or not, I must say I'm getting more than a bit tired of wearing this silk thing."

Chapter Seven

"Mr. MacDougal, that outfit the princess is wearing looks damnably similar to recently acquired garments in my wardrobe." Caleb stared as the two women came on deck the following morning clad in breeches, shirts, and woolen coats.

"Oh, aye? I was just making a similar observation about her lady maid's getup. Her attire looks a wee bit like purchases I made during our last stay in port."

Turning on his mate, Caleb caught the twinkle in the Scotsman's eyes.

"Damnation, Dunc…!"

"They had to have something to wear, and since we had no female garments aboard…"

"So I'm to understand we've each contributed our best new clothing to enhance their wardrobe?"

"That would appear to be the case, sir." Duncan MacDougal leaned closer to the ship's master and lowered his voice. "And don't they make a right fetching pair, thusly garbed?"

"Perhaps in your eyes, Mr. MacDougal."

The mate's amused chuckle served to further rankle him.

"That maid is a dab hand with a needle and thread, isn't she?" his friend continued, grinning. "Didn't take her but a single evening to alter those getups to fit. Had to snip off bits and pieces here and there, she told me when I met her in the companionway this morning, but she made a right fine job of it."

"Snip? You mean my clothing is forever altered for that twit who calls herself a princess?"

"I believe such is the case. Apparently there was no choice. They'd not fit decently otherwise…so I was told."

"I'm surprised you didn't give them a pair of my best boots to rip apart."

"No need. Look at what they're wearing on their feet. They came aboard decently shod. The princess has a pair of good, sturdy shoes, her maid half boots. Those will serve them well for the time they're with us."

"Strange footwear for a princess." Caleb's brow furrowed. "I'd have thought satin slippers."

"And what would you be knowing of ladies' footwear, Captain, sir?" Duncan cast him a roguish glance. "I've always fancied your interest in ladies rested higher up their lovely bodies."

"I'm not a complete roué," he snapped. "Unlike you, I do take time to admire a dainty foot and a well-turned ankle."

"A thousand pardons, sir."

"Enough. I'm simply grateful their feet are decently outfitted. I paid a fine sum for my newest boots."

"Now, now, Captain, you'd not go begrudging a few small sacrifices when you're making such a fine profit from them."

"Argh!" Caleb swung away and headed for the hatch at the rear of the vessel. "See that they're put to work at once, Mr. MacDougal," he yelled back over his shoulder. "These decks need swabbing."

****

"Now what does that daft pair think they're about?" Caleb came up on deck the following morning to see a goodly number of his crew leaning against the bulwarks and staring toward the rear of the ship, where the princess was bent over a bucket while her maid rubbed soap into her hair. Both were wearing their male attire, the princess's bottom enticingly displayed as the breeches tightened across her behind.

"They declared they must wash their hair." Duncan straightened from where he'd been leaning against the mainmast and came to join the captain. "They demanded water, buckets, and soap."

"And you obliged! Bloody hell, man, they're causing a spectacle! You lot!" The captain swung on his gaping crew. "Get back to work. There's a fair breeze blowing. Get canvas into it, and be smart about it!"

"Shouldn't you be allowing me to relay orders to the men?" Duncan quirked a corner of his mouth as the men turned away to do his bidding.

Caleb rounded on his mate. "Not if your recent actions speak of your ability to command authority, Mr. MacDougal. Demanded water and buckets and soap, did they? Did you not have the guts to deny them? You two!" He headed toward the women, shouting, "Get below! You've not been given permission to display yourselves about my decks."

"Would you be having us living in filth, Captain, sir?" The maidservant paused in washing her mistress's hair and turned on him with a saucy, belligerent smirk. "Her highness will not be denied cleanliness."

The princess straightened and waited while her

companion wrapped a length of drying linen about her head. *No doubt supplied by my besotted mate.* Her royal highness looked at him with narrowed eyes, guessing, he assumed the content of their confrontation.

Bollocks, but she's pretty, like something out of a fairytale. He fought down the thought. *Get on with it, man, just get on with it. Don't let them weaken you like they have Dunc.*

"Get below…now!"

"Her highness's hair has to be rinsed, and she had decreed that when I've finished with her, I shall wash my own." The maid stuck out her chest and chin, planted her hands on her hips, and faced him. "If you insist on us leaving the deck before all this is accomplished, you will have to remove us bodily. I doubt such a spectacle will sit well with your crew. In their eyes you will appear a man who cannot manage a couple of poor, captive women without the use of brute force."

The truth of her last comments struck him with all the insult of a dish of stew thrown into his face. He had to retain his crew's respect. A few who'd sailed with him before, like Doucet and Munro, knew him to be a fair and just man, but the others were new under his command. Dragging two women below deck would sully his reputation no end. Stymied, he paused.

"Very well, finish your ablutions, but be smart about it. We're heading into weather, and I've no desire to see either of you washed overboard with your head in a bucket."

He turned and strode to the quarterdeck. There he brushed the helmsman aside to take the wheel.

"I suppose you've run us miles off course, gaping

at that display," he snapped at the man. "The masts need oiling. Get to it."

"Aye, aye, sir." The man scuttled off.

"Aw, Cal, it's but a bit of innocent relief for the men." Duncan sauntered up to join him. "They're no fools. They know those two are untouchable."

"Yes, well, this is the last we'll have of such incidents. You, Mr. MacDougal, will see to it. Understand?"

He swung the wheel sharply and was rewarded by a squeal from her highness and a bawdy expletive from her companion as the bucket in which the princess was rinsing her hair overturned onto her servant.

"When they're finished," he bellowed to his mate, who had begun to walk away, "take them to the galley and introduce them to Higgins. They can begin working for him. God knows, he needs all the help he can get."

Chapter Eight

"Bloody hell!" Ginny stared around the dark, dirty galley. "This place isn't fit to prepare food for rats."

Annie silently agreed as a brute of a man, his head shaven and his shirt sleeves rolled up to reveal hairy arms, swung away from the stove toward them. His broad face, red and sweating in the heat, contorted with anger as he leveled an angry, one-eyed glare at them. A black patch covered his right eye.

"And just who might you be to go thumbin' your nose at my galley?" he snarled.

"Captain's sent them to help you," replied the sailor Munro, who'd brought them below deck.

"Oh, aye?" As the giant stepped forward, Annie repressed a shudder. In the dark, dingy galley, his appearance, except for the bald head, reminded her of drawings of great apes she'd found in books in Lord Mannering's library.

"Aye." Ginny stepped forward to confront the glowering man. "If you'll move aside, we'll get to the task of setting this pigsty to rights."

"It will give me great pleasure." He slammed a pot down on the stove. "You can have the whole damned place. I never signed on to cook for this bunch. I'm a fightin' man, not a cursed scullery maid."

He shoved the two women aside and limped out of the crowded galley.

Munro grinned. "It's all yours, ladies. The men expect food in two hours. You'd best set to work." He turned and left.

"Dear God!" Annie breathed. "What a miserable hole! And the smell!" She lifted the cover on a barrel near the door and wrinkled her nose. "Salt meat."

"Well, we've no choice." Ginny rolled up her sleeves. "Let's get to it. First we clean, then we cook. Maybe if we produce half-decent meals, the men will side with us and we can provoke a mutiny if needs be. I've heard the way to a man's heart is through his stomach." She moved about the cramped space inspecting barrels and containers. "Potatoes, flour, dried peas, cheese, and even butter. We'd best use up some of this lot before it starts to spoil."

****

Caleb got up from behind his desk and stretched. Looking down at the figures scratched on a bit of paper on its surface, he let a satisfied smile curl his lips. He'd spent the better part of the morning calculating the cost of outfitting his ship as a privateer against the payment His Grace had given him and found he had more than enough to make the *Jenny Jones* a first class fighting vessel.

Whistling, he went out of his cabin and climbed the ladder to the deck. He wanted to share the results of his calculations with Duncan. Maybe it would lessen the Scotsman's apprehension about the value of shanghaiing that annoying pair.

"Mr. MacDougal…" He started to speak to the man standing amidships, hands on his hips.

The remainder of what he'd been planning to say died in his throat at what he saw.

Strung between the main and mizzen masts was a length of rope. Blowing in the wind along its length were several blankets, the two dresses his passengers had worn at the time of their abduction, and a small assortment of female undergarments.

"Bloody hell!" he roared. "Mr. MacDougal, what is the meaning of this?"

"The maidservant said they had to have clean bedding and clothing." The mate turned to him with a shame-faced grin. "They washed them in that small barrel yonder. Munro and Doucet strung a bit of rope for drying."

"Good God, man! This is a merchant ship, not a cursed laundry barge! Order those two on deck and have them remove that abomination immediately!"

"Perhaps a bit later." Duncan spoke softly to his captain. "They're making a meal just now, and from the smells issuing from the galley, I'd say it's going to be a right tasty one. Anyway"—he returned his tone to normal—"what's the harm? My cabin's getting a first-rate cleaning, and while they're engaged in tasks they're not bedeviling us."

"Bah!" Caleb gave a flapping blanket a crack with the flat of his hand and headed back to his cabin. Maybe looking over his favorable finances again would help to sooth his annoyance.

****

Caleb came up on deck to find his mate engrossed in watching the horizon through a spyglass. The *Jenny Jones* knifed through the water at a good clip while the sun shone warm on his back.

"A fine morning, is it not, Mr. MacDougal?" He slapped his friend on the shoulder in a spirit of *bon ami*.

"We're making excellent time. I calculate we'll soon be offshore from that convent, where we can deposit part of our cargo late this afternoon."

The moment the words were out of his mouth a small, nasty sensation fluttered in his gut. Even though he was loath to admit it, the past weeks with better-than-normal food served on a freshly scrubbed table with clean dishes, accompanied by decent coffee served in well-washed mugs, had mellowed his feelings toward the women. They'd further pleased him by staying out of his way. And today the infamous clothesline between the masts hung empty.

"Aye, if we make it." Duncan lowered the glass and handed it to him, a frown furrowing his forehead. "Take a look, Captain." He swung his arm to the northeast.

Good humor fading into apprehension, Caleb accepted the instrument and focused across the water in the direction his mate had indicated.

"Damnation! It can't be!" He lowered the spyglass and turned to stare at his friend.

"I had a hard time believing my eyes, too, Captain, but sure as I'm a sea dog, it's a pirate ship. What in blazes can they be doing, coming after us? We've nothing aboard but pots and pans and farm implements and…"

"And sabers and pistols and muskets with ammunition. Bugger all! We'll have to make a run for it. With no cannon aboard, the only way we can make a fight of it is with sabers and pistols if we're boarded."

He swung to his men standing alert about the deck. Their expressions told him they'd caught wind that something was amiss. "Get up every inch of canvas, men. We're about to make a dash for it," he bellowed not waiting to relay the order through his mate. "And," he continued as they rushed to obey, "keep your belaying pins handy. We may be in for a fight. Doucet, Munro, fetch swords as well as muskets and pistols. See that every gun is primed and ready."

A chorus of, "Aye, aye, Captain," came in enthusiastic response.

"They're ready and more than willing." Caleb raised the glass once more to his eye. "I chose well. They're some of the best fighting seamen London had to offer."

"Let us hope they prove to be worthy of the title." Duncan turned away and bellowed more orders. Above them, sailors scrambled into the rigging. Sails billowed in the wind as the *Jenny Jones* took off on a run for her life.

"What about our passengers?" Duncan came back to the captain.

"Order them to stay below deck. I don't want them underfoot making a nuisance of themselves. With luck, we can outrun those bastards."

Chapter Nine

Below deck, Ginny Tart staggered and sat down with a plunk on the mate's sea chest as the ship heaved to port.

"Damn it!" she snapped. "Doesn't the man or that great brute of a mate know how to steer this tub? I could have fallen. I could have hit my head..."

"Instead of landing safely on your bum." Sitting on the bed, her feet pulled up, arms clasped around her knees, her companion grinned. They were taking a small reprieve from cooking and cleaning after the men's early morning hunger had been satisfied.

"Scoff all you like, Mistress Pudden. I'm right sick and tired of those two." She crossed her arms on her chest and scowled.

"I'd advise you to keep such thoughts to yourself, my girl. We're still miles at sea, I reckon, and they're our only hope of seeing dry land again."

"Very well." With a heaved sigh of resignation, Ginny started to get to her feet again only to be once again thrown onto the trunk as the *Jenny Jones* heaved to starboard.

"Argh!"

"Ginny, I wonder..." Annie swung to put her feet on the floor.

"Wonder what? If we'll survive this topsy-turvy trip?" She rubbed a hand on her hip.

"No, I wonder if we're being pursued. Nothing like this has previously occurred. We seem to be racing with the wind. Ginny, I think another ship is chasing us…another ship with a crew intent on rescuing us. Just listen to all that activity on deck. They're getting ready for a fight."

"Why in bloody hell would anyone want to rescue us? God knows there're lots more girls ready to be pressed into service where we came from."

"Not us as such but what if they believe Princess Cassandra is aboard? Perhaps they started out before they realized she was safe and sound at Rannoch Manor. There was a storm brewing when we were abducted. Quite possibly the princess was forced to stay at the manor for the night, and when they discovered she was missing…"

"A farfetched tale, at best." Ginny looked down at her work-coarsened hands clasped in her lap. "The other servants would have known the truth."

"Well, what other explanation do you have? From what we've seen, this is a merchantman, full of manufactured goods bound for North America."

"Pirates!" Ginny jumped to her feet only to be promptly thrown back onto the chest as the ship lurched once more to port. "You've hit on it, Annie! This ship is carrying a load of merchandise. I overheard the men talking about the cargo the other day. What better target for pirates?"

"Oh, God, you're right! That makes much more sense. I've heard the waters off North America are fairly teeming with them. Ginny"—she grabbed one of the belaying pins from its hook on the wall—"prepare to help defend the *Jenny Jones*…and ourselves."

"Ladies!" Duncan MacDougal's voice interrupted their talk. Dismayed, Annie clasped a hand over her mouth.

"He didn't hear you," Ginny reassured her, "what with all the noise on deck."

"Ladies, open the door."

"All right, all right!" Ginny dropped the bar to let him in. "What is it?" Her words trailed off as she stared at the man revealed.

A sheathed sword hung at his side, a pistol stuck into his belt, and his shirt opened to reveal an expanse of broad, hard chest, Duncan MacDougal was the epitome of a handsome, charismatic warrior. Annie saw an expression of awed admiration spread over her friend's face.

"We're being pursued by pirates. The captain orders you to stay below and bar the door. Are you listening?" he barked at Ginny's stare.

She nodded.

"Relay that order to your mistress...however you do it." He turned and headed back for the ladder to the deck as she gazed after him.

"Ginny, come out of it!" Annie grasped her arm. "We have to make ready for battle. Grab that belaying pin and prepare to head for the deck!"

"Bloody hell, Annie, you can't mean..."

"Exactly what you're thinking. If we're to get these two to take us on as privateers, we have to show them we can fight."

"But, Annie..."

"It won't be all that hard." Annie plucked a belaying pin from its peg by the bed. "Just imagine these pirates are any of the many lads who tried to run their hand up your skirt…or pin you to a wall."

"All right." Ginny drew herself up and reached for the other weapon. "It'll be good to let some bastard feel my wrath."

****

"Argh!" Caleb fell to the deck, blood spurting from a gash in his forearm. Before he could right himself, a pirate loomed over him, sword pulled back, ready to plunge it home in the captain's chest. Struggling to gather his strength to lunge upward, Caleb sucked in his breath.

A dull thud stopped him. The eyes of his enemy widened before he slumped unconscious to the deck. Through the gunsmoke, Caleb saw the princess standing over him, feet planted apart, belaying pin still grasped in both hands until she held down a hand to him.

Too astonished to realize what he was doing, he accepted her offer and staggered to his feet. She whirled as another pirate rushed at them, and landed a hearty blow into his belly. Before the man could recover, Caleb had taken over the fight and flattened him to unconsciousness with a blow to the jaw.

A cry from the woman made him whirl to see a pirate charging across the deck toward them. Bellowing a battle cry, the outlaw wielded a sword. Suddenly he was lifted off his feet and flung flat onto his back. The clothesline, nearly invisible in the haze of gunpowder, had caught him across the throat.

Damned thing finally proved useful. Caleb felt a corner of his mouth quirk upwards.

****

"Easy there." An hour later, with the defeated

pirates, many of them wounded, sent off on their disarmed ship, Caleb screwed up his face while Annie stitched the slash in his arm. As she fought a roiling in her stomach, she wished she'd learned to sew. Her handiwork was crude, at best. The man would have a nasty scar that Ginny's skillful needle could have lessened.

She paused and held up the laudanum bottle, a question in her expression.

"No, we've little to spare." He shook his head. "Some of the other wounded men need it more than I do."

With a nod, she returned her attention to her stitching.

"You acquitted yourself well out this day," he surprised her by continuing. "You and your friend proved yourselves worthy companions to my men in that fight. Even your bloody clothesline came in handy. Surely took one of those bastards out of commission in short order."

She raised eyebrows in what she hoped was a puzzled fashion.

"Ah, bloody hell, you don't understand a word I'm saying, do you? But on the off chance that you can get the drift, I'll explain what you saw on deck just now. This ship's crew is composed of fighting men, something those picaroons didn't expect to find on a merchantman. Once we'd gotten the better of them, my men dumped those bastards' supply of cannons, muskets, pistols and gunpowder overboard before we let them sail away. They'll pose no further threat to British shipping until they can restock."

Keeping her attention focused on what she was

doing, she completed her task, wiped blood away from the wound, and wrapped a cloth about it. When she'd finished, she drew in a deep breath.

When she began to gather up her medical supplies, he got up from where he'd been sitting beside her on his bed and continued his explanation. "Taking them as prisoners would only slow us down and make more mouths to feed."

She paused in her work and gazed up him, hoping her expression resembled that of a puzzled spaniel. When she continued to stare at him, wide-eyed, he heaved a sigh. "No need to favor me with such puzzlement, Your Highness. It's hopeless. You don't understand. Go and join your friend. The rest of my bruises and cuts will heal on their own. Your nursing skills are needed elsewhere." He held out his good arm toward the door.

She inclined her head to indicate she'd interpreted the gesture, but as she was about to leave the cabin, his voice stopped her.

"Thank you, Your Highness. You've done good service this day." His remarks, issued in a respectful tone, astonished her. He favored her with a quick bow.

With a solemn nod that could have acknowledged any softly spoken words and not her pleased satisfaction, she left the cabin. Amidships, she found Higgins bent against the bulwarks while Ginny stitched a great rent in his pants. Several sailors who weren't awaiting treatment grinned as they moved about doing their tasks.

"What are you doing?" Annie drew her away to hiss into her ear. "There are wounded men waiting, and here you are stitching trousers!"

"I'm dressing a wound." Ginny drew herself up defiantly.

"Dressing what wound?"

"I had to sew up a long gash in his backside." Ginny's face flushed red. "And these stupid buggers"— she waved a hand to indicate the chuckling sailors— "seem to think it's great sport. Since he's wearing his only pair of half-decent breeches. I had to mend them to cover the wound."

"Oh."

"Yes, oh."

"I'm sorry, Ginny." Annie smothered a chuckle. "I'll help with the others."

"I'll be right grateful, Annie. Blimey, but I'm getting plumb tuckered. I'll be glad when I get the last of this lot sewed up and set to rights. By the time I've finished, I reckon they'll be looking for victuals again. Working at the manor house was a good sight easier than this."

"We'll soon be done," Annie whispered. "Take comfort in the fact that the captain just thanked me for our services. Perhaps what happened today will weigh heavily on his decision when you approach him to take us on in his privateering venture."

"Me? Why me?"

"Because I don't speak English, remember?"

"You and your daft ideas." With a sigh, Ginny turned her attention to yet another wounded sailor approaching her with a bloody arm.

"How long until we get fed?" he asked holding onto his wound.

With a resigned, I-told-you-so shrug Ginny pursed her lips. "You'll get fed when we're finished patching up you lot. You're lucky to be getting any decent victuals, what with fresh water running to the dregs on this tub."

Chapter Ten

"Only a few more hours and we'll be rid of them once and for all." Caleb leaned back in his captain's chair and drew a deep breath. "Over a month cooped up with them aboard this vessel has sore tried my good humor." He picked up the mug from his desk and swirled the liquid inside. "It will be more of a relief than having a boil on my backside lanced."

Sitting opposite him, his mate remained silent, his expression pensive.

"Well, come on, man, what is it?" Caleb snapped. "Don't tell me you'll be sorry to see them go."

"I'd be lying if I said not at all." Duncan stared down into the tankard he held cradled in his hands. "The meals have been 'way better, the table and plates clean, and rum and limes measured out exactly as they should be." He chuckled. "Atop all that, they've had a way of livening things up aboard, and no mistake. Why, I fair have to laugh when I remember your expression the afternoon you discovered them washing their bonny locks in a bucket. And when you saw their pantalets flapping in the breeze…"

"Oh, and being first mate on a fine ship like the *Jenny Jones* previously bored you?" Caleb was on his feet, glaring down at the man.

"No, no, not at all, Cal." Duncan pulled himself up straighter in his chair to meet his friend's ire. "It's just that they've spirit and courage. You'll remember how they joined in the fight against those pirates and never batted an eyelash when it came to treating the wounded."

"Spirit and courage, is that what you call it? I call it brazen bravado that they've no right to possess. I'll grant they pulled their weight and were helpful with the wounded, but in such a manner no lady would ever attempt. You do recall that so-called lady's maid getting Higgins to drop his britches to fix a wound on his backside?"

"She stopped the bleeding and sewed him up right proper. You and your blasted idea of ladies. I doubt you'd know a genuine one if you fell over her. Anyway, it's all arranged for tonight, and that will be the end of it." He drew a deep breath and squared his shoulders.

"I sure as hell hope so. I'm weary of their antics."

"Do you want me to go over the plan again?" Duncan looked over at his friend. "Tonight we slip a goodly dram of laudanum into their supper wine. Once they're asleep, we'll deliver them, safely trussed up, into the woods on the grounds of that French convent Doucet told us about on the southeast coast of New Brunswick. We're nigh on there now. If we can't find a well to put them beside, we'll place them a decent distance from the privy. In either location, the good Sisters will discover them early in the morning.

"It will take the nuns a fair length of time to figure out what our former passengers are saying, what with them being French speaking, the lady's maid, English, and her royal highness spouting God only knows what gibberish. By then, we'll have sailed with the tide and hopefully a good, stiff breeze."

"Almost too easy to be trustworthy."

"Bloody hell, Cal, stop looking for trouble. You're starting to sound like an old woman...a nervous old woman." He chuckled. "My only fear is that the princess's maid will treat those religious ladies to a collection of words they'd be better off not hearing."

****

"Well, that's that." Caleb stood in the darkness on his deck and waited while Duncan, Doucet, and Munro climbed back over the bulwarks to join him.

"Aye." Duncan came to stand beside him. "They're finally gone."

"Mr. MacDougal, I hope that wasn't a sigh I hear in your voice." He waved the two sailors back to their regular duties.

"It's been a long voyage, Captain." Duncan put his hands on his hips and stared off across the water in the direction they'd taken the women. "There's a village with a tavern, a few miles farther up along the coast. Logerville, Doucet informed me it's called. Being from this area, he knows the lay of the land. It's English, he says. It's only fair to give the men an evening's shore leave. And we do need fresh water. Only this morning our former cooks informed me the casks are near dry."

"Bloody hell, man, we need to get away from here as soon as possible."

"Nothing is going to happen tonight. We'll sail at first light. It could be days, maybe even weeks, before news of those two castaways gets to that village."

Caleb hesitated. His crew had had a long voyage. They'd worked hard and fought off a pirate attack. Furthermore he was reasonably certain they'd guessed their passengers were of such importance as could put them in prison or on the gallows if they were intercepted. The princess's clothing when he'd first brought her aboard had indicated she was a lady of consequence, but they'd remained unquestioningly loyal, nevertheless.

And, as his mate had informed him, they did need fresh water.

"Very well. An evening in the village. But, mind"—he let his words follow the mate as the man, grinning, swung away to inform the crew—"make certain you and everyone else are back on board at sunrise."

"Oh, aye." Duncan strode down the deck. "You lot," he yelled to the sailors on deck, "Get a move on. The captain has authorized shore leave in Logerville tonight."

****

"Ginny, Ginny, wake up!" Annie shook her friend as the first rays of dawn grayed the sky.

"What…what in bloody hell do you want?" Confused and disoriented, her friend struggled to a sitting position and rubbed her head. Coming further awake, she stared about at their surroundings and the malodorous building beside them. "Annie? Where are we?"

"Somewhere on dry land behind what I can reasonably assume is a large privy."

"What happened?" Coming fully awake and sitting upright, Ginny stared at her with wide, confused eyes.

"I believe those two drugged us with laudanum." Annie drew a deep breath. "That's why the captain was so sparing with it after that pirate attack. He was planning to use it to get rid of us. He never planned to deliver us to a convent. All he wanted to do was throw us ashore at the first opportunity."

The sound of someone clearing her throat made the two women whirl to look to their left. Standing beside the building was a tall, austere-looking woman in black, a snow-white wimple surrounding her stern face.

"Bloody hell, you were wrong, Annie." Ginny turned to her friend. "He did deliver us to a convent. We're behind the Sisters' privy!"

The nun spoke, and Annie listened. French. She understood French.

By the time the Sister had finished speaking, asking how she and Ginny had come to be there, Annie Pudden had a plan in mind. A bold plan that would get her and her friend back aboard the *Jenny Jones* and on the way to becoming rich as privateers.

****

"You're daft, Annie Pudden, you know that!" Ginny hissed as she walked through the woods beside her friend, following the Reverend Mother and two nuns. "Force them to marry us! Good God, as if I want to marry that great lout of a Scotsman!"

"I can't imagine you'd find the prospect so daunting." Annie tossed her a sardonic grin. "I've seen the way you look at him."

"He is an eyeful, and that's a fact." Ginny relented momentarily before she snapped back to the moment. "But, hell and damnation, Annie, admiring the bottle don't mean I'll like the wine. What makes you think they'll agree to marry us anyway?"

"I've told the good Sisters that they seduced us." She let a triumphant smile cross her face. "They're taking us to the nearest village to swear out a warrant for their capture. If they're caught, they'll have a choice of either marrying us or facing a long time in prison. Given those alternatives, I think they'll agree."

"And what makes you think they'll be captured? By now they're probably miles away."

"Perhaps, but with their water supply all but gone, I'm guessing they'll have to hove in for water at the village for which we're headed. It takes time to fill the casks. Then, too, correctly assuming the nuns speak only French, you only English, and myself some foreign tongue, they'll take it for granted it would take some time for us to make our true plight understood. Furthermore, knowing your Mr. MacDougal, I'm venturing to suppose he'll be pressing for shore leave to visit the nearest tavern."

"He's not *my* Mr. MacDougal. Annie, this is the daftest plan you've had yet. I think we should stay here, go back to the convent with these good women, and, after we've rested, go on from there."

"Go on to what?" Annoyed, Annie paused and caught her companion by the arm to turn her toward her. "We have nothing beyond the clothes on our backs, and we know little about this country. We could be attacked by wild animals or savages or highwaymen. I've no desire to be beaten or raped, or both, and then probably killed."

"And what makes you think those two bastards to whom you're planning to marry us off won't beat and rape us?"

"Ginny, think." Annie started off again in pursuit of the three women in black. "They had ample opportunity during the voyage. In my opinion, neither of them is the kind of man who would have to resort to violence against a woman to get his way. It would be beneath their dignity to have to resort to force. I think I can safely say we can expect a platonic marriage as long as we wish it."

Head held high, she lengthened her stride, a sly smile on her lips.

Behind her, she heard Ginny mutter something that reeked of exasperation as she hastened to catch up with her.

Chapter Eleven

Mid morning found Caleb pacing his deck, a scowl wrinkling his brow. Ten members of his crew had yet to put in an appearance after their night ashore. He should have known better than to go along with Duncan MacDougal's daft idea of shore leave. These men might be fine fighters, but they also had a strong taste for rum and the riotousness that generally went along with it ashore. He was glad he'd made the men replenish the water casks before he'd released them. The *Jenny Jones* was ready to sail on a moment's notice.

Damn you, Duncan MacDougal! You could charm Satan into giving you your way! By now we should be well out into the gulf.

He paused at the rail to scan the ragged excuse for a village in search of evidence of his men's returning figures. It was then he saw them. A militia officer and a half dozen soldiers bearing muskets marched onto the Logerville wharf and halted with military precision.

"Duncan MacDougal, Caleb Cameron?" the officer squinted up at him.

"Captain Caleb Cameron, at your service, sir." *Good God, what now? Have those daft bastards gotten themselves arrested? Will I be expected to pay a handsome fee to get them out of the village jail?* "What can I do for you?" He forced himself to sound affably agreeable. It never paid to challenge the law, not even in an outpost like this excuse for a settlement.

"Is a man named MacDougal on board?"

"Aye." Something in the officer's demeanor started a nasty suspicion coiling in Caleb's belly.

"Summon him to the deck." Now Caleb knew something was definitely wrong. There was no attempt at civility in the sergeant's words.

"Mr. MacDougal." He bellowed over his shoulder.

When there was no response, he yelled again.

"Jumped ship perhaps?" The sergeant's words had a nasty ring.

"No, sir, sleeping off a night in port." Caleb struggled to keep what he considered a civil tongue in his head.

"Aye, aye, what is it?" Duncan MacDougal's tangled curls appeared out of the door below the quarterdeck. "This better be life-and-death important, Cal." He fumbled into full view, clothes rumpled, eyes bloodshot as he peered into morning light, rubbing his fingers through his hair.

"This gentleman, who, by the way, has yet to introduce himself beyond the appearance of his uniform, wishes to speak with us." Caleb indicated the officer.

"Sergeant Joshua Miller, sir, of His Majesty's 42nd Fusiliers," the officer snapped in response to Caleb's acknowledgement of his lack of proper protocol. "Gentlemen, I order you to disembark immediately. You're both under arrest."

"Oh, aye." Rubbing his temples, the mate came to join the ship's master at the rail. "If it's about that small set-to in the tavern last evening, I've already made restitution with the landlord. And no one was hurt…much." He lowered his hands to frown down at bruised knuckles.

"Enough talk." The officer glared up at them. "Disembark immediately, and come with us."

"Bloody hell," Caleb heard Duncan mutter. "All this because of stealing a kiss from a tavern wench who happened to be another man's doxy."

"Sweet Jesus, Dunc." Caleb's words came out in an exasperated exhale as he headed for the gangplank.

"Sorry, Captain." His mate's apology as he followed him did nothing to alleviate his annoyance.

"May I know the charge against me? I spent the entire night on my ship." On the wharf Caleb stopped close in front of the sergeant, facing into the officer's liquor-fouled breath.

"Seduction, sir, as serious an offense in this country as it is in England."

"Seduction?" The name of the offense bellowed from Caleb. "Seduction of whom? When…"

"The seduction of one Princess Cassandra on your part, sir, and of her lady's maid, on MacDougal's."

"Seduction of that bit of boot-tough leather?" Duncan MacDougal stared at the officer for a moment, then burst out laughing. Just as quickly he stopped and grabbed his head. "Bloody hell. Goddamn cheap rum."

"No laughing matter, sir. Taking advantage of two defenseless ladies while they're trapped aboard your ship is a heinous crime."

"Good God, man, this is absurd," Cal snapped. "There's absolutely no truth…"

"We're to doubt the word of the good Reverend Mother of Sisters of Charity at St. Jean de Baptiste Convent? It is she, not those defenseless young ladies, who has laid charges. Her highness and her maid were too much in fear of the pair of you to do any such thing. The Reverend Mother said she had to proceed without their permission because she felt so strongly about their accusations. She and the defiled ladies walked for hours through the woods to Logerville to lodge charges. She suspected you'd put to shore here, the nearest place where you could replenish your water casks."

"I assure you, Sergeant, those two 'ladies,' as you've termed them, are as pure as they were when they left England. My involvement was simply to transport them into the care of the Sisters. I don't know what tales they've fed you, but I assure you there's not a drop of truth in any of them."

"Then you'll not mind coming along to the magistrate to be confronted by them."

Nudged along by the bayonets on the soldiers' muskets and under the curious eyes of bystanders, they were forced from the wharf and along the village's single street toward a log cabin at its end.

"A fine pickle we're in," Caleb muttered.

Shame at their present position chaffed him like a hair shirt. He'd always prided himself on being a respectable mariner. Now, before the eyes of this backwoods village, he was being marched off at gunpoint to possible prison, on a scurrilous charge.

"Aye." Duncan walked by his side, waving occasionally to the crowd, who yelled back warm support for the pair and derision for the sergeant and his company. "But as you may recall, it wasn't me who got us involved with that troublesome pair."

"Damn it, Dunc, don't you think I remember?"

"I'm certain sure you do, but not to worry. As soon

as we come face to face with them, I've no doubt they'll see the folly of telling lies about two men who have behaved as perfect gentlemen toward them. Take that bloody scowl off your face, man, and smile at the people. If all else fails, we may need the populace to break us out of whatever type of cage it is they call a jail. So far it looks as if they're on our side, and the sergeant and his men are not in their good graces."

****

"Get in there!" The sergeant nudged Caleb in the back with his bayonet as he hesitated before the plank door of the small log building.

He yanked open the door and stepped inside. The air, swarming with dust motes and flies, reeked of stale tobacco, sweat and rum. A fat, blurry-eyed man sat behind a rough-hewn table littered with soiled documents. His neckcloth hung limp and dirty, his waistcoat stained with food and drink.

To one side stood the two villains who were the cause of their present predicament. A black-gowned nun, her expression stern and haughty, hands thrust up the wide sleeves of her robe, stood ramrod straight before her two cringing female companions. A pair of nuns stayed humbly in the background.

"Sweet Jesus!" Cal muttered.

"So these are the two rogues who defiled a couple of innocent young women." The magistrate drew a hand across his mouth. He paused to belch. "'Scuse me, Reverend Mother. Well, we know how to deal with such rubbish in this port. Although it should be a hanging offense, in my opinion, the best that it's in my power to hand out is several years in the provincial jail. What do you think of that, you bastards? Pardon,

Reverend Mother." He glanced up at the austere woman. "Damned good thing you don't understand English. Jenkins!" He jerked his head toward one of the young officers. "Translate…without any language unfit for the lady's ears."

"Aye, sir." The young officer turned to the nun and spoke in what sounded to Caleb to be fluent French.

"Jenkins has a French mother," the magistrate said. "He'll keep negotiations clear between all of us."

"And how would the Reverend Mother be knowing anything of their so-called plight?" Duncan asked. "Does she understand English?"

"No, but that lady here"—the magistrate gestured at the princess—"speaks French."

"Bugger all!" Caleb glanced over at her. *Damn me. I should have thought of it. Most of the European aristocracy speaks French.*

Meanwhile the Reverend Mother and Jenkins had been engaged in a conversation, part of which included nods toward Caleb and Duncan.

"Sir." The young officer finished his talk with the woman and turned to the magistrate. "The Reverend Mother says she's spoken with the ladies and together they've come to another solution to this problem."

"Aye, and what might that be? If it will save me any trouble, I'm eager to hear it." He burped and excused himself once again to the nun.

"Seeing as how their reputations have been forever ruined, they've agreed to let the captain and his friend marry them."

Chapter Twelve

"Good God! Marry them?" The impact of the idea hit Caleb like an uppercut to the jaw.

"It sounds like a simple and sensible solution." Duncan MacDougal's words further shocked him. "I'll consider the offer as soon as I know who I've the privilege of addressing."

"Jacob Lock, magistrate for this county, but I hardly think it necessary to introduce myself to the likes of you."

"Of course not, sir, of course not."

Caleb could only stare at his mate. *Has the man taken leave of his senses?*

"So you're willing to entertain the proposition, MacDougal... Is that your name?" Jacob Lock squinted down at a paper on his desk.

"Aye, Duncan MacDougal, your humble servant, sir." He bowed. "If you'll do the honor of presiding over our nuptials, we can get right to it."

Sweet Jesus, what...! Caleb sucked air into his lungs so sharply he choked.

"Sounds like a sensible solution." Jacob shifted his wide bottom on the chair to allow him to face the young officer, and wheezed his relief. "Jenkins, tell the Reverend Mother these men will wed that pair and pass the information along to the French-speaking lady. We'll await their decision."

"I beg permission to speak to my companion in private conference." Coming out of shock, Caleb spoke.

"I'll grant it provided you're accompanied by two officers." The magistrate pulled a bottle from beneath the table that served as his desk, unscrewed the cap, and took a long pull. "'Scuse me, Reverend Mother, but I'm terrible dry this day. Jenkins, explain it to her."

"Outside, and be quick about it." The sergeant nudged Duncan with his bayonet.

"No need to prod, laddie, no need to prod." The mate held up a hand.

"Get along, you bit of flotsam, or I'll give you something to whine about."

Followed by the officer and one of his men, Duncan and Caleb were herded out of the room.

Once the door had closed on the sound of Jenkins putting forth what he guessed was an explanation of his mate's daft proposal, Caleb swung on their guards.

"Step off and let us have privacy," he snapped. "You can't seriously expect us to try to escape with two muskets ready to fire leveled at us."

They moved away a few paces but kept their weapons trained on the pair.

Caleb grabbed Duncan by an arm and swung him to face him.

"Are you mad, man?" he hissed. "Have you taken leave of your senses? Marry that pair? Stuck for life with one who can't speak English and another who can't stop?"

"Calm yourself, Cal." Duncan removed his captain's hand from his arm. "Did you get a good look at that drunken lout of a magistrate? Any marriage he'll perform will be as legal as piracy. We'll go through the motions, then take our lovely brides on to the next convent, dump them in the dark of night, and be gone before another Reverend Mother can bring us to task. Think about it, Cal. We have to get out of here. We can't afford to leave the *Jenny Jones* unattended much longer, or she'll fall victim to vandals. Without us to lead them, our crew isn't much good."

"Sweet Jesus!"

"You can swear all you like, Captain Caleb Cameron. You can even go to provincial prison if you choose, but I'm going to marry that foul-mouthed vixen and leave this blasted village in my wake on the next tide."

"Oh, so if I don't go along with your mad plan, you'll steal my ship." Caleb's outrage was reaching fever pitch.

"Not steal, take to safety. As soon as you've served your time, probably after the war and when our chance to make our fortunes is over, I'll come back for you."

"You? Master of the *Jenny Jones*?" Caleb caught an all-too-familiar taunting in the Scotsman's tone and countenance. "You'd run her aground before you got three leagues toward sea."

"Hardly. You've taught me well."

Caleb heaved a deep sigh and stared out toward the wharf where his ship was moored. *What a bloody pickle. And I have no one I can honestly blame but myself. Much as I'm loath to admit it, this mad scheme of Dunc's just might get us out of here. Bloody hell, I can't think of any other solution.*

"Very well, Duncan MacDougal. I'll go along with your insanity. I hope to hell you're right about the illegality of that old bastard's marriage ceremony. I don't fancy being tied for life to a creature who's as haughty as a queen, an all-around pain in the backside, and to top it off cannot say a single word in my language."

"Better than my fate with cne who knows far too many." Duncan's mouth quirked at one corner. "Now let's get to it. The sooner we get this over with, the sooner we'll get back to the *Jenny Jones*."

****

"Well?" Back inside the dirty building, Jacob Lock faced the pair. "What's your final decision?"

"We'll…marry these…ladies." Caleb could barely force out the words as he looked over at the princess, who stood glaring at him.

"Good, very good." The magistrate shuffled about among the soiled papers on his desk. "The Reverend Mother is convinced it is the best solution, especially given the possibility that there may be…er… consequences." He struggled to his feet and rounded his desk. "I've no formal marriage document, but I reckon writing a sentence or two to the effect that I've married the pair of you on this day in the year of our Lord such and such and all four of you sign it, that will be sufficient. The Reverend Mother and her ladies can serve as witnesses." He drew himself up and stuck out his belly. "Stand before me. First you, MacDougal, or whatever you call yourself, and the lady of your choice."

"Just a bloody minute." The lady's maid stepped forward. "I'm having second thoughts. "Perhaps I'll return to the convent and take the veil."

"Take the veil?" The magistrate, clearly becoming weary of the whole business, snapped at her. "By your own testimony, early this day, you're damaged goods, young woman. I'd advise you to take this man up on his offer to make a respectable woman of you and be sharp about it."

She glanced over at her mistress. Something Caleb couldn't interpret but which must have advised consent passed between them.

"Very well." She marched across the room to join Duncan, who was already standing in front of Jacob Lock. "Say the words."

It took only a few sentences as Duncan and his lady stood before the magistrate.

"Sign here." The magistrate, swaying on his feet, shoved a paper toward them. "I'll fill in the required words above your names later."

After a sly wink at his bride, Duncan bent over the desk, took up a quill, dipped it into a stained inkwell, and scrawled on the paper. When he'd finished, he handed it to the dark-haired woman by his side.

"Not having second thoughts, are you, my love?" he grinned when she hesitated.

She swallowed hard, then drew him down that she might whisper into his ear. Caleb saw his mate listen, then nod and whisper something back to her. He bent and wrote again before handing her the quill.

She's making an X, I'll wager. Can't read or write. Duncan surely is getting a gem.

"There, done and done." The magistrate sucked in a great breath that puffed out his chest. "Next."

He turned to Caleb and indicated he was to come before him.

"Not quite finished, your honor." Duncan swept his bride into his arms to cover her mouth with his, to half-lift her off her feet in a passionate embrace. An astonished audience fell silent. The bride offered no protest but, to Caleb's astonishment, seemed, after a moment to melt into her new husband's arms. When the kiss continued, Jacob Lock lost patience.

"All right, all right, enough of that!" The magistrate put a stop to it. "You other two. Get up here before me."

Duncan slowly released his bride, a sly, suggestive grin crossing his features as he looked down at her. Seemingly mesmerized, she gazed up at him..

"I said enough!" the magistrate, weary of the proceedings, bellowed. "You other two. Get over here."

When Caleb moved into position beside the princess, he caught the mate's lustful expression as he watched his bride come to her senses and sashay away, hips swinging.

"Bloody hell, man!" he hissed at Duncan as he stepped past him. "Don't even think about it."

"As a married man, I have my rights, Captain."

"Damn you for a fool, Duncan MacDougal!"

"You, young lady, get beside your man." Jacob Lock was rapidly losing patience with the affair that was keeping him from his bottle. The princess looked blank.

"Bugger all! Jenkins," he bellowed. "Speak a language she understands and get her up her beside this bastard— Excuse me, Reverend Mother, but this quartette is fair driving me mad."

The young soldier did as he was bidden, but the princess remained where she was. Her face stern, the Reverend Mother took her firmly by an arm and led her to stand beside Caleb. She gave a solemn nod to Jacob

Lock and stepped away.

Short minutes later the deed was done, and Caleb bent over the desk to sign the filthy bit of paper. The princess drew herself up regally as he handed her the quill, gave him a withering look, then added her signature to the document.

"Do not expect me to behave as my randy friend," Caleb snapped when she straightened and turned to look at him.

Green eyes flashed contempt up into his blue ones.

"Enough, enough." The magistrate grabbed up their marriage document and folded it clumsily. "I'll fill in the rest of the nonsense required by law later and hand it on to the good Reverend Mother for safekeeping. Now get out of my sight. I've had enough bloody trouble for one day. 'Scuse me again, Reverend Mother."

Chapter Thirteen

Captain Caleb Cameron strode up the gangplank of his ship, the two women behind him, Duncan MacDougal bringing up the rear. He'd once heard a drunk in a tavern refer to his wife as a ball and chain, and that's exactly what he felt he was dragging behind him.

Free. Half-assed free. Bloody hell, I can't wait to get to another French convent where I can dispose of my so-called wife and her foul-mouthed companion once and for all.

But when he stopped on reaching the deck and turned on her, he felt his body react. *She is beautiful, so damned beautiful—slim, with a shape that thickens in all the correct places. And it's been a long time since... Stop it, man. Just stop it. Otherwise you'll find yourself behaving as that great fool MacDougal, who's even now watching his bride saunter ahead of him with all the subtlety of a tomcat.*

Princess Cassandra tilted her head to one side and favored him with a defiant glance as she walked past. His crew, standing about, watched, curiosity apparent in their expressions.

"Gentlemen." The maidservant paused and cast her most disarming smile over the men. "I have an announcement to make. The princess has, this fine morning, married your captain, and I have wed the

Jenny Jones' first mate, Mr. Duncan MacDougal. I hope you'll be wishing us well."

"Sweet Jesus!" The curse was a mutter as Caleb glared at the dark-haired woman.

Surprise apparently rendering them silent, for a moment the crew didn't respond. Then Munro pulled off his cap and threw it in the air. "Three cheers for the captain, Mr. MacDougal, and their ladies!" he yelled.

As the cries of hip-hip-hurray rose in the air, Caleb stifled the urge to hustle the pair below deck, thrust them into their cabin, and slam the door. Instead he acknowledged the men's good wishes with a nod of his head and the best attempt at a pleased expression he could muster.

"Thank you, gentlemen," he forced himself to reply when the cheers subsided. "Now I see that during our absence the errant among you have returned. We'll be getting underway directly. Mr. MacDougal, set things in order while I take our ladies below."

"Aye, sir. Men, to work. The breeze is freshening. No time to waste."

"Ladies…" As his mate strode off, bellowing orders, and the crew scattered to do his bidding, Caleb swung out an arm to indicate the way to their living quarters. "Your cabin awaits."

"Our cabin!" the maid servant snapped. "I think not, Captain. The princess, as your wife, will be sharing your living quarters. Your officer will be sharing our former lodgings with me."

"Don't be daft, woman!" Caleb confronted her. "I'll not be sharing my quarters with a woman I married to avoid prison, and neither will Mr. MacDougal."

"Don't you dare order us about." Her dark eyes

sparked defiance as she hissed at him and bristled. "You'll do exactly as I say, or her highness and I will disrupt this vessel with more wailing and screaming than you will know how to handle, you great bit of flotsam!" She stepped forward to stand inches in front of him, hands on her hips, eyes narrowed in threat as she glared up into his face and spoke in a soft, threatening murmur. "There must be at least one among your rowdy crew who has compassion for women and will incite others to come to our aid. They've all had mothers, some sisters, some even sweethearts and wives. You'll have a mutiny on your hands, Captain."

"Argh!" With more than one reason for frustration rushing hot and chaffing up through his body, Caleb herded them toward the hatch.

****

"Captain."

Caleb emerged onto the deck after seeing the pair ensconced in their respective cabins. He was intent on checking his ship's readiness to set sail when an unpleasantly familiar voice hailed him. Looking down to the wharf, he saw the Reverend Mother and the two Sisters, accompanied by Sergeant Joshua Miller and a pair of soldiers. The nuns carried sacks.

"Aye, what is it now, Sergeant?" He paused and grasped the rail in both hands, struggling, out of respect for the religious women, to keep the annoyance that still rankled him to the bone from spilling over. Watching the princess critically perusing his cabin had been enough to drive a man to jump overboard.

"Clothing." The officer squinted up at him. "The good Sisters have gathered together clothing for the women. They believe it's sinful for them to continue to go about clad as they are in men's apparel."

"Aye, well, that was thoughtful. Murphy," he bellowed to one of his sailors busily coiling ropes. "Get down there and free the good Sisters from their burdens."

As the man scuttled to do the captain's bidding, the Reverend Mother looked up at Caleb, bright eyes berating him with the intensity of their stare.

"*Merci*, Reverend Mother." He used one of his few French words to try to lessen the strength of her condemnation.

A disgruntled grunt was her response as she turned away, and her companions, freed of their burden, followed. Apparently even his marrying the princess hadn't been enough penance to put him in her good graces.

"Cast off those mooring lines," the sergeant ordered. "And get out of here. You've caused me enough trouble. I won't be happy until I see your wake disappear in the distance."

"We're of a mind, Sergeant." Caleb watched his men freeing the *Jenny Jones* from the wharf as Duncan continued to pace about the deck giving orders.

****

"So we're married to those two creatures." Annie plunked herself down on a chair in the captain's cabin. Ginny had come to join her and they'd donned the shapeless cotton nightshifts the nuns had provided. "Now they'll have to take us along on their privateering venture and let us get rich along with them."

Night had fallen with the *Jenny Jones* rocking steadily forward.

"That they will," murmured Ginny, curled up like a

kitten replete with cream on the master's bed. A soft, vacant smile turned up the corners of her mouth and softened her brown eyes.

"Ginny, what is wrong with you? You're acting addled. You do realize we'll have to be prepared to keep those louts at bay? They've now got legal rights to our beds. We definitely don't want to end up with child."

"I'm not so sure I want to keep Duncan MacDougal out of my bed." The smile spread and grew even more absentminded.

"Ginny, what in God's name...?"

"Oh, Annie, that man is pure magic." The words sounded like a contented purr. "I've never felt anything like that kiss. It set me all a-tingle, head to toe. And when he thrust me against his body..."

"Ginny!"

"I know, I know." She flashed out of her dream state. "He and his friend took us prisoners, forced us on this voyage, but..."

"But?"

"They've behaved as gentlemen. We've been treated with respect. And they deposited us at a convent where we'd have been safe and cared for."

"Good God! The man's seduced you with a single kiss. Ginny, I thought you were stronger, I thought..."

"Well, you thought wrong, Annie Pudden...or I should say, Mrs. Caleb Cameron. I'm a flesh-and-blood woman, and Duncan MacDougal has made me feel like one from the tips of my toes to the top of my head. Maybe, if you gave the good captain half a chance, he could do the same for you!"

"Ginny...!"

"Annie, don't let's quarrel." Ginny stood and walked across the cabin to put an arm around her friend's shoulders. "I promise my first loyalty will always be to you."

"Please, please, be very careful, Ginny." Annie stifled her annoyance in concern for her friend and put a hand over hers. "I've nothing against your enjoying any of the pleasures your husband may have to offer, but I suspect he's a bit of roué. I don't want you getting hurt."

"Trust me." Ginny gave her friend's fingers a squeeze before returning to her perch on the bed. "I'm no fool. Now we'd best be quiet. I hear your lord and master coming down the ladder."

Chapter Fourteen

"Out!" Caleb pulled open his cabin door and bellowed the order at the maidservant perched on the edge of his bed. Her mistress sat in a chair by his desk. Both she and the princess were attired in the bag-shaped cotton nightshifts he presumed the nuns had provided, gray woolen shawls likely from the same source about their shoulders. The pair appeared to have made themselves at home.

"What!" The servant jumped to her feet. "You can't go ordering us about! This"—she pointed to the princess—"is your wife. And I'm her lady's maid, here to assist with her toilet."

"Well, now you've obviously assisted, so be off with you! You've a place to go only a few feet from this cabin, thanks to the generosity of that rogue who is supposed to be your husband."

The saucy wench stood, glanced at her mistress, and shrugged before sauntering to the door he held open.

"Mind you treat her well." She tossed him a brazen glance. "She is a royal princess. By the by, I've been curious about a heavy door at the bottom of the ladder that leads down to this dungeon you call living quarters. From its position, I'd wager it's an opening to the cargo section of this great tub. I also noticed it is barred with a great thick plank. This floating bucket isn't a slaver, is it?"

"Don't talk daft, woman. You'll find no manacles or restraining chains aboard the *Jenny Jones*. That plank simply keeps cargo from bursting into this living area during rough weather. What would give you such a mad idea?"

"Well, my princess and I *are* your prisoners." She faced him, chin stuck out, shoulders back. "I wanted to make certain you didn't, at some point, plan to cast us into a dank, miserable prison if we failed to do your bidding."

"Argh!" His farewell was a snarl as she sauntered past him.

"Now." He slammed the door behind her and swung on the princess. "I've work to do. You will oblige me by being quiet." When she raised questioning eyebrows, he muttered an expletive. Out of the corner of his eye, he saw her shrug, then begin to roll up a blanket to make a division down the center of the bed. Glancing toward her moments later, he saw she'd settled herself for the night at the rear of the bed beyond the barrier, her back turned to him.

"Bloody hell." He crossed the cabin and took another look at the princess before turning his attention to a section of the mahogany wall in front of him. Putting his fingers on a rise disguised in the paneling, he pressed. A small room slid silently into view. His log book and other ship's documents lay on a shelf inside. He stepped inside, gathered up the former and retreated, easing the secret door shut after him.

It always amazed him how well hidden the compartment was and how he'd discovered it one night when, staggering as a storm tossed his ship, he'd chanced to stumble against the release point. When he and Duncan had purchased the *Jenny Jones* at auction, they'd had no idea of its existence, but he'd been quick to make use of it as a safe place for his most valuable documents. Perhaps the former owner had used it for smuggling. He didn't care. It came in handy for hiding valuables like his log book and insurance documents. And if he'd been married willingly to a lady, he'd have stored their marriage lines there, as well. As it was…

Sitting down at his desk, he glanced at the woman in his bed. A soft snore assured him she slept. He glanced over at the gleaming copper tub he'd had installed in a corner after his last voyage. It was an indulgence, he knew, but he did enjoy soaking in warm water after a hard day's work. Now with this creature in residence, he'd have scant to no opportunity to use it. With an exhale that was half exasperation, half relief, he bent over the journal and began to write.

A half hour later, he stood, stretched cramped shoulders, and moved to return his log book to its secret hiding place. With it once more restored to safekeeping, he paused to gaze at the golden hair spread out over the pillow on his bed. Finally, with a shrug, he pulled his shirt over his head and began to loosen his belt. He'd never enjoyed sleeping fully dressed and never did so except in bad weather when he could be summoned on deck at any moment.

"Hell and damnation, Ginny, hold your tongue! It's our one chance to get away from this life of 'yes, milady, no, milady, yes, sir, no, sir.' These two great louts are our ticket to freedom, don't you see?"

His breath caught in his throat. *The woman is talking English.* He stared down at her, too astonished for a moment to be outraged. *Spouting it like a scullery maid…or a dock girl…calling Duncan and me great louts.*

"Princess, are you? With the tongue of a bloody servants' hall wench?" He caught her by a shoulder and shook her.

Eyes snapping wide open, she stared up at him. After a moment's hesitation, she burst into a tirade in the type of dialect she'd been spouting whenever she spoke since they'd met.

"Stop! Stop it! You were talking English in your sleep…tavern English. Exactly who are you, *Princess Cassandra?*" Outrage scalded over every inch of body and soul. *Bloody hell, what kind of awful mistake have I made?*

She pulled herself to a sitting position and heaved a sigh that reeked of annoyance.

"Very well." She squared her shoulders and looked at him with an unfaltering gaze. "My name is Annie Pudden, and my friend is Ginny Tart. I assume you were commissioned to kidnap the real Princess Cassandra and her lady's maid. You made a mistake. We took advantage of your blunder."

"No, no, no!" The words came out in an exasperated gush of shock. "That cannot be! You were dressed as a princess, and your hair…"

Then the thought hit him.

She understood when I warned her to silence on the night we took them from the manor house. Damn me for a fool not to have remembered!

"You may as well know." She heaved an exasperated sigh. "I was lady's maid to the princess. My friend was a parlor maid."

"But you were in the princess's bedchamber, dressed in her clothes... Your hair..." Words tumbled out, although he hardly knew he was mouthing them. *Good God, the trollop has the audacity to be looking up at me as if I'm beneath her contempt!*

"There was a soiree at a manor house several miles away. All the gentlefolk had gone. Ginny and I thought we'd take advantage of the situation to enjoy a bit of dressing up shenanigans. You and your great brute of a friend simply chose the wrong moment to kidnap the princess and her maid."

"Ah, bloody hell!" He swung away from her and began to pace the room.

"Sir, since you now know the truth, I'd be most grateful if you'd put on some clothing and refrain from blaspheming. Although I'm not a princess, I expect appropriate decorum."

"*Decorum?* You have the temerity to expect decorum? A serving wench who has falsely represented herself to inveigle her way into my life, and who, worst of all, has gotten herself married to me?"

"Very well, if you're going to be difficult, we'll talk in the morning. Perhaps a good night's sleep and a hearty breakfast will mellow your mood." She turned her back to him and settled once more for sleep.

He stared. Confident she was in control of the situation, the bold wench was cool as a winter's frost.

"Bollocks!" Unable to stop blaspheming as she'd called it, he flung himself into the chair behind his desk and put his head in his hands. *What a bloody mess.*

Then, as another aspect of the situation trickled into his mind, a bit of his ire eased. By now, William might possibly be married to the horse-faced princess who couldn't speak a word of English. He smirked.

Serves the wimpy bastard right, always relying on me to get him out of scrapes.

He glanced over at the woman. She sighed, apparently unperturbed by the situation, seemingly lost in sleep.

Bugger all. I'm married to the biggest mistake of my life. Annie Pudden. Good God, what a ridiculous name...as ridiculous as this entire situation.

With a warm, contented-sounding sigh, she snuggled deeper into the bed. *Contented as a cat full of cream.* He couldn't take it. He stood, pulled his shirt back on, grabbed up his coat, and strode out the door, banging it shut behind him in the hopes of disturbing her tranquility.

On deck, he found his mate standing amidships, hands on his hips, his gaze focused on the lightly ruffled sea beyond the ship's bow, his enjoyment in the moment obvious in his expression as the *Jenny Jones* rose and fell rhythmically with the swell. Above the wind-inflated sails, a black velvet sky adorned with a sparkle of stars surrounded a slip of a new moon.

Normally Captain Caleb Cameron would have joined Duncan MacDougal in the enjoyment of this perfect night, but with mind and spirit at odds with any semblance of peace, he strode to his mate's side, ready to be belligerent with the man to ease his annoyance.

"Mr. MacDougal," he addressed the man. "I've matters to discuss with you."

"Oh, aye." Aroused from his thoughts, Duncan MacDougal turned to face him. "Right bonny night, eh, Cal. Lets a man know he's chosen the proper way to spend his years."

"It might be if it were not for those two creatures to whom we've ended up wed."

"What now? I have to say, Cal, I'm getting right weary of your bellyaching about those women. Might I remind you, getting us mixed up with them in the first place was your doing. Never mind. We'll be rid of them soon enough. We should be nearing the mouth of the Restigouche by dawn. Afterwards, all we have to do is head for that other convent Doucet told us about and drop them on its doorstep."

"It would be closer to leave them somewhere up the Miramichi River than sailing miles farther north," Caleb snapped. "I can't wait to be rid of them."

"Aye, but you know as well as I that area is well settled by English. In all likelihood there's a militia unit stationed there, and there'll be a number of ocean-going vessels capable of giving pursuit. Doucet assures me the convent at the mouth of the Restigouche River is small and relatively isolated. With the river shallowing not far from its mouth, it's unlikely there will be any vessels in the area capable of taking out after us, he says. It's a river best suited to canoes."

"Might I remind you that this plan is a near mirror image of our previous one? Have you forgotten how that turned out?"

"Aye, but this time I've been right careful with the details. I'll see to it that their supper wine is even better dosed with laudanum. They'll never expect us to try the same thing twice, especially since they now consider themselves our lawful wives.

"Once they've fallen under its influence, we'll truss them up and row them ashore. Doucet has relatives near the mouth of the Restigouche. He'll go to one of their houses and engage a young lad to watch over them until dawn. Once they're awake, he'll pretend to happen upon them and offer to take them to the safety of a nearby convent. We now know the princess can speak and understand French, but by the time she's told their story to the good Sisters, we'll be far out in the gulf, well on our way to Saint John and an outfitting as privateers, ready to obtain those letters of marque and reprisal."

"Princess!" Caleb could contain his outrage no longer. "Nothing could be further from the truth. The *princess* has just confessed her true identity...in servant's hall English!"

"Whit?" Duncan MacDougal stared at him. "No, it cannot be." His tone dropped to soft disbelief.

"The princess—who, by the way, has commandeered my bed—talks in her sleep...in the King's own English. Her companion, your wife, is a parlor maid."

For a moment his mate stood staring at him in the light of moon and stars.

"Well, well, they're a cunning pair!" A chuckle sounded deep in his throat. "Snookered both of us clever bastards. In truth, it's a blessed relief. We might not swing for taking away a couple of serving girls. Good God, Cal, what a whale of a mistake!"

"I'm glad you can find humor in the situation." Caleb's anger boiled over into sarcasm. "I reckon you could no more read what yours scrawled on the marriage paper any more than I could decipher the so-called princess's signature. That drunken sod who married us didn't bother to check names...just 'do you take this woman' and 'do you take this man.' At this last bit you'll remember, your doxy nudged the so-called princess to nod. What actors! The wench understood every word."

"Aye, aye." Duncan stifled mirth.

"For God's sake, man, stop snickering!" Caleb's annoyance was being exacerbated by his mate's taking it all as a joke. "I assume that yours whispered to you that she couldn't write and you recorded her name while she signed with an X. What moniker did yours ask you to write for her?"

"Sophia Mannering."

"Bloody hell! And you didn't find that strange? That the woman once reputed to be one of the most notorious in England and now dead, had fallen into our clutches in the guise of a maidservant?"

"Who?"

"Ah, you great ignorant lout! Don't you read the newspapers? Your bride is no more Lady Sophia Mannering than I'm a horse's rear end! Her real name is Tart, Ginny Tart."

For a moment Duncan stared at his captain. Then he burst out laughing again, doubling over in his mirth.

"And what's your beloved spouse called?" he finally managed. "Betsy Bun?"

"Pudden, Annie Pudden."

"Holy Mother, Pudden! This just gets better and better." Again the mate gave himself over to mirth.

"Argh!" Caleb ground his teeth. "I can see there's no talking sense to a great oaf like you. You're about as capable of finding a solution to this mess as a rum-soaked guttersnipe. I'll talk to you in the morning."

"Wait, wait." Duncan brought himself under control. "There's no need to go getting your tail in a knot. I'll make sure and certain the plan isn't foiled this time."

"Fine. But that doesn't remove the fact that we're still married to them."

"Of course we're not." Duncan moved closer and spoke softly so that the helmsman couldn't hear. "Since you say my bride definitely isn't Sophia Mannering, and I didn't sign my actual name on that dirty piece of paper that sodden old magistrate made out as marriage lines, there's no binding contract."

"What! You didn't sign your own name?" Caleb stared at his companion.

"You did?"

"Of course. I'm a reasonably honorable man. How, may I ask, did you identify yourself? That sergeant knew your true name when he came to summon us."

"I felt right certain that drunken lout wouldn't bother to look over what we wrote. He was too eager to get rid of us and the good Sisters and get back to his bottle. Furthermore, I was damned sure he was too far gone in his cups to be able to focus on anything by way of written words. So I signed myself as John Cake in a messy scrawl. Good God, Caleb, I didn't think I had to instruct you in the art of subterfuge, not at your age and with your past."

"John Cake? John Cake? Johnny Cake? Argh!"

"The name just came to me. I've always been right fond of johnny cakes. Did you know they were so named because they travel well in saddlebags—journey cakes—but some people think they were named Shawnee cakes because of the Indian tribe that taught white settlers to make…"

"Bugger all, I don't need a blasted history lesson!"

Another galling thought flashed across his mind as he turned to go back to his cabin.

"You're not planning on sleeping with the so-called Mrs. MacDougal when your watch is over, are you?" He moved close enough to hiss at his mate, below the hearing of the helmsman. "Because, even if her name and station do suggest..."

"Ah, Cal, what do you take me for?" Duncan MacDougal became deadly serious. "I'd not do any such thing when we're planning on abandoning her and her companion. I slung a hammock in my cabin while she was making herself comfortable in my bunk. I've not the luxury of a large room and bed such as you. I'm assuming you'll be playing the gentleman, as well?"

"Do you have to ask?" Caleb strode to the bow, where he watched the *Jenny Jones*'s prow cutting smoothly through the light swell. Throwing back his head, he drew a deep breath of salt-tinged air. He needed time to regain his composure before he returned to his cabin and the trouble it contained. This was the place to do it...with the sea and ship he loved.

Chapter Fifteen

"Ginny, wake up!" Annie Pudden eased open the door of Duncan MacDougal's small cabin and hissed at her friend.

"Wha...what?" In the light of a lantern, a dark-haired head turned on the pillow, and eyes of the same color struggled open.

"I followed the captain onto deck just now and hid behind a cask." Annie ducked under the hammock strung parallel to the bunk and sat down on the edge of the latter. "He was so annoyed at being forced to marry me, I reasoned he'd have yet another plan to rid himself of us. I overheard it. Oh, Ginny, for heaven's sake, pay attention! One of them might come at any minute. It's our future I'm talking about."

"Right, right." Ginny pulled herself up and placed her shoulders against the wall at the bunk's head. "So what is their scheme this time? I thought we were secure, that we'd sail with them as their wives." Rubbing sleep from her eyes, she yawned.

"Hardly. Even before I talked English in my sleep and the captain discovered we weren't who we've been pretending to be..."

"Bloody hell! You talked in your sleep? Now we're well and truly boiled."

"They would have found out eventually." Annie tried to dismiss her faux pas. "Of course the captain was furious and strode out. I guessed he'd want to discuss his discovery with his mate, so I followed, hid behind a water cask on deck, and listened." She drew a deep breath before continuing.

"I've known something was wrong since I realized we were heading north, not south toward Saint John. The story the captain told when I confronted him, something about their having to deliver goods in that direction before we could proceed to the destination where they'd get those licenses to privateer had the ring of a lie to it. I was right! Ginny, we're on our way up the coast of New Brunswick to a river called the Restigouche, where they plan to leave us trussed up on the grounds of another French convent."

"You mean they're going to try the same trick again?" Wide awake, Ginny Tart stared at her companion. "Do they take us for fools? They must be daft! Or do they think they can turn us into blinkin' nuns?"

"I don't believe they thought that far ahead into our futures." Annie drew a deep breath. "They just want to be rid of us. What the good Sisters do with us isn't their concern. They also think we'll never suspect them of trying the same thing twice."

"A plague on the pair of them." Ginny slammed her fisted right hand into the palm of her left. "If I were a man…"

"But you're not. And do keep your voice down. We must rely on our wits. Now listen, here's what I propose."

****

"Becalmed out in this damned bay! What rotten luck! At this rate, any number of ships will get to Saint

John ahead of us and apply for letters of marque. Bloody hell!"

Captain Caleb Cameron paced the deck as the *Jenny Jones* rested peacefully on the mirror-like surface of Chaleur Bay—the mouth of the Restigouche, where they planned to rid themselves of the women, still miles away. Moonlight illuminated the great sails hanging limp and impotent above him.

"Keep your voice down, Cal." His mate leaned against the butt of the mainmast. "If it's as you said, that this country without a navy is looking for every able-bodied man and ship to fight the Americans, there'll be no problem getting a license. Did you ever see such a perfect silver moon? Relax and enjoy the night. The rest of the men are."

Indeed they are, the lazy layabouts. Caleb looked around at his crew lounging about the bulwarks toward the bow of the vessel. With the ship riding at anchor as it awaited a breeze, even the helmsman had deserted his post and was sitting on the edge of the quarterdeck.

Suddenly, from somewhere near the bow, the sound of a female voice reached him. A woman was singing a beautiful old folk song he hadn't heard since childhood.

"...close by the window young Eileen sits spinning..."

"What the hell..." Startled, he followed Duncan, who was already moving toward the music.

Leaning against the rail, dressed in the emerald green gown she'd been wearing when he'd stolen her from the manor, golden hair flowing over her shoulders, a vision in the moonlight, Annie Cameron nee Pudden stood singing while Munro sat on a keg playing accompaniment on a battered guitar. When the song came to the chorus, he joined in.

As if transfixed by a siren call, the entire crew followed their officers in the direction of the sounds that seemed magical in the moonlight.

"...to her lips lays a finger..."

Caleb had stopped, mesmerized as the others by the beauty of the song and the woman in the sensuous shadows. She had the appearance and voice of an angel.

"...a frightened glance turns to her drowsy grandmother."

She had seen him and was moving toward him, a mesmerizing silhouette in the moonlight.

"Noiseless and light, through the lattice above her..." The words of the old folk song had never sounded so sweet, so filled with magic.

"The maid steps and leaps to the arms of her lover."

At its finish, she paused in front of him and held out her hand, dropping into a deep curtsy.

Whoops and whistles of approval burst from the crew. Caleb remained immobile, transfixed by the woman and her song. She locked up at him. In the starlight he saw she was smiling, a smile of suggestive invitation. The cheers and shouts increased.

"Three cheers for the captain's lady!" And so it went while he remained in her thrall, his hand somehow finding hers and holding it, drawing her upright.

Sweet Jesus, the woman's a raving beauty, a vision. Enough! Bloody hell, be strong, be strong. She's but a serving wench.

With an effort, he snapped back to the moment.

"What do you think you're doing, woman?" He

stepped close to her and hissed into her ear. "Up on deck in the night when you should be sleeping."

"Your crewmen are fine fellows." She cast a dazzling smile over her audience. "They deserve to be entertained during this mind-numbing calm."

Wide, emerald eyes feigning innocence (he believed) gazed up at him. Slowly, sensuously, she raised a hand to run her fingers down his jawline. Annoyance chafed him to the core as he felt his body react. He'd been at sea over a month, and now this woman was daring to tease and torment him.

But then she was stepping back, still gazing up at him with a coyness that left his heart pounding, his body raging. His men's cheering snapped him back to his senses, and he managed to move away to arm's length.

Good God, she's enchanted me.

"That will be enough, gentlemen." He found his voice, but to his shame, it sounded shaken, lacking authority. "To duty or your rest, whichever is your current station."

They moved to obey, their soft chuckles rankling him to the core.

"See what you've done!" he hissed.

"Sir, I must say I cannot understand your annoyance." She smirked up at him. "I could have sworn you enjoyed the moment. I know the men were pleased with being entertained."

"But it's not the province of the captain's wife to do so." He took her by an arm more forcefully than he'd intended and headed her toward the hatch. "By the way," he leaned close to mutter into her ear. "Where's your friend? She's usually a part of your infamy."

"She's not feeling well."

"Never try to tell me she's seasick. She's not had a twinge on the voyage, and now the water's still as glass."

"Womanly troubles, if you must know." She flashed him a demeaning glance. "Not that it's any of your business."

"Oh."

****

"Just what did you think you were about, singing and flaunting yourself on deck before the men?" In his cabin, Captain Caleb Cameron confronted her.

"As I told you, we were simply entertaining your crew during this miserable calm." Annie Pudden faced him, arms crossed on her breast. "Are you such a great tyrant that you would deny your men a little relief in these blessed doldrums?"

"It's been but twelve hours. I doubt they're dying of boredom. In fact, this is a respite for them."

"Ah, yes, a respite." She swung about and sashayed across the room, swinging her curving hips. "But any respite is made better with pleasant entertainment."

"Not when it's provided by the captain's wife, a woman who is expected to behave with dignity and decorum. And as for throwing yourself upon me in front of the crew…"

"Throwing myself upon you! I merely caressed your face."

"Caressed in invitation, more like!"

"You expect quite a lot of me, especially when you give so little in return." She strode back to him, eyes flashing emerald fire. "Well, let me tell you, Captain, if you and your bloody mate don't start treating my friend and me as we deserve, we'll scream rape and brutality at the very first port we enter! And if we don't manage to do it at that one, then at the next or the next or the next. You can't keep us trussed up forever, and as you've experienced, we're not easily disposed of through any of your nefarious schemes."

"Don't threaten me. The areas where we dock aren't easily disturbed by a woman's fishwife accusations concerning her husband. You and your friend are supposed to be our spouses, you'll recall."

"Yes, but we weren't given much choice in the matter, were we? The Reverend Mother and that drunken magistrate all but held pistols to our heads. We'll tell the whole story, and with the right embellishments, I'm sure the horror of our fates will be believed."

"Argh!" Caleb swung away from her self-satisfied smirk. "What exactly is it you want?"

"Ginny and I want to privateer with you." Annie faced Caleb full-on and made the demand. "We want a chance to make a fortune that will free us from being servants for the rest of our lives."

"Good God!" Caleb stared at her. "Privateer with us! Woman, have you taken leave of your senses?"

"No, Ginny and I came to them after you kidnapped us. After we overheard your plans to outfit this fine vessel as a privateer with your ill-gotten gains from our abduction, we saw the opportunity to turn your mistake into our good fortune.

"You've seen us fight, and you've seen us treat the injured," she put forth in argument. "You know we're capable of holding our own in battle. And God knows you need someone who can prepare decent meals and keep a reasonably clean galley. Now, since we are obviously the wounded parties in all of this…"

"Wounded! You've been well treated aboard this vessel and then given the chance to make respectable lives for yourselves in a new country. Since you've chosen not to avail yourselves of these possibilities…"

"Possibilities! What future is in a nunnery? Don't be daft!" She was inches from his face now, green eyes sparking anger, hands on her hips. "We want a life, a real life, with a fine house and gowns and food and…" She paused.

"Go on."

"And a couple of strong, handsome men who can satisfy all our desires." A sly, seductive glance accompanied her words.

He looked down at her, every bit of his body tightening, desiring—with an intensity such as he could not remember previously ever experiencing—this defiant woman standing before him. Visions of taking her into his arms, of sliding that silken gown from her perfect shoulders, of putting his mouth to her neck, of letting his lips slide downward to those round, ripe breasts…

"Bugger all!" With a supreme effort he forced himself to turn away from her.

"So what's your answer, Captain?" She turned and swaggered across the cabin.

Bloody hell, the twit is as cool as a winter's day…after she's left me all but weak-kneed in lusting after her. How many other men has she teased and tormented? How many have called her bluff?

"It's a daft request." Running his hand through his hair, he began to pace the cabin.

A thought struck him, and he stopped abruptly. Why not agree to the woman's brash demands? Tomorrow night she'd be gone. Keeping her quiet for the immediate future was all that mattered.

"Very well, mistress." He swung on her and held out his hand. "You have an agreement."

Looking up at him with what he interpreted as suspicion, she hesitated.

Clever wench. She's rightly thinking I acquiesced too readily.

He felt a surge of relief when she took the proffered hand. Her touch revived his former feelings. He released it, as quickly as if he'd grasped a hot poker, and strode out of the cabin, hoping to cool his ardor in the night air on the deck. The *Jenny Jones* had begun to roll, indicating a breeze. He'd give orders to get the ship underway as fast as it could travel toward the Restigouche and freedom from the misery the woman he'd once thought was a princess was causing him.

Chapter Sixteen

"They're asleep." Duncan came up onto the deck as Alphonse Doucet and Harry Munro eased the anchor into the midnight river. On shore, a large black building stood silhouetted in the moonlight. Two other seamen slowly lowered a cutter into the water.

"Good. I trust their supper wine was spiked with a goodly dose of laudanum?" Caleb faced his friend on the dark deck. Not a single lantern burned on the *Jenny Jones*.

"Spiked it well and good." Duncan drew a deep breath. "Both of them were fast asleep with their heads on your desk, which they were using as a dining table. Their cups had been drained. My lovely bride was snoring lustily when I went to check on them. They're wearing those garments the nuns provided. Good God, those dresses are ugly sacks. Their only pretense to female attire is those bits of cord that draw the cloth in at the waist. They make the pair of them look like inmates of a workhouse."

"Never mind how they're arrayed. Let's get to it. The sooner we're rid of them the better. Truss yours up, and I'll get mine. Take care you cover her mouth. In case the drink wears off, we want no blasphemous screams disturbing the good Sisters at this ungodly hour."

****

The captain and his mate deposited the pair a quarter mile from the convent. For a moment Duncan stood looking down at his bundle.

"You know, Cal, I'll miss her."

"You can wax sentimental all you like once we're back on board and the *Jenny Jones* catches the tide. We have to move quickly. This time there will be no stopping for shore leave until we hit Saint John. Now come on."

"Sure, sure." Heaving a sigh, Duncan MacDougal bent low and followed his captain back into the shadows in the direction of the shore.

On the beach they paused to wait for Doucet, who'd scuttled off to include his nephew in the plan and give the young lad a generous payment for his part in the scheme.

Duncan pulled a flask from his vest, took a long swallow, and handed it to Caleb.

"What's this, Mr. MacDougal?" He jerked his head in the direction of Higgins sitting in the cutter, ready at the oars to row them back to the *Jenny Jones*. Caleb had a hard and fast rule about drinking in front of his crew and never beyond a dram or two at a time even in the privacy of his cabin when at sea. "You know my thinking on such conduct."

"Aye, aye, Cal." The words were a mutter in the darkness. "But this is an exceptional night, you'll have to agree." He shook the flask in front of his captain.

Caleb hesitated, then turned into the shadows beyond Higgins' sight and knocked back a goodly swallow. Returning it to his mate, he muttered, "Illicit though it may be, I believe exceptional circumstances require exceptions. Damn it, what's keeping Doucet?"

****

A half hour later Doucet joined them on the beach.

"What in hell delayed you, man?" Caleb's greeting mirrored his annoyance.

"I haven't seen my uncle and aunt in three years." The man hung his head as he stood before his captain. "And…"

"All right, all right. Get aboard the cutter. The sooner we return to the ship and declare an end to this business, the better."

Once back aboard the *Jenny Jones*, Caleb wasted no time on relaying orders through his mate. "Higgins, Murphy, hoist the anchor. The tide's turning. It'll be at full flood shortly."

"Come on, move your arses!" Duncan followed up Caleb's orders. "The faster we get away from here the better."

"You appear a tad touchy, Mr. MacDougal." Caleb turned to his friend as a cloud drifted away from the moon and he was able to see his companion's face. "And scowling, as well."

"I've no taste for what we've done this night, Captain. Our conduct is unbecoming of gentlemen. Leaving two ladies at the mercy of the elements…"

"Those two! Ladies! At the mercy of the elements! They're both as tough as shoe leather, and it's as fine a summer's eve as you could wish. Furthermore, Doucet's nephew has promised to watch over them and take them to the convent at first light. Mr. MacDougal, I'll thank you to get your mind back to the task of getting this ship out of the river and into free sailing in the bay as soon as the tide warrants."

"Aye, aye, sir." The mate turned away, but the

stiff, stubborn set of his shoulders told Caleb he was far from being in agreement.

"Dunc." He called him back, and when his friend rounded to face him, continued, "I apologize for involving you and the crew in the operation. I had no idea it would turn out to be such a fiasco. Fortunately it's over and done. Now we can head for Saint John."

"Aye." Duncan glanced back toward shore. Caleb caught a note of wistfulness in the man's tone.

"Good God, you *are* missing that woman!"

"Just a tad." He turned to his captain. "What about you? I'll take nothing but the truth."

"I'll admit the one who called herself my wife was a brave—or perhaps I should say brazen—little wench. But there's the rub. Brazen wench. Once we make our fortunes in the war, as wealthy men, we'll have our choice of women…women of birth and manners. Women who don't swear like drunken sailors or swing belaying pins like bloody picaroons. Women who know how to behave in polite society."

"Women who know how to order their maids to dress their hair and squander a king's ransom on clothes and jewels, women who have all the brains and courage of a field mouse? Bah!" The mate strode off to join the helmsman.

Caleb watched him for a moment, then went to the bulwarks to stare down at the river.

Tide's moving like cold molasses. A sailor passing wind would give a better breeze than what we're catching. I could put the men to the sweeps, but I don't want to wear down the crew unless it's absolutely necessary. Stop looking for trouble. Those two are safely trussed up until morning. There's no way they can get to us like they did last time. And no more shore leaves to make us vulnerable. Might as well take advantage of the time to catch a few moments' respite.

He drew a deep breath as he headed down the hatch to his cabin. His cabin. His alone. No more sharing a bed...and not even half a bed at that...the shameless creature had taken more than her portion behind the blanket barrier. No matter that it was well after midnight, he was going to take a bath in the privacy he now had.

"Munro, bring heated water to my cabin. Fill the tub. Now."

"Aye, aye, sir." The man hurried off as Caleb descended.

A hot bath and a dram of my best whisky, free of the danger of interference from those two annoying females. Ahhhh. At the moment I cannot imagine Heaven offering more in the way of comfort.

He strode the short distance to his cabin door and shoved it open. His breath reversed and snagged in his throat.

Chapter Seventeen

Standing beside his bed, her back to him, in the seductive shadows cast by swaying lanterns, stood a woman. Stark naked, she rubbed a length of drying linen through a fall of golden curls.

"Sweet Jesus! What are you doing here?"

"I have returned to my husband." She cast him up a coy glance from beneath lowered lashes as she swung the toweling about her with such skill he got only a glimpse of round breasts and curving hips before she'd turned to face him. "Did you think I would so easily desert you?"

"How…what…" Words tangled on his tongue. *Good God!*

"I overheard your plot to dispose of us…again." With a deft sweep, she fashioned the cloth about her body in a sarong-type garment such as he'd seen women wearing when he sailed in the south seas. "Stupid, really, using the same scheme twice. We are not about to be so easily denied the opportunity to become ladies of wealth and stature. We pretended to drink that dangerous wine. We feigned unconsciousness until you left us poorly trussed up near that convent…apparently you were confident it would be some time before the effects of drink wore off…and we quite easily escaped our bonds."

"How did you get back to the ship?" He remained

just inside the door, too flummoxed to move.

"We're both strong swimmers. Fortunately, Doucet's visit to his relatives gave us ample time. We removed our clothing, tied the lot about our waists—we were not about to cast aside perfectly good garments—and headed for the ship."

"There was supposed to be a young lad watching over you..." He struggled to suppress a stutter.

"Well, if there was, he was late arriving. We encountered no one."

"How did you manage to get aboard? How...?"

"While I was amusing you and your crew with a song and shameless display of lust for the captain of the *Jenny Jones* last evening, Ginny let a rope ladder down near the stern." She swaggered close to him, casting him a sideways glance from beneath long lashes. "Tonight, while you tarried ashore, we swam back to the ship. Your man on watch had fallen asleep amidships. It was easy to slither over the rail and across the deck when clouds hid the moon."

"You won't get away with this!" He came back to fighting form. "I'll cast the pair of you overboard."

"Oh, that would be most unwise, Captain." She started toward the bed but paused to throw him another tantalizing look over a bare shoulder. "The crew has become quite fond of Ginny and me. We cook, we clean, we tend the sick and injured, and I entertain. Also, they've been given to understand we're your wives. You could find yourself with a nasty mutiny on your hands if we were suddenly to disappear. Therefore, you should be grateful for our return. Now, if you'll excuse me..." She continued across the cabin. "I'm cold and tired. Sleep well ..whenever you choose to come to your couch."

She picked up her nightgown lying across the blankets. "I'd be grateful if you'd play the gentleman and have the good grace to turn away while I don my sleeping attire." Again the sly, taunting glance, again the eyelashes lowering seductively.

"Argh!" He whirled and strode out of the cabin, slamming the door behind him. In the narrow corridor he bumped into his mate coming out of his sleeping quarters.

"From your expression, I take it you've met with a similar surprise." Duncan MacDougal chuckled. "You have to hand it to those two. They are as sly as vixens."

"Bugger off, Dunc. They're a bloody nuisance. They stick like burrs in a horse's tail. But," he threw back over his shoulder, "even burrs can be gotten rid of."

****

"A fair, stiff breeze, is it not, Captain?" The following evening Annie came up on deck and joined him as he stood facing forward, watching his ship slice through the wind-ruffled Northumberland Strait. "We're making good time, I'd estimate."

"Aye." He tendered her but a brief glance before turning his attention back to the sea.

"The *Jenny Jones* is a fine vessel." She grasped the rail to steady herself against the ship's progress. He loved the craft, she'd come to realize. It was time to take advantage of this weakness. It would be so much easier if she and the captain had a truce of sorts. Bickering and engaging in a battle of wits was failing to profit either of them and wasting time better spent on plans for their future.

She felt confident she could bring about an agreement, not only because she and Ginny had bested him and his mate on two occasions, but because of the look she'd seen in his eyes when she'd approached him after her siren song. The man might pretend indifference, even annoyance, but that look told her he was a long way from insensible to her charms as a woman.

"We'll arrive in Saint John on Thursday if this keeps up." Although he failed to look at her again, she caught a softening in his demeanor.

"You love sailing, don't you?" She gripped the rail as the ship rose and dipped with more vigor.

"Aye. There's nothing quite like racing before the wind in a gale in a good ship…unless it's racing across the moors on a fine horse. And even that falls a far second."

"I can ride. Rather well, in fact." She tossed him an impudent glance and came to a decision. Now that they were far from England, she'd tell him of her past. Perhaps it would help toward his agreeing to keep them on as privateering partners. "My former mistress, Lady Sophia Mannering, often requested I ride with her instead of one of the grooms."

"Lady Sophia Mannering? You were her servant?" He turned to her, eyes widening with surprise. "*The* Lady Sophia Mannering? She had a notorious reputation. It was rumored she may have been involved in robbing coaches…she and a companion about her own size."

"Aye, a companion about her own size." She looked up at him, green eyes twinkling.

"Nothing was ever proven against her, to the best

of my knowledge." He continued to stare at her. "That companion…was you?"

"Perhaps." She ignored his look and kept her gaze focused on the rising and falling swell before the ship. "I'm not about to confess to anything that could put me in prison or worse, even this distance from the scene of such deeds."

"Now things begin to make sense." He drew in a deep breath. "That's where you learned to fight, to plot, to…"

"To make myself a worthy adversary, Captain?" She let a grin curl her lips as she avoided meeting his astounded gaze.

"No, I was going to say that's where you learned to be an accomplished outlaw."

"*If* Lady Sophia did relieve a few wealthy individuals of a bit of their ill-gotten gains, she saw that it went where it was most needed…to the poor on various estates." She gave her head a defiant toss.

"And did she?" He looked down at her, his tone demanding a truthful answer.

"I said 'if.' Even though she has passed, I'll not go condemning her."

He was startled to see a gleam he believed to be tears in her emerald eyes.

"And 'if' she did, on occasion, act the highwayman, or woman, was her lady's maid by her side?"

"A lady's maid owes her mistress unswerving loyalty."

"And after her death?"

"After her death, her husband wanted to be rid of everything that reminded him of her. He'd tolerated her antics, even lied for her on several occasions. Revealing her duplicity would have ruined his standing, might even have cost him his seat in Parliament, but once she was gone, he burned her gowns, sold her horse, and shipped her lady's maid off to the first vacant position he could find among his peers' households. He wanted no reminders of her left about the estate."

"Thus you ended up in Willie's establishment?"

"Willie?"

"Well, since we're now thousands of leagues from England, I'll tell you my story." As they stood on the starlit deck, he told her of his life and of his association with the Duke of Haverbrook. He ended the tale by explaining how he and Duncan MacDougal had abducted the wrong pair of women.

When he'd finished, he paused, looking into her face for a reaction. For a moment she gazed back, then burst out laughing.

"A wonderful trick to play on such a pompous ass as the duke. Oh, it does amuse me no end. Lady Sophia would be delighted."

And suddenly they were both laughing, joined in mirth over the schemes they'd perpetrated on their so-called betters.

"When did you link your fortunes with your present friend?" he asked finally. "Surely she wasn't from your days with Lady Sophia."

"I met Ginny at His Grace's manor. She was a parlor maid there. After Lady Sophia's death, Lord Mannering foisted me off on his friend the Duke of Haverbrook, who needed a maid who could speak French to accommodate his newly arrived future wife, the Princess Cassandra. Her own servant had died on the voyage to England. Ginny and I became friends, with a dream to escape the drudgery that our lives appeared destined to be, but until you conveniently kidnapped us, we had no real plan."

"So you're telling me I was a catalyst to your future ambitions?"

"My, my, Captain, you do toss big words around." Back under control of her emotions, she slanted him a teasing smile.

"I've told you I attended Cambridge." She saw he was relaxing as he leaned against the bulwarks beside her.

"Where did you join forces with Mr. MacDougal? Judging from his accent, I doubt it was at Cambridge."

"Hardly." He drew a deep breath, grasped the rail, and looked out across the sea. "I finally got disgusted with bailing Willie out of messes and took off. I went to sea. Over the next few years I rose to the rank of captain, eventually obtaining my master's ticket. But I wasn't satisfied. I wanted to own a ship of my own. That's where my first mate came in.

"I met Duncan MacDougal in a London tavern. He'd been instrumental in relieving a few British aristocrats of their purses in the north of England. We got to talking. My ambitions came out, and I told him that in spite of saving over the years I was still a fair bit short of the purchase price of a fine vessel—this one, in fact—that I had my eye on to buy.

"Dunc surprised me by telling me he'd laid aside a fair sum with a similar ambition. He'd done a bit of sailing as a young lad and had learned to love the life. He'd only taken to the ways of a highwayman to raise funds for a ship of his own. Since his takings were still far from sufficient, he'd all but abandoned his dream.

"We did some calculations and discovered that with our two fortunes combined we could just manage the purchase. We made a deal: I'd captain the ship, and Duncan with his lesser investment and experience at sea would be mate. The partnership has proven to be an excellent one…even if he has, by times, gotten us into a few scrapes."

"Oh, and I suppose you've been entirely blameless, Captain?" She cast him a sideways glance, struggling to stifle the grin that threatened to curl her lips.

"No, I'd never say I wasn't responsible for a few incidents that put us in a bit of harm's way. We're well matched, you see. A pair of rogues."

The expression in his eyes when he turned to her made her suck in her breath. For a moment time seemed to cease as they gazed at each other in the starlight on the gently rolling deck. When he drew her into his arms, she went willingly, mesmerized by the man and the night and the stars.

In that instant she understood what Ginny had told her about tingling from her toes to the top of her head…and so much more. His mouth covering hers, his tongue seeking entrance shook her to the roots of her being. When he drew her full length against his body, hard and powerful and desiring, she swirled away into an erotic vortex such as she had never known and would never have believed existed. Her arms went about his neck, and she pressed herself to him, allowing him his wishes.

"Now you'd best be getting below." As suddenly as he'd embraced her, he released her and stepped away. "The wind has taken on a sharp chill. I don't want you becoming ill. A sick crew member isn't something that goes well aboard."

Stunned, she had to grasp the rail to keep from staggering. A coldness that had nothing to do with the stiffening breeze enveloped her.

"As you wish." To her ears, the words sounded squeaky and unnatural. *Good God, what is the man playing at?* "I'll probably be asleep by the time you come to the cabin, Captain, so I'll bid you good night. I will see you in the morning."

With an effort more than anything she could recall previously exerting, she turned and walked to the hatch.

Is he watching me? What is he thinking? What was *he thinking?*

Inside his cabin, she sank into a chair and covered her face with her hands. She'd just let the man know he had the power to seduce her. *Stupid, stupid, stupid!* She'd planned it to be the other way around.

"Annie, are you awake?" Ginny eased open the door and stuck her head inside.

"Yes…yes. Come in. Where is Mr. MacDougal?"

"In our cabin, in his hammock, snoring like thunder. I thought I heard your door open. Where were you?"

"I was on deck…with the captain."

"Oh."

"What do you mean 'oh'?"

"Just that there's something about you…your lips. I'm thinking you've been tasting the captain's charms." She slanted Annie a sly look as she went to curl up on the captain's bed.

"Oh, God, Ginny, he kissed me, and…"

"Oh."

"Stop saying that! Stop sounding so all knowing."

"Well, perhaps I am. Remember how I told you I felt when Mr. MacDougal kissed me after our wedding? I'll wager Captain Cameron treated you to a dose of the same pleasure."

"Good God, Ginny, we can't let those two seduce us! Think of how they tried to rid themselves of us! Think of how…"

"Think of how they've been becoming attached to us, maybe even to admire and desire us?"

"Don't be daft, Ginny."

"I'd dare say I'm thinking way more sensibly than you are right now. So what if we're enjoying those two rogues and might allow ourselves to enjoy them even further? I'm sure, knowing the pair of them, they're equipped to take their pleasures without the danger of getting us with child."

"Ginny, that's disgraceful thinking!"

"You've only just had your first encounter with the captain and a small taste of what he has to offer." Ginny stood and headed for the door. "Once you've had time to reflect, you might come to other conclusions."

She went out, closing the panel softly after her.

Chapter Eighteen

The *Jenny Jones* sailed smoothly into Saint John Harbor. With Caleb's hands on the wheel, she swung alongside the dock. Shore men scuttled to catch the lines her crew cast.

"Ahoy, the *Jenny Jones*!" one of them bellowed, grinning up at Duncan, who stood on the port side supervising her docking. "We've heard news...news of a double wedding! Seems you and your captain got yourselves good and caught!"

"Damnation!" At the wheel, Caleb overheard the jest.

"How would the likes of you be knowing such tidings?" Duncan shot back.

"A militia man arrived from Logerville only yesterday. He told of a rare wedding...a double wedding between two officers for the ship *Jenny Jones* and a princess and her lady's maid, no less."

"Don't go believing everything a drunken soldier tells you." Glancing back at the captain's scowl, Duncan replied jovially. "They're known to exaggerate...and not just tales of their great courage in battle."

"Ah, but he claimed the Reverend Mother from the convent had been a witness. Challenged any of us to ride up there and ask her."

"Well, then." Caleb left his place at the helm as the

ship was made fast to her moorings. "I suppose we can deny it no more. Ladies…" He turned and called across the breadth of the deck to where two figures dressed in dull gray woolen gowns, their hair done up on the back of their heads, had emerged from beneath the quarterdeck. "Come and let us introduce you to these gossip mongers."

Annie came forward, smiling. Ginny followed.

"Gentlemen, allow me to present Mrs. Caleb Cameron and Mrs. Duncan MacDougal."

He drew Annie forward with an arm about her waist and forced what he hoped appeared to be a besotted smile as he gazed down at her. Duncan likewise brought Ginny to the group's attention.

"Well, well, this is a fine tale." One of the older men sporting a growth of gray stubble grinned up at them over gaps in stained teeth. "Never thought you two would end up with balls and chains. Just goes to show, don't it? A pretty face and a comely form can capture even the most wily critters."

A roar of laughter went up from the men. The man who'd spoken raised his hat and shouted, "Three cheers for the captain, his mate, and their ladies. Hip…hip…hurray."

"It seems you two are well liked in this port." Annie cast Caleb a sideways glance as the shouted approval went up. "And that you've been quite a pair of lads…in your day."

"In our day?" Caleb began to protest, but his bride was moving away, throwing a smug smile back over her shoulder at him as she headed back toward their quarters.

"We'll be going ashore directly," she informed him

as she walked. "It's been some time since we set foot on dry land…at our own choosing."

"Just a damned minute." As the cheers on the dock subsided into chuckles and good-hearted ribald remarks, he halted them with a mutter below the hearing of their audience. "You can't go traipsing about Saint John in those sackcloth gowns. People believe you're my wife, our wives." He shot a look at his mate, standing a few feet away, arms crossed on his chest, an amused grin crinkling his weathered face.

"Our wardrobe is extremely limited, sir." She looked up at him, a bold taunting expression further chafing his annoyance. "Aside from what we were wearing when you brought us aboard, we have only the male outfits we made and these gowns the good Sisters provided…which, with all due respect to their generosity, look like clothing for inmates of a debtors' prison. Of course, we could don the clothing in which we arrived aboard, but those outfits might provoke a number of questions you'd rather not answer."

Stymied, Caleb paused.

"Might I offer a solution, Captain?" Duncan MacDougal stepped forward.

"Oh, aye. It might prove amusing." Sarcasm colored Caleb's words.

"Let us delay unloading the *Jenny Jones* a few hours. We can leave Munro and Doucet to guard her while we take our ladies into the town to purchase some much-needed clothing."

"Delay the unloading? Man, are you daft? I want to get rid of this cargo and head for the Court of Vice Admiralty to get those privateering licenses. Afterwards, there will be outfitting to see to…"

"But first I suggest we see to the outfitting of these ladies." Duncan advanced to the group and crooked his arm to Ginny. "Milady?" He grinned down at her.

"Sir." She hesitated only a moment before bobbing a curtsy and accepting his gesture.

"Ah, bugger all. Very well. Give orders to the men. Tell them if so much as a single teacup is removed from this vessel before we return, they'll live to regret it."

****

Two hours later, the four stepped back out into summer sunshine from the depths of Madame Marie Roi's Maison des Robes. The men carried bundles and packages. The women wore new summer gowns of sprigged muslin. Fitted in under the bodice, the garments dropped straight to the toes of dainty slippers and were complemented by straw bonnets arrayed with ribbons that matched the outfits.

"My, my, these gowns are so much cooler and more comfortable, are they not, my dear?" Annie took Ginny's arm as they started down the street back toward the harbor. "The short, puffy sleeves are so pretty, too."

"Sure and certain," her companion replied, a grin curling her lips. Leaning close to her companion, she whispered, "Hell's bells, Annie, we sure enough ran up a pretty account in there…and with more to come once that mad-mosell finishes sewing up the rest of what we ordered."

"Not to worry, my dear." Annie tossed her head as they strolled along. "Our men have a cargo to sell, and I've a feeling they aren't poor, by any means. Oh, look!" She turned aside to a street lined with vendors. "Raisins and oranges." Affecting a wifely tone, she turned to the burdened captain following in her wake. "My dear, we really must have some decent food after that dreadful voyage of spoiling stores and salt meat. Here are baskets just made for shopping. Come, Ginny. Take one and join me. Let us gather the means of making a fine dinner. Those vegetables and that excellent-looking meat, venison perhaps, are exactly what we need to make a lovely repast. And will you look at that butter and cheese…and milk and bread!"

As she set about making selections and filling the baskets she and her friend had taken into possession, she smirked as she heard her husband breathe an expletive.

"I'll be in debtors' prison before this day it out!" he muttered.

Chapter Nineteen

"I still can't believe it, Dunc!" Caleb strode across his cabin, perused the bottles held in a box on a shelf, and selected one. "That dolt of a magistrate denying us letters of marque and reprisal! Bloody hell, this colony has no navy. They should welcome every able-bodied ship willing to come to their aid. Such a slap in the face cries out for a shot of my best brandy to numb the disappointment."

He proceeded to pour a hefty measure into each of a pair of tankards.

"The command to deny it did come from the Prince Regent himself." Duncan slouched down in his chair and accepted the drink his captain handed to him. "Not much we can do about it."

"And who would have the power to incite His Royal Highness to make such a request and have it sent on the fastest ship available to get here ahead of us? Sweet Jesus, if I could just get my hands around Willie's rotten little neck! No thanks to that pair of hussies who call themselves our wives. If we hadn't been delayed by two attempts to rid ourselves of them, we might have been here before that blasted declaration."

"And what good would that have done?" Duncan drew a long breath. "Even if we'd sailed with the licenses, they'd have been revoked and any prizes we captured and sent back into port would be ruled illegal. You've got to stop blaming any and all misfortunes on the ladies. They didn't ask to be shanghaied."

"Argh!" Caleb threw himself into his chair and scowled down into his drink.

"Sir." A knock sounded on the cabin door. "Sir, there is an officer on deck requesting to see you."

"Hell and damnation! What now?" Caleb's response was a mutter. "Are they about to cart us off to prison? That's about the only misfortune left to befall us."

"Send him down." Duncan made the reply, and when the sound of retreating feet marked the sailor's leaving to obey, continued, "We may as well find out what he wants. We're tied to the dock, most of the crew is ashore, and the tide's slack. There's no chance of running."

Caleb muttered again but got to his feet to greet the red-coated sergeant as he entered the cabin.

"Captain Caleb Cameron?" the man asked.

"Aye. What can I do for you, Sergeant?" Realizing belligerence would only serve to exacerbate the situation, Caleb struggled to give an affable response.

"I come from the lieutenant governor of the province of New Brunswick," he said crisply. "The Honorable George Stacey Smyth is commandeering your ship and crew to take him to a ball in Halifax to be given to welcome the new lieutenant governor of Nova Scotia, Sir John Sherbrooke, and his lady."

"Good God, what next!" Caleb tightened his jaw in exasperation. "Does the *Jenny Jones* look like a bloody pleasure craft?"

"Word has reached the lieutenant governor that you

have your wife and another lady aboard," the man replied. "Since Mrs. Stacey Smyth will be traveling with her husband, he believes it's best that there be at least one other woman aboard aside from her own maid."

"Those two again!" Caleb knew his words sounded like a snarl, but he couldn't help it. "Is there no end to the misery they can cause me!"

"When can you be ready to sail?" The officer stood rigidly impassive. "The ball is Thursday next. The lieutenant governor wishes to leave as soon as possible. He has other business to conduct in Halifax, and he'd like to complete it before the festivities. In way of recompense, he has instructed me to give these to you."

He handed one envelope to Caleb, the other to Duncan.

"We can sail with the tide day after tomorrow." Duncan stood and addressed the officer. "We've nearly finished unloading our cargo. It will take us but a short time to replenish the *Jenny Jones*'s victuals, and then we can be off."

"Very well. With the tide day after tomorrow." With a curt nod, he left.

"Argh!" Caleb slammed down his mug. "Reduced to submitting to the whims of a lieutenant governor whose lackey of a judge won't consent to give us a damned license that would allow us to make a living…and largely because we have that precious pair aboard!"

"We're making a living now, Cal. What we wanted in seeking that consent was to get rich. Look at the bright side. Maybe after we do the governor this favor, he'll listen to our entreaties and order the judge to revoke that order."

"A colonial lieutenant governor revoke a royal decree? Hardly."

"It won't hurt to give it a try."

"You know what this means to our living arrangements, don't you? I'll have to give up my cabin to the governor and his lady. Our so-called wives will share your cabin, and you and I will have to sleep on deck. I'll be damned if I'll hang a hammock among the men."

"If we get underway early in the morning with a good, stiff breeze and every inch of canvas up, we could be in Halifax by evening. None of our sleeping arrangements need be disrupted."

"Aye, well, it's possible." Caleb felt some of his annoyance relax for a moment at his mate's words before it returned and he continued sharply, "But I don't plan to spend my time shuffling fat, rich government officials around, any more than I expect to end my days as a merchantman. I want a fine house and a fine…"

"I know, I know. A fine house and a fine lady." The mate's words reflected his weariness with his captain's dreams as he opened the envelope the sergeant had handed him.

"Sweet mother!" The two words were an intake of breath. "Cal, this is an invitation for my lady and me to attend the lieutenant governor's ball in Halifax."

"What?" Caleb ripped his open and stared down at it.

"Imagine two merchant seamen being invited to such a grand affair. Fine recompense, for sure."

"An honor, that's certain." Caleb stuffed his

invitation into his vest. "We'll attend, dressed as the finest of gentlemen. It's an excellent opportunity to meet someone who can assist us to get those licenses—denied in New Brunswick but perhaps not in Nova Scotia. But," he continued softly, "not a word of this to our so-called spouses. Can you imagine the commotion they'd cause, the orgy of spending they'd effect in an effort to array themselves, if they thought they were invited to a grand ball? I shudder to think what those two scoundrels have cost us already." Caleb leaned back in his chair and frowned at his friend. "And you, Mr. MacDougal, did not a thing to stop them."

"Ah, leave off your bellyaching, man." Seated across from him, Duncan flung his invitation onto the captain's desk and grinned over at him. "They looked right fetching in their new finery, and that meal they conjured up tonight was fair fit for royalty. Forget your purse strings and savor the moment."

"Don't think you won't be paying your fair share of today's spending spree. Half of the problem belongs to you."

"I'm more than willing to pay." Duncan MacDougal quirked a grin. "But I'm not the one who got us into this situation. Anyway, isn't it supposed to be Scotsmen who are tightfisted when it comes to spending, not greedy Englishmen?"

"Greedy!"

"Aye, greedy. I don't see any indication that you plan to return His Grace's money, even though you failed to carry out the appointed task."

"I'm not about to waste time sailing back to England on such a fool's errand. Even if I did, I'm dead certain Willie wouldn't accept the return of his coin in recompense for abducting the wrong women. Nothing short of seeing me hang would satisfy him. By now, he's probably miserably married to the real princess, with the charms of Lizzie Harrison only hot night dreams, and he's condemning me to Hades with each breath he takes."

A knock on the cabin door interrupted.

"Aye, what now?" he barked.

"Your wife and Mrs. MacDougal," he heard Annie reply.

"Come in." The words held no warmth of invitation.

"Good evening, gentlemen." Annie glided into the cabin and across to the bed to perch daintily on its edge. "Do join me, Mrs. MacDougal." She patted a place beside her, and her companion tried to obey in like fashion, her lack of training as a lady obvious in her movement. "How did you enjoy your meal?"

"Top notch, Mrs. Cameron." The curl at the corner of the mate's mouth irked Caleb. "Our compliments to the cooks. Would you be sharing a wee dram of this fine brandy with us, as our way of showing thanks?"

"That's most kind," Annie smiled, demurely folding her hands in her lap. "Mrs. MacDougal?"

"I'd not say no. I haven't had a good quaff in a dog's age."

Caleb heard his mate chuckle as Duncan stood to serve the women. *At least I can thank God that one isn't mine and that Dunc has the sense of humor necessary to deal with the creature. Bloody hell, I hope they didn't overhear our talk of the Halifax ball.*

"Next time I'd be most grateful if you waited for an invitation to join us." His words snapped out as

Duncan took down a pair of mugs and poured brandy into them. "Mr. MacDougal and I were discussing business."

"If that is what you wish." Annie cocked her head to one side and slanted him a taunting glance. "We wouldn't want to catch either of you in a state of undress, would we, Ginny?"

"That's for sure and certain." Her friend grinned. "It might be more than a lady of my refinement could take."

Caleb guffawed.

"What did that soldier want?" Annie asked. "We heard Munro announce him and then the murmur of voices from this cabin, one of them unfamiliar to us— that of the officer, we presume? Not about to pull you off to the stocks, was he?"

Caleb scowled at his wife. "Hardly. A small commission for the lieutenant governor, nothing more."

"Ah-ha. Delivering a package somewhere along our route back to sea?"

"You could say that."

"When does this fine tub go into drydock to be refitted as a man o' war?" Ginny turned on Duncan.

"No time soon." Duncan glanced at Caleb. "And the *Jenny Jones* would have become a privateer, not a man o' war at the king's beck and call. Cal, they may as well know the truth."

"Truth? What truth?" His wife turned on him.

"We were denied privateering licenses today." Caleb stood and went to help himself to more brandy. "It seems His Grace the duke is visiting his revenge on my shanghaiing the wrong ladies. He's had the Prince Regent send an emissary with orders that we're not now nor ever to receive such a commission."

"Bloody hell!" Ginny jumped to her feet, brown eyes blazing. "Does that mean we've suffered you two for nothing? That we'll not have an opportunity to get rich from the spoils of war?"

"It would look that way." Duncan drew up broad shoulders in a large intake of breath. "Unless you fine ladies can concoct a plan."

"Don't be facetious!" Annie snapped. "But"—her words slowed and her eyes narrowed—"perhaps we can think of something."

"Annie's right clever at coming up with plots and plans." Ginny's brown eyes sparkled in a way that made Caleb wince.

"In my wildest imaginings, I cannot come up with any situation in which you and your friend could secure such permissions for us."

"Give me time." Her initial annoyance apparently cooling, Annie stood and began to stroll thoughtfully back and forth across the cabin.

"You mentioned we had a commission to perform." Ginny turned to the captain while her friend paced slowly 'Where might it be taking us?"

"To Halifax. A short jaunt to deliver New Brunswick's lieutenant governor and his lady to a …social event. Now, mind." He hurried on as his wife paused to glance at him. He didn't like that look, not at all. "There's to be no high jinks while they're aboard. You're to play the roles of my wife and Mrs. MacDougal your maid servant with dignity and all the respect due the old bastard and his spouse."

"My, my, such language." Annie pulled in her chin and batted her eyelashes at him.

"He denied our request for letters of marque and reprisal." Ignoring the seductive look, Caleb took a larger than normal drink of brandy and pulled his lips back.

"Well, speaking disrespectfully of him and being rude to the man won't increase your chances." Annie's expression became a frown of concentration. "Have you never heard the old expression about getting more flies with honey than vinegar?" She turned her back to him to run her hand slowly along the edge of his desk in a gesture he, for some nebulous reason, found highly sensuous.

"And you can get a whole swarm with horse manure." Caleb snapped in a sudden, mad effort not to imagine those fingers stroking him intimately. "Now, enough. You'll both behave yourselves while the man is aboard. Once we deliver him and his lady wife to Halifax, that will be the end of it. We'll be going..."

"To a ball...the lieutenant governor's ball!" Whirling back to face him, Annie held up the invitation Duncan had left lying on the captain's desk. "Ginny, we're going to a fancy ball!"

Chapter Twenty

"What? No, no, no!" Caleb grabbed the embossed card from her. "Only Mr. MacDougal and I will be going. It will cost more than enough to attire ourselves, never mind you extravagant creatures."

"But won't the lieutenant governor think it strange for you and Mr. MacDougal to arrive *sans* ladies?" Annie taunted.

"He can blasted well think what he likes. I'm not dressing the pair of you up for one night in refined company where I've no doubt you'll do something outrageous."

"Very well." Annie swung away with regal disdain. "Come, Ginny. We've no desire to be taken to a place where it's already been determined we'll shame ourselves…and our oh-so-respectable husbands."

Head held high, followed by her companion, Annie Cameron swept out of the room.

"Sweet Jesus, Dunc, now you've done it. How could you have been so dumb as to have left that invitation in plain sight? What do you want to wager they're already setting some scheme to accompany us to that blasted ball?"

"Without coin to buy gowns, hire someone to dress their hair or rent a carriage? Talk sense, Cal."

****

"Wasn't it fortunate we chose to stroll through the

township today?" Annie grinned at her companion once they were back in the mate's cabin. "Now we know exactly where to go to purchase ball gowns. There won't be time to have any especially fashioned, but I saw a ready-made pair of quite lovely ones with matching slippers and shawls that should fit us right down to the ground."

"And just how do you expect us to pay for such grandeur? We've not a shilling between us."

"From our recent excursion about the commercial section of this town, we've become recognizable as the wives of two prosperous merchant seamen. Tomorrow, while our loving spouses are busy arranging for the *Jenny Jones'* restocking to return to sea, we'll take a walk into the town and purchase those gowns...on our husbands' credit. I'm sure the seamstresses whose shop we graced with our trade already will be able to give us the name of someone who can fittingly dress our hair."

"Oh, Annie, you are a conniving little wench. But," Ginny continued more slowly, "are you sure such an escapade won't simply drive them to other schemes to rid themselves of us?"

"We're known as their wives now, in this British port. It would seem mighty strange if we both turned up missing, wouldn't it? At any rate, I'm still convinced they're men of basically good character, not about to leave us destitute or dispose of us in a cruel fashion. Furthermore, once we appear on their arms at that ball, we'll forever be remembered as their beautiful, refined spouses."

"Going to that fancy ball may fit your style, Annie Cameron. You learned to dance and cavort among the gentry when you were Lady Sophia's partner in her antics, but I'll stick out like a sore thumb. I'll open my big mouth and cuss like a sailor or fall over my feet into the punch bowl."

"No, you won't. I'll teach you to dance, and then, if you just mind your tongue, you'll be fine."

****

"Now, remember what I've told you." Annie carried the basket she'd purchased the previous day to transport foodstuffs and whispered to her friend similarly burdened as they headed out onto the dock where the *Jenny Jones* was being unloaded. "We're going into the township to buy stores for the voyage to Halifax, items we'll need to serve the lieutenant governor and his lady in the manner to which they're accustomed."

****

"A bit more wine, sir?" Annie, wearing one of the sprigged muslin dresses that had become part of her wardrobe, placed her hand around the bottle on the captain's desk as the *Jenny Jones* rocked steadily toward Halifax.

"Don't mind if I do, m'dear." Lieutenant Governor Stacey Smyth held up his glass. "I must say, that was a fine repast you provided. I'd never expected such elegance on a merchantman. My compliments to you and your lady, Captain Cameron."

The stout official gave Caleb a commending nod as Annie replenished his drink.

"Aye, well, my wife does know how to entertain." He narrowed his eyes as he gave Annie a glare. God only knew what that meal of beef with all the trimmings had cost him, not to mention the fine wine that had accompanied it. And caviar! Good God, where had the woman obtained such a thing this side of the Atlantic? He shuddered inwardly as he tried to dismiss his horrors at the price it must have fetched in the Saint John market.

"More tea?" Annie turned to the lieutenant governor's lady. The tall, skeleton-thin woman had come aboard, her nose in the air, obviously ready to disapprove of everything about this merchantman she'd been obliged to take as transport. Now, after a fine meal and expertly brewed tea, she smiled at the captain's wife.

"That would be lovely, Mrs. Cameron. You do make a fine cup."

"Thank you." She bobbed a slight curtsy in acceptance of the compliment.

Again Caleb frowned at her. She hadn't made the tea. It was Ginny, relegated to the galley, who had produced the pleasing meal and its aftermath. She'd had to be hidden, since the wives of mates weren't allowed to be aboard their husband's ship. Annie, as the captain's wife, had taken on the position of hostess. Munro, to whom the previous day she'd given a swift training in how to behave appropriately, had served the meal, acting as footman.

Caleb had had to suppress a chuckle when he'd seen the burly sailor dressed in a clean white shirt, tan breeches, stockings, and polished shoes. His wife's years with the notorious Lady Sophia had left her with a wealth of skills. But his mirth had been short lived.

Later he could barely keep from gritting his teeth at his mental calculations of the cost, although he wasn't such a fool as to not recognize the effect Annie's grace and charm were having on the vice-regal pair. He realized there was but faint reason to hope, against a royal decree, but he couldn't quite squash the thought that maybe, just maybe, the lieutenant governor, under the influence of a highly agreeable experience aboard the *Jenny Jones*, might be influenced to advise the judge at the Court of Vice Admiralty to change his decision.

****

"As pleasant a voyage as I've ever experienced, Captain Cameron." The lieutenant governor extended his hand as he and his lady prepared to disembark in the soft dusk of the summer's evening a half hour later. "Swift, as well. You took advantage of every breath of breeze. It was as fine an example of seamanship as I've ever seen. I trust I'll be seeing you at the ball tomorrow evening?"

"Of course, sir." The lieutenant governor's praise reviving his hopes, Caleb bowed in acknowledgement.

"I'll look forward to seeing you there as well, Mrs. Cameron." Vivian Stacey Smyth smiled at Annie while behind her back Caleb shook his head at his wife. "You've made this, as my husband has said, one of the most pleasant voyages we've ever experienced."

"I'm happy you enjoyed it, ma'am." Annie curtsied. "It's been delightful having another lady with whom to chat."

"Of course, my dear." She leaned close but without any real effort to avoid Caleb's hearing. "It must be trying, to be alone at sea for so long with men as your only companions." She straightened and spoke again in normal tones. "And I don't recall when I've taken such pleasure in spending time on deck during a voyage. It wouldn't have been possible if you hadn't placed me in a comfortable position out of the wind and wrapped your lovely cashmere shawl about me."

"Cashmere?" Again Caleb mouthed a word at Annie behind the woman's back. *Good God, more expense! Does the woman think I'm made of money?*

"A gift from my devoted husband." She further chafed on his humor by smiling at him in a besotted fashion. "Captain Cameron is a most generous man."

"Go along, my dear." The lieutenant governor indicated the carriage with the provincial crest on its side awaiting them on the dock. "See to your lady, Rose," he continued to the maidservant who had accompanied them on the voyage. "I'll be along in a moment. Captain Cameron," he continued in a lowered tone as the girl hurried off with her mistress, "a word in your ear."

"Yes, sir." Caleb stiffened. Surely no complaints about the voyage, not after the rare and expensive treatment the man and his wife had received.

"You and your lady wife have provided us with a lovely day, sir." He leaned close to the captain. "A genuine pleasure cruise. I'd like to repay you in some small measure."

"That's not necessary, sir." Caleb smothered the urge to suggest recompense in the form of a letter of marque and reprisal. "Our invitations to the ball tomorrow evening will more than suffice."

"Still, I'd like to do something for you." He sucked in a deep breath that pulled in his paunch. "I know that order to repudiate your request for a letter of marque came from His Royal Highness, but I will endeavor to have it repealed. Now," he hurried on as Caleb opened his mouth to express his gratitude, "I doubt it will do any good, but still one can but try, eh, Captain?"

****

"He said he'd try? Lieutenant Governor George Stacey Smyth said he'd try to have the order against us rescinded?" Duncan MacDougal stared at his friend as, together with their wives, they sat in the captain's cabin minutes later.

"That's exactly what he said." Caleb's face was so bright with hope Annie hated to rain on his joy, but she felt it necessary.

"He said indeed just that," she said softly. "But he also said he didn't hold out much hope."

"Hush your nay-saying, woman." Caleb was too buoyed up to be disheartened by her response. "A chance is a chance. Bloody hell, you spent a fortune to impress the old bastard and his wife. Don't go telling me it was all for naught."

"No, no, definitely not." Annie made her tone as placating as she could. "But he's only a colonial official with little clout at Court. Now, the person I reckon to go after is the lieutenant governor of this province of Nova Scotia. Sir John Sherbrooke is a war hero, knighted by the king himself. He has a reputation as long as my arm for bravery and service to the crown. I heard of his feats of daring spoken of most highly when I served Lady Sophia. Lady Sophia only met him once, but she was impressed."

"If you were so wise as to who holds the reins of power in this area, why did you spend a king's ransom trying to impress that bloody twit and his wife?" Caleb swung on her, his face making thunderclouds look friendly.

"We must inveigle ourselves into the upper

echelons of society in order to get introduced to Sir John. George Stacey Smyth and his lady will do just that. One must think ahead."

With a swish of her gown, she left her husband staring after her.

****

"My, my, aren't we the fine pair." Duncan MacDougal turned to his friend the following evening as Caleb finished adjusting his cravat before the mirror in one of the two rooms they'd rented at a Halifax inn. "All dandied up, we're quite the lads." He glanced down at the formal evening attire he wore, then grinned over at his friend, similarly dressed. "If we weren't a couple of happily married men, I swear we'd sweep all the ladies off their feet tonight. Wipe that frown off your face, man, and prepare to enjoy the evening."

"I could if my gut wasn't telling me to beware some nefarious little scheme my wife may be plotting. Did you notice she said 'we' when she mentioned getting an introduction to Sir John Sherbrooke?"

"Ah, come on, man. Stop imagining trouble. I swear, that woman's got you suspicious of your own shadow. They're both in their room next door, most likely preparing for bed. It was clever of you to engage two rooms, one for them and one for us."

"Gave us a chance to dress in peace, didn't it, without any nagging about how they want to go to the ball." Caleb brushed an invisible speck from his dark sleeve. "At any rate, they've nothing appropriate to wear to such a soiree."

"True, true." Duncan drew in a deep breath, and, glancing over at him, Caleb had to admit his mate looked every inch a handsome gentleman in his formal attire. "They'd hardly try to fashion something out of bed sheets."

"Hardly." Caleb let a corners of his mouth rise at the ridiculousness of the response. "Fancy a wee dram downstairs before we head off? The carriage won't be here for another half hour."

"Just the ticket." Together the pair made their way downstairs.

****

"I still can't believe we're leaving our wives here at the inn with not a whisper of protest from either of them," Duncan remarked as they turned into the common room.

"They're coming to know their place and who is in charge of the *Jenny Jones* and all who sail on her." Caleb swaggered to a table and sat down in a lordly fashion.

****

"Bloody hell, will you look at that!" Duncan MacDougal jerked alert as he stared past his friend. His hand holding the whisky tankard let it drop to the table as others in the common room followed his gaze and gaped.

"What?" Caleb didn't bother to turn. "Some drunken lout about to make trouble?"

"No, no, definitely not a drunken lout."

The aghast expression on his companion's face made Caleb swivel in his chair. And choke on the whisky he'd put into his mouth. Entering the room, causing all heads to swing in their direction, resplendent in glittering ball gowns, their hair piled artistically about their heads and intertwined with ribbons and flowers, were their wives.

Chapter Twenty-One

"Sweet Jesus!" Caleb stumbled to his feet, knocking over his chair. Too astonished to speak further, he stared as the pair of beauties made their way toward them, fluttering ivory-handled feather fans in the stuffy heat of the room. Delicate lace shawls lay draped about their shoulders; snow-white gloves stretched to above their elbows.

"Good evening, gentlemen." Annie paused in front of her husband, cast him a radiant smile, and dropped him an elaborate curtsy. "So kind of you both to absent yourselves from our room and give us time to prepare for the ball. Now we'd best make haste. The landlord has informed us our carriage awaits."

She slipped a hand through her husband's arm. Still beyond any ability to find words, Caleb allowed himself to be led out of the inn and into the waiting conveyance, barely aware that his friend and his wife followed.

****

"You look right fetching, Mrs. MacDougal."

Once in the carriage, Duncan was the first to find his voice. He grinned down at the dark-haired beauty by his side.

"Thank you, kind sir." She smiled demurely behind her fan. "You don't look too shabby yourself. And you've no need to be concerned regarding my behavior at the ball. Annie has taught me to how to dance. She's also advised me to keep my trap shut."

"Ah, well done, Mrs. Cameron." Duncan winked over at her. "If that last bit holds true, you will have accomplished a minor miracle."

Ginny made to protest, then catching the twinkle in her husband's eye, chuckled. "It would appear so, Mr. MacDougal…if she's succeeded."

"Those…outfits." Caleb found his power of speech returned. "Where did you get them? How much did they cost? Who dressed your hair, and at what…?"

"Ah, Captain, let us not dispute such mundane matters this lovely summer's eve." Duncan took Ginny's hand in his and smiled at her. "Let us just enjoy the beauty which our wives have gone to so much trouble to effect, and the fine affair to which we're destined."

Caleb grunted and turned to stare out the window into the thickening twilight of the summer's evening.

****

Caleb hadn't expected the reception the two couples would receive on their entrance into the ballroom. As they paused at the top of the stairs before descending to be presented to the lieutenant governor and his lady, all attention turned to them. Only then did he realize what a handsome foursome they must make. He and Duncan looked dashing in their formal attire, but it was their ladies who caught everyone's eye.

His wife and her companion, in flickering candlelight, had to be the most beautiful women in the room. Where had the ragamuffins he'd had running about his deck in cut-down men's clothing gone? How had they managed to transform themselves into utterly beguiling creatures? Lady Sophia Mannering. That was it. Under her former mistress's tutelage, Annie Cameron nee Pudden must have learned the art of formal dress...no, more than that, spectacular formal dress.

"Captain Caleb Cameron and his lady." For a moment after the announcement he stood without moving, staring down with a sudden new appreciation for the woman at his side.

"Captain," she whispered. "Come. They've called our names." She nudged him with her hand beneath the crook of his arm, and he found himself moving down the steps with an enchantress guiding him.

At the bottom of the staircase, he received another surprise. Annie dropped an elegant curtsy to the lieutenant governor and his lady, one so flawlessly executed it appeared she'd been doing it for years. When he glanced back, he saw his mate's wife doing the same...with just a tad less polish. They were making an outstanding impression on the crowd of dignitaries, and the evening had barely begun.

A sudden pride blooming in his chest, Caleb led Annie across the room to a seat among a group of finely gowned ladies. One of them immediately stood, introduced herself as Lady Margaret Henderson, and accepted Annie and Ginny, who had followed with Duncan, into their ranks. The men were free to move off and join the rest of the males at the gathering.

****

"Making a right fair shine of it, aren't they, Captain?" Duncan, a taunting grin turning up the corners of his lips, leaned close and muttered in Caleb's ear a half hour later as the two men stood near the far end of the ballroom, watching the proceedings. Their ladies appeared to be the belles of the party. Certainly, Caleb had to admit, they were the most eye-catching.

"It would appear they haven't yet brought us to ruination with outbursts or behaviors unbecoming ladies." Caleb swirled the whisky in his glass. "But I do notice yours is imbibing a fair amount of champagne."

"Ah, Cal, let her have some pleasure. She's had little enough in her life, I'd hazard a guess." He moved away, smiling in his wife's direction.

"That minx in the pale green dress is quite an addition to this soiree." Grinning, a young officer, glass in hand, paused beside Caleb and jerked his head in Annie's direction. "She's already got a bevy of admirers buzzing around."

Looking in his wife's direction, he saw it was indeed a fact. A group of young men had gathered around Annie, seeking to engage her attention. In response, she smiled and fluttered her fan demurely. She glanced over at him with a coquettish batting of eyelashes.

Bloody hell! Just what I need...a flirt.

"Think I'll join the group." Smirking the officer gave Caleb a nudge. "Who knows, the lady might have a taste for a captain of the guards. What say, sir? Do you think she'll surrender to my charms?"

"I sincerely hope not, Captain." Caleb's words were a growl. "The lady is my wife, and I'd have to be calling you out if you were so unwise as to practice your charms on her."

"I beg your pardon, sir." The younger man faltered and reddened as he looked into Caleb's scowl. "I meant no disrespect. I had no idea..."

"Well, now you do, so I'd advise you to abandon any amorous intentions you may be entertaining with her in mind. Is that clear?"

"Of course, sir. Certainly, sir." All but stumbling, Captain Donner backed off a few feet before turning and hurrying away into the crowd.

Caleb grunted his satisfaction, then turned his attention back to his wife.

There was no doubt she was the belle of the ball. A mix of pride and jealously flooded his gut. Would the woman never leave his innards to settle into peace?

As the music once again began, Caleb was amazed to see Lieutenant Governor Stacey Smyth heading toward Annie. The group surrounding her drew back to allow the official a path. When he reached Caleb's wife, he honored her with a deep bow, then offered a gloved hand. After a demure hesitation, she accepted it.

Sweet Jesus, he's asking her to dance. Even that old twit is fascinated by her.

As the couple took their place at the head of the line of dancers, another thought flashed through his mind.

She'll have half an hour with him as her partner. Maybe, if that pleasured expression on his face is any indication, she might charm him into getting us those letters of marque and reprisal. She's as anxious for them as I am.

Pleased with the thought, he strolled down the side of the ballroom and, smiling, nodded to his wife and her partner. He paused to admire her as she moved gracefully through the dance.

"Bloody hell, look what you've done, you daft bugger!" The outburst behind his back burst his pleasant contemplation and made him whirl. Only one female in this company would blast out such a statement.

Ginny MacDougal stood confronting a blushing young officer who apparently had spilled his champagne down the front of her gown.

"This outfit cost my husband a bloomin' fortune!" the tirade continued. "Ruddy, clumsy bastard!"

As Caleb was about to seize her by an arm and propel her out of the room, a short, stocky, middle-aged man, his dress uniform glinting with medals, stepped forward. Recognizing him as their host Sir John Sherbrooke, to whom they'd been presented on their entrance to the ball, Caleb felt his heart plummet.

Sweet Jesus, she's brought the wrath of the lieutenant governor himself down on us.

"Allow me to help ya, mistress." His Honor swung on the flustered officer. "You, there, lad. Look sharp. Get the lady a cloth. And a fresh glass of champagne." As the young man fled, he turned to Ginny. "Trip over his own spurs that one, I reckon, what? Name's John Sherbrooke, me dear. Sir John, it is now. I believe we met briefly when you arrived this evening. Glad to hear someone that can speak as they feel, none of this foolish high-falutin' talk. We're not in the king's court now, are we?"

"Your...Honor." Ginny bobbed him a deep, awkward curtsy and would have pitched over forward if Sir John hadn't caught her by an elbow.

"There, there, me dear. No need for such bugger-all formality. Hell of a thing, all this bowin' and scrapin', what? Will ya do me the honor of shakin' a leg with me in the next dance? My bride doesn't wish to participate in such antics." His weathered face was all-out grinning.

"Aye, sir." With a smile spreading across her countenance, Ginny accepted his hand.

"Guid, guid. It'll be a pleasure to chin wag with someone who speaks a decent lingo."

Glancing across the room, Caleb saw Sir John's wife, his bride of four months, glowering at the couple. Tall and spare, with a long, narrow face, her lips pursed into wrinkles of disapproval, she glared as her husband and Ginny inveigled their way in among the dancers.

Caleb swallowed the last of his whisky, placed his empty glass on the tray of a passing waiter, and took a flute of champagne.

That doxy's vulgar tongue will be the end of us, and every randy buck in the room is lusting after my wife. What a hellish night! Nothing to do but get damned good and drunk.

****

By the time Annie and the other lieutenant governor had finished a second dance, over an hour later, Caleb had downed more glasses of champagne than he'd bothered to count. If he hadn't been a man who could hold his liquor, he'd have been more than a bit unsteady on his feet.

What he couldn't hold in check was his desire to take the beautiful woman who was his wife away from the rigidly formal man in military uniform who represented the king in New Brunswick, to show him and every man present that he, Captain Caleb Cameron, was the man who would be taking the vivacious, charming woman back to his room for the night.

****

"Good God, Captain!" Annie swung on him the moment they were in the room at the inn she was sharing with Ginny. "What is the matter with you! You all but pulled me away from the lieutenant governor and pranced me out to a carriage! Do you realize you left Mr. MacDougal and my friend to find their own way back here?"

"Duncan MacDougal has been finding his way back to his bed with women for a goodly number of years. Tonight won't be any different."

"If you're thinking Ginny will consent to…"

"Consent? I'd be more inclined to say welcome the man into her bed. I've seen the way she looks at him, the way they look at each other. And tonight, with your friend full of excellent champagne…"

"You think Ginny will welcome a drunken tumble?" She drew herself up to face him. "Well, sir, you'll learn you're quite mistaken. You'll learn…"

She got no further. He pulled her into his arms and covered her mouth with his. Struck still with surprise, she didn't react. By the time she realized what was happening, it was too late—he had her in his thrall. Melting into his arms, she allowed his tongue to explore her lips, then her mouth. His hand slid to her bottom and thrust her so firmly to him she could feel his desire straining toward her. Her hair cascaded about her bare shoulders. Somehow he'd managed to free it from pins and ribbons.

"Ann," he breathed against her temple when he finally released her lips. "You're the most beautiful woman I've ever seen." He slid the gown from her shoulder and nuzzled her neck.

"Captain," she murmured. His lovemaking had set

her senses swirling.

"Caleb," he muttered as his mouth slid lower. "My name, Mrs. Cameron, is Caleb."

"Caleb." The word was a gasp as he gathered her into his arms and carried her to the bed.

Chapter Twenty-Two

Annie Cameron woke, stretched, and yawned. Sunshine flooded into the room. A sensation of absolute satisfaction and contentment permeated her from head to toe. Why? *Oh, good Lord!* Memory washed back in a warm, all-encompassing wave as thoughts of a night of passion such as she'd never imagined possible flooded back.

Caleb. Caleb, her husband, her lover.

She turned in the bed to greet him, languid and happy. The place where he'd lain was empty.

"Captain?" She voiced his title even though a glance around the room found it deserted.

Where had he gone? Had last night been a mistake...on his part, the result of too much champagne?

A knock on the door made her heart lurch. He'd come back! Pulling the bedsheet to her chin to cover her nakedness, she sat up. "Come in."

"Annie, are you all right?" Ginny Tart, dressed in a white cotton gown, greeted her as she entered and closed the door. "I was right worried when Mr. MacDougal told me he'd been ordered to keep me from our room last night. The great oaf told me all was well, that you'd agreed to such an arrangement. In the clear light of day, now, I realize I shouldn't have trusted him, but last night I had a tad too much of that bubbling wine…"

"It's all right, Ginny." Annie jerked a blanket across the bed to hide the evidence of their lovemaking. "He didn't force himself on me. I was quite willing to go along with whatever he…suggested."

"And?" Ginny sat down on a chair to face her, eyes bright. "Was it wonderful? Did he make your head spin and your toes tingle?"

"Ginny, you sound as if you speak from experience." Annie narrowed her eyes as she looked at her friend.

"Aye, well, perhaps…yes." She jumped to her feet and came to join her friend on the bed. "Annie, he was… Oh, I'm not like you. I don't have a lot of fine words to describe Mr. MacDougal and his charms, but let me just say this—he knew what he was about, without doubt."

"So you slept with him?"

"Much more than slept, Annie my dear, much more than slept." Ginny's brown eyes sparkled. "What a lot I've been missing."

"Rightly or wrongly, our husbands appear to have given us both a night of pleasure." Annie drew a deep breath as she moved to the edge of the bed to reach for undergarments on the floor beside it.

"Rightly or wrongly? What are you on about, Annie Cameron?" Ginny's eyes narrowed suspiciously. "Wrongly? Annie, the man did take precautions…?"

"No."

"Oh, Annie!"

"Oh, indeed." She struggled into the retrieved clothing, then went to the washstand and poured water from the ewer into the wash basin.

"Annie, I thought that in your years with Lady Sophia she must have told you how to avoid getting in a family way."

"She did." She turned to her friend, washcloth in hand. "Only it all happened so suddenly, so passionately…and I'd never…"

"Oh, God." Ginny flung back the bed covers and stared at the evidence. "You'd never had a man before."

"No." The word came out barely above a whisper.

"And this one is handsome and no doubt skilled in the ways of lovemaking." Ginny heaved a great sigh. "Well, there's only one thing to do now…hope and pray there are no results. But, Annie, I find it hard to believe a woman as clever and cunning as you…"

"I know, Ginny. I was a fool. I take it you and Mr. MacDougal were wiser?" She returned to her ablutions, trying to sound casual.

"Aye." Ginny looked seriously at her friend before a twinkle brightened her eyes. "Even though it did interrupt a most pleasurable moment…for a moment."

"Ladies, breakfast." A knock at the door and Duncan MacDougal's voice stopped their conversation. "We'll await you downstairs." There was a pause, then a sly continuation, "Mrs. MacDougal, I assume you've a hearty appetite this fine morning?"

"Aye, Mr. MacDougal." Ginny grinned up at Annie. "As I'm sure do you. We'll be with you directly."

As footsteps told of his retreating, Annie finished her washing and reached for one of her recently purchased gowns for day wear and pulled it on.

"Button me up, you shameless creature," she said, turning her back to her friend. "And help me do up my hair. We're about to face our lovers in the harsh light of day. God knows how that will turn out."

****

"Mrs. MacDougal." Duncan stood as the two women made their way into the common room. Caleb followed his example more slowly. *Damn, but I wish I hadn't quaffed so much champagne.* His head beat an annoying tattoo. *But on the other hand...* He looked at his wife looking lovely and fresh as a summer's breeze in a soft, white gown. *It was an amazing night.*

She smiled, and he felt his lips responding in like. That smile told him exactly what he wanted to know, what he'd been longing to know ever since he'd left her bed. Last night hadn't been a mistake...by either of them.

"Mrs. Cameron." He stepped around the table and drew out a chair for her as Duncan did the same for his wife.

"Thank you, sir." Again the smile, only this time coy and intimate, making his body react, even in its state of overindulgence. *Good God!*

"The landlord has seen fit to serve us before you arrived." Duncan cast out a hand to indicate the table laden with cheese, cold meats, bread, and a pot of coffee. "I'm sure all that dancing...and such"—he grinned at Ginny—"has left you fair to middlin' hungry. I know I'm ready for a hearty meal."

"Aye." Ginny reached for a plate of ham and smirked in his direction. "Let us get to it."

Something in her remark brought a deep-throated chuckle from Duncan.

That pair is shameless.

Caleb looked across at Ann, as he'd decided to call

her, helping herself to steaming coffee. She caught his glance and smiled…a demure lady's smile.

"Coffee, Captain Cameron?" She moved the pot along the table in his direction with a graceful movement.

"Thank you, Mrs. Cameron." As he accepted the coffee, he recalled how often he'd seen her behave as a lady. But then she could also fight and cook and clean and scheme…

"Captain Caleb Cameron?"

Caleb looked up from pouring steaming liquid into his cup to see an officer in red tunic standing beside their table.

"Aye." *What now? Bloody hell, can't these redcoats ever leave us in peace?*

"The lieutenant governor has requested your presence at the Court of Vice Admiralty within the hour, sir. I'm to inform you he's not to be kept waiting. He's a busy man."

"Did he give a reason for this summons?" Apprehension knotted his gut.

"No, sir, only that he won't tolerate tardiness. You're to bring your first mate, as well. I have a carriage outside. I'd be obliged if you'll finish your breakfast and come with me."

"We'll come immediately." Caleb stood as Duncan followed suit. "I've lost my appetite."

****

"Good God, Annie!" Ginny's face blanched. "You don't think it's because of something I said to the man? I did have a tad too much champagne."

"Hardly. If you were guilty, you'd have been summoned also. Let us just hope and pray that, whatever grievance Sir John has against our men, we don't shortly learn they've been incarcerated."

****

"Mrs. MacDougal, open the door! At once!" The mate's banging on the panel made both women jump two hours later as they sat in Annie's bedchamber.

Exchanging an apprehensive glance with her companion, Annie moved to obey. Ginny turned from where she'd been watching their husbands' arrival from the window and gave her friend a nod of consent when she paused before removing the bar.

The moment she did, Duncan MacDougal burst into the room and strode across it in long strides to capture his wife into an embrace, all but dropping the bottle of whisky he carried.

"You bonnie wee lass!" he whooped. "You've worked a miracle!"

"What?" Ginny staggered as he allowed her to stand once again and went to place the bottle on a chest of drawers near the window. "What are you talking about, you daft Highlander?"

"Mr. MacDougal is merely trying, in his crude way, to thank you for being responsible for our getting letters of marque and reprisal." The captain entered the room at a more dignified pace, carrying four mugs and a sheaf of papers. "To which I'll add my gratitude, Mrs. MacDougal." He honored her with a deep bow.

"What...how?" Annie stared at the documents in her husband's hand.

"It appears Sir John so enjoyed Mrs. MacDougal's company last evening that, bright and early this fine summer's morn, he ordered the Court of Vice Admiralty to grant our wish."

"But how did he know…?" Annie still couldn't understand.

"It seems Mrs. MacDougal, after more than a few glasses of champagne, decided to tell Sir John all about how those 'rotten old sods' at the court in Saint John had refused her husband and his captain a means of making a decent living for her and her friend. Apparently Sir John had once found himself at odds with such a judicial system and has little sympathy for any perceived injustices committed by them. Furthermore, if his words of this morning are true, he's quite taken with you, Mrs. MacDougal. He actually went so far as to say something along the lines of 'If both of us weren't married,' and, 'If I'd only met that girl six months ago.' "

"Ginny, you've worked a miracle!" Annie rushed across the room to hug the still-dazed woman. "You and your colorful tongue."

"Aye, well, don't get carried away with one good result." Caleb placed the mugs on the chest of drawers beside the whisky and crossed his arms on his chest. "I consider this incident, as my good wife has described it, a miracle. There was a great deal more to it."

"And what might that be?" Annie demanded.

"We had to deposit a bond of two thousand pounds with the Court of Vice Admiralty to ensure we abide by the terms of commissions." He walked across the room and at the window turned back to its three other occupants. "This means all captures we take must be brought in and submitted to a prize court's decision. Only if the seized vessel is found to be enemy property unprotected by license or permit can the detention be condemned and sold for our benefit. If it doesn't prove a lawful prize, we'll be liable for damages for having interfered with it."

"Bloody hell! I hope that's all of the conditions." Ginny's expression clouded.

"No, there's more." Caleb drew a deep breath and continued. "We're forbidden to take ransom for vessels, goods, or prisoners of war. We're required to report enemy movements as observed, to submit log books of our daily activities, and never molest ships carrying women and/or children."

"They're making it difficult for us because the governing powers believe that every shilling of privateer prize money is stolen from the white silk breeches of commanders of the Royal Navy," Duncan said. "They're permitted to privateer, also."

"Well, I guess we must regard all this as small cheese." Ginny sank down on the edge of the bed. "Annie and I were afraid the pair of you were about to be arrested...again."

"They might have done just that, but the results would have had to be different this time." Grinning, Duncan took her hand and drew her to her feet to stand in front of him. "The authorities can only marry a man off once."

He started to take her into his arms, but Caleb's words brought him up short.

"Save your passion, Mr. MacDougal. Right now we have to get to the docks and start the outfitting of the *Jenny Jones* as a privateer. War was officially declared last week, and we want to be among the first at sea, ready to take prizes."

Annie moved to put her back against the door. "But before you set out, *we've* agreements to reach."

"Agreements? Good God, woman, what are you talking about?" Impatience reeked from Caleb's every word.

"As you will remember, we've expressed a desire to go privateering with you, to share in the spoils as regular crew members.. And since if it hadn't been for us, especially Mrs. MacDougal, you still wouldn't have your coveted licenses, we have a claim on your planned adventures."

"Bloody hell, woman!"

"She does have a right good point, Cal." Duncan was grinning at Ginny. "If it weren't for my wife and her saucy tongue, we wouldn't have succeeded today. And," he continued, "I'm not certain sure your lady didn't have a hand in it as well, what with her treating that old blighter Stacey Smyth and his wife like royalty on the voyage here. Her favoring him with a pair of dances last evening didn't hurt, either. You'll recall he was standing beside Sir John, nodding his approval, when Sir John advised the judge to grant our petition. There was no way his honor was about to deny two lieutenant governors."

"Mr. MacDougal, I'll thank you to keep your own counsel where matters involving my ship are concerned." He swung on his mate.

"Now, there you'd best watch your words, Captain." Duncan MacDougal became suddenly serious in a way Annie had never before seen when he was addressing Caleb. "I own a third of the shares of the *Jenny Jones*, and I say we hear our ladies out."

"Damnation." Caleb drew a deep breath and crossed his arms on his chest. "Very well. What are your demands?" He narrowed his eyes as he looked down at his wife.

"That we sail with you at all times and that we get our fair share of any prizes your ship and crew are awarded." Although his towering over her, blue eyes as hard as sapphires, made her cringe inwardly, she drew herself up and faced him. "In return, we'll do the cooking and cleaning and tend your sick and wounded. We'll also fight by your sides..."

"Stop right there." He wet his lips. "I'll agree to your duties as stated, but when it comes to actual battle, the pair of you will take to my cabin and bar the door. Wartime engagements are brutal and unpredictable. I don't want my men or my mate and me distracted by trying to protect you two. I'll also expect you to assist Munro in performing any amputations that might be required after a battle. He's by way of being the best excuse for a surgeon we were able to hire aboard." He narrowed cold blue eyes as he waited her response.

The first shaft of apprehension she'd had in months shot through Annie as he stated the last condition. Telling herself she would do anything rather than return to a life of servitude, she willed her churning innards to be still. She'd demanded seamen's rights, and if this was part of acquiring them, so be it.

"Agreed." She forced herself to stand strong.

"Furthermore, and most importantly," he continued, "if enemies see women aboard, they'll think us weak and vulnerable, distracted by your care and protection. Such assumptions will greatly weaken our power. Therefore, you're to stay out of sight at all times when we're encountering another vessel." He drew in a deep breath before continuing. "Also, there will be no further intimate relationships between the married couples in this agreement until such time as we cease privateering."

Chapter Twenty-Three

"Whit!" Duncan whirled on him. "What manner of daft condition is that?".

"The women will go back to sharing your cabin, Mr. MacDougal." Caleb avoided looking at his wife as he continued. "Mr. MacDougal, you can sling your hammock in my quarters. It would not look right for a married man with his wife aboard to sleep forward with the crew. Munro alone will be permitted in our living area, and he will be sworn to secrecy about the sleeping arrangements. Understood?"

"Good God, Cal!" The mate's response was an outburst. "We're husbands and wives. We have rights. And I, for one, am willing to take all necessary precautions to avoid the circumstance you fear."

"Even the best of precautions have been known to fail." Caleb faced him and the two women standing behind the first mate. "We cannot risk bringing a child into our present conditions. Would any of us want a son or daughter to be born on a warship, a warship where their innocent lives will be in danger from birth...possibly even before?"

"You're absolutely correct." Annie stepped forward, hand extended. "A child should not be born on a battleship. We agree to your terms, Captain...all of them."

She thought she glimpsed astonishment tinged with

a slight shade of disappointment as he accepted. *Ah, ha. That took him by surprise. Did he expect me to protest, to declare I couldn't bear to be without his desires in our bed?*

She glanced at her friend. Ginny MacDougal looked appalled.

"Annie, it could be weeks, months…"

"Ginny, it makes absolute sense. Remember the wives of husbands involved in whaling are often separated from them for years at a time. Surely we can do as well."

"Hell and damnation, very well."

Captain Cameron went to the chest of drawers. He picked up the bottle of whisky, pulled the cork, poured a good measure in each of the four mugs, and handed them around. When they all held drinks, he faced the three and raised his.

"To the success of our future endeavors."

"To the success of our future endeavors," they echoed and drank.

"Very well, then." He turned to Duncan. "Now to work. You ladies"—he glanced from one to the other— "can begin among the merchants, purchasing provisions. You know what the galley requires." He pulled a piece of paper from his pocket and scribbled a sum on it. "This much and no more." He handed it to Annie. "And, mind, no champagne or caviar."

"That wasn't really caviar I served the lieutenant governor and his lady." Annie's eyes twinkled. "It was salmon eggs darkened with blueberry juice."

"Good God, may they never find out!" Captain Cameron favored his wife with a stiff bow, turned, and strode out of the room. Duncan paused before Ginny to run a finger down her cheek, blue eyes soft with regret.

"May this damned war end soon," he muttered, then strode after his captain.

****

Caleb and Duncan watched as laborers put the finishing touches on the *Jenny Jones* while she stood in a slip high out of water, their brushes moving to conceal her former black sides with a coat of white paint. The change of color, Caleb had declared, would make her worthy of the new name he'd chosen for her. From that day forward the *Jenny Jones* would be known as the *Lady Ghost*. Five cannon had been installed on her deck. Three hundred of roundshot and four hundred weight of gunpowder had been purchased to store in her magazine, along with twenty-five muskets and forty cutlasses to supplement the weapons already in their possession.

"She'll be sliding into the water tomorrow, if all goes well," Caleb said, hooking his thumbs into his wide belt.

"Aye, but those two conditions you didn't share with our ladies will prove major pains in the arse." Duncan squinted up at the vessel. "Flying that flag they've so rightly named a Red Jack to indicate we're privateers will be like going duck hunting with a brass band. And that provision about our only being able to apprehend and seize vessels belonging to France, when it's American ships we were planning to go after…"

"Do you seriously think I've wasted money painting our ship to be next to invisible, refitting her from stem to stern, and posting that usurious bond only to be tied down by a couple of ridiculous regulations?"

"Damn it, Cal, you're wearing that devilish grin I

know only too well. You realize the risk we'll be taking by ignoring those regulations, don't you? You realize…"

"I realize that with this war brimming over, the Court of Vice Admiralty will soon be only too happy to rule American prizes legal. Now, come on, man. With the *Lady Ghost* about to slide into the water, we have to check on what our wives have been purchasing. I can only hope and pray there's no caviar, champagne, or French lace among their wares."

****

"Where are they? I sent a carriage for them an hour ago." Caleb paused in pacing the deck of his newly painted, renamed, and refloated ship the *Lady Ghost* to glower up the street that led down to the docks from the inn where they'd been staying. "I told them we sail on the noon tide."

"They'll be here, never fear, Captain." Duncan MacDougal stood by his side, hands on his hips, a good-natured grin curling his lips. "They're not about to risk their chance to become rich."

"Aye, well, we'll see. It's taken way longer than I'd anticipated to outfit and rig up the *Lady Ghost*. I never thought we wouldn't be putting to sea until September."

"Ah, unless I miss my guess, here they come now." Duncan pointed at the approaching carriage. It came out onto the wharf and halted at the gangplank. A pair alighted.

"What the….?" Caleb's mouth gaped open.

Stepping from the conveyance were his wife and his mate's spouse attired as never before. Both wore close-fitting tan breeches, knee-high boots, white shirts, wide belts, and black leather jerkins. Their hair tied back into queues, they looked as sea ready as the best of sailors.

"Now, will you look at that!" His friend's amusement and appreciation came out in his words as the pair took canvas bags the driver handed to them and headed for the gangplank. "Right fetching, I'd say."

"If you have a taste for such nonsense," he muttered.

"Well, Captain, what do you think?" His wife paused in front of him as she gained the deck and dropped her burden. She turned slowly before him in what he saw as a seductive move.

"I suppose if it's what you and Mrs. MacDougal have decided upon, my opinion matters little. Mr. MacDougal!" He swung on his mate. "Get the *Lady Ghost* underway. We've been delayed long enough."

"Aye, Captain. Ladies, stow your gear and take up your duties." With a sly, amused grin at his wife, Duncan turned away and began to bellow orders to the men.

"Come, Mrs. MacDougal." Annie picked up her luggage and headed for their quarters. "We've work to do."

Caleb tried not to watch as she walked away from him. Her shapely hips encased in those breeches were far too distracting.

****

"Mr. MacDougal, you'd best take a look at this." Caleb handed the spyglass to his mate, his tone reflecting rising excitement. "If I'm not mistaken, our first prize is looming on the horizon."

"Bloody hell, Captain, you're right." Duncan

squinted through the instrument as the sun, appearing over the horizon, glinted on the lens. "A big one, too. What ruddy luck! Only seven days out, and now this! Bugger all, I'm up for a fight. These days of remaining celibate with my wife aboard are fair straining at my nerves."

"I told you the Georges Banks was the place to be." Caleb grinned at his mate. "Full of pickings, with American ships heading home and trying to strike soundings off the coast. She's coming dead at us." He took the glass from his mate to further peruse their proposed victim. "Good God, she must be six times the size of the *Ghost*, probably brimming over with cargo, from the way she's sunk in the water. Ah, she's swinging with the wind." He put the glass back to his eye. "I can see her broadsides, and not a single cannon in sight. Her name is the *Middlesex*." He lowered the instrument and pulled in a deep, satisfied breath. "Didn't I tell you lying off here with our sails furled and that cursed red flag stowed would yield us a nice prize? Order the men to get ready. When she comes within range, fire a ball across her bow and hoist our flag. Unless they dare to risk being blown out of the water, they'll heave to without any further persuasion."

****

"Bloody hell! Coal, salt, earthenware, and a mess of other sundry items!" Duncan leaned against the mainmast and watched as the *Middlesex* prepared to get under way for Halifax with Samuel Poole, one of the *Lady Ghost*'s prize masters, and ten of their men aboard. "We're not going to get rich this way. And they were travelling under license from the British government. I can still see that arrogant prig of a captain fluttering it under our noses. We may not get a farthing out of this, once he shows that bit of paper to the Court of Vice Admiralty."

"Maybe we will, maybe we won't." Caleb wasn't about to let his mate's exasperation get the best of him. "We'll have to wait and see. It looks as if Mr. Poole and our men are about ready to get underway. The last of their sea chests have been loaded."

"Our first prize!" His wife emerged grinning from the living quarters, her friend close behind her. "And only a single shot fired. Excellent work, Captain, Mr. MacDougal."

"Thank you, ma'am." Duncan bowed and grinned back as Caleb scowled.

"You're supposed to stay below deck when we're in action," he snapped.

"Well, we're not in action now, and it's stifling below deck," she countered.

"Sweet Jesus, Cal, look!" Duncan who'd been gazing out to sea, away from the captured vessel, waved out an arm. "Sails. Coming straight at us again!"

"Another American seeking soundings, I'll wager." Excitement tingled over Caleb. Something in his gut told him here was a real prize. "They probably think the crew of the *Middlesex* and this vessel are both American ships paused to have a chin wag." He swung on the two women. "Get below deck. We're headed into action again, and this time it may take more than a single cannonball to bring about a surrender!"

"Come along, Mrs. MacDougal." Annie caught her friend by the arm. "It is part of our agreement."

"Your orders, Captain?" Duncan's voice reflected his master's eagerness as the women scuttled to obey.

"Let them come in until, like the *Middlesex*, they're close enough for us to skip a ball across their bow." He raised his spyglass. "Aha, she's swung a bit in the wind. She's named the *Factor*, and again, no cannon in evidence. Maybe we can take this one without a fight too."

****

Two hours later, Caleb watched exuberantly with his mate as another of his prize masters and twelve of his crew took possession of the *Factor* and headed her, side by side with the *Middlesex,* ahead of the *Lady Ghost* toward Halifax.

"Now, this second one has promise." Duncan grinned as he stood beside the captain. "Loaded with wine from Portugal, bags of silver dollars stashed in the captain's cabin, and not a bloody license in sight. I don't see how the Court of Vice Admiralty can fail to rule this one a legal prize. What a day!"

"Wine and silver?" Annie, followed by her friend Ginny, came out onto the deck in time to overhear the mate's description of the ship's cargo. "A prize indeed!"

"Aye, it well might be." Caleb let a self-satisfied grin crease his face. "My main concern is that our prize master will be able to keep the men from drinking up a hefty share of the booty. Now for Halifax and presenting the accounts of our seizures to the Court for ruling."

Chapter Twenty-Four

"Hell and high water, Cal, I never thought we'd be back at sea two days after depositing our prizes and papers with the Court in Halifax." Duncan stood on the rolling deck in the sunshine of a clear autumn morning as his captain scanned the horizon with his glass.

"And I never thought we'd be sailing for a week without sighting a single prize." Caleb lowered the instrument with an exasperated sigh. "Things have got to pick up, and soon. It could take the court months to rule on our first two prizes. We're burning up supplies to no good purpose and, as yet, with no income for our efforts."

"But maybe not for long." His mate grabbed the glass and put it to his eye. "Look, to the nor'east. A rare-looking vessel. She's low in the waist and high at both ends like a sway-backed horse. An old Spanish trader, I'd swear." He handed the instrument to Caleb, his voice hot with expectation.

"I concur, Mr. MacDougal. Give the orders. She could be weighed down with all manner of valuables."

An hour later, Samuel Poole and his prize crew were sailing off aboard the *Marengo*, the ship loaded with her cargo of wine, coffee, dyewoods, and other merchandise intact. The crew had given up without a fight after the *Lady Ghost* had lobbed a cannonball mere feet before her bow. There had been no way they could retaliate. The *Marengo*'s old brass cannons had been stowed in the hold for ballast.

"We'll follow her in to Halifax, Mr. MacDougal," Caleb advised his mate. "She's got the look of a valuable, easy prize. We can't risk losing her to others of our ilk."

"Aye, Captain." Duncan MacDougal was all-out grinning.

"When we put back to sea, we'll be heading for Cape Cod. I've a feeling the pickings will be good down there."

"Cape Cod! Hell and damnation, Cal, that's right in the Americans' dooryard."

"Exactly. They won't expect privateers so close. The *Lady Ghost* is fast. We'll be in and out with our prizes before they can raise the alarm."

****

"October has been a good month." Caleb leaned back in his chair in his cabin and let his mouth quirk in a self-satisfied grin. "Four prizes taken in five days between Cape Cod and Cape Ann."

"Something well worth bragging about, Captain." His wife smiled over at him as they sat in his cabin with Ginny and Duncan.

"The cargos they carried will fetch a right decent sum." Duncan, from his place in a chair across the cabin, looked up at Ginny. "You'll soon be living in luxury, Mrs. MacDougal."

"Gin, peppers, hops, sugar, oil, lumber, corn, flour, salt, earthenware, vinegar, cheese, cotton-duck, bonnets, and dry goods…" She canted her head to one side as she saucily recited the list of some of the spoils they'd taken. "And even rice, cotton, leather, and shoes from Carolina."

"So why are we now heading back into Halifax at such speed?" Annie asked. "We still have enough men on board to take another prize before we return. Ginny and I have seen to it we have provisions aplenty."

"You may not have been counting the days, Mrs. Cameron, but I have." He looked up at her and was surprised at the startled expression that crossed her face. "It's been sixty days since we obtained that provisional license. It's about to expire. Now I want an outright commission against the Americans. With that in hand, the Court of Vice Admiralty will be much more generous in awarding our prizes legality."

****

"You've got to tell him, Annie," Ginny hissed once they were back in the mate's cabin. "It's all his fault. He has to take responsibility."

"And get me put ashore and not allowed to sail again until after...and maybe never? No, I can manage. It's cold, and he won't notice, what with me wearing a coat most of the time. I won't give up my dream to be rich and have a fine house, especially now that there's someone else concerned." She ran her hand over her belly.

****

"We're iced to the limit, Captain." Duncan MacDougal stood beside Caleb on the heaving deck, slick with frozen spray and snow as he hunched his shoulders against the blizzard that assaulted his back. "I don't mind saying, I'm glad we're not far off Halifax. A chair by a fire will be more than welcome."

"Poole had orders to rent us a house when I sent him in with that prize last Friday." Caleb had to shout to make himself heard above the roar of wind and water. "We'll not put to sea again until March. I won't risk smashing the *Ghost* against a rogue iceberg."

"Agreed. I reckon as how our wives will enjoy playing housekeepers for a bit."

"Captain." Her cry above the screams of nature made him turn toward the hatch.

"Mrs. Cameron, don't come out!" His yell reflected his fear. "The deck is slick…"

Before he could finish, she'd stepped onto the icy surface. With a sharp yelp, she lost her footing and catapulted backward down the ladder and into the companionway beneath.

"Ann!" His shout mingled with her cry in the wind before she was horribly silent.

****

"A child?" Caleb stared at his mate's wife. "She's lost a child? How? When?" He stood in the heaving companionway outside his cabin, shock consuming him as never before.

"I'm sure you know how." Ginny faced him, her face contorted with anger. "The when was the night of the ball in Halifax…when you were too full of champagne to have the brains to protect her. Now…" She turned away, he guessed to hide tears.

"But she'll be well, won't she?" His consciousness tossed with a madness that had nothing to do with the motion of the storm-racked ship.

"She must be." She swung back on him, wiping her eyes with the backs of her hands. "She is my dearest friend, the best friend I've ever had."

"We'll be in Halifax by morning." He began to come out of the horror of it enough to become practical.

"I'll get her the best doctors. Now, I must see her."

He started to move past Ginny.

"No!" She blocked his way, eyes flashing with outrage. "You've done enough! She needs rest."

"Damn it, woman, I am her husband, the father of the child she's lost." His words, which began loud and angry dwindled over the last. He put a hand to his forehead and rubbed it, trying to restore reality to the situation. *Dear God, a child, and Ann badly injured...*

"Very well." Relenting before his reaction, she stepped aside to allow him entrance to where Annie lay. "But mind, only for a few minutes. She's very weak."

"Aye, aye." The consent was a mutter as he opened the cabin door.

He closed it behind him, then looked across the room to the woman lying in his bed.

"Captain." The word came out barely above a whisper.

"Mrs. Cameron." The words hurt his throat as he stood frozen in place. He didn't know what to do, what to say. *Dear God, she's white as death.*

"Our babe..." She held out a hand. Tears trickled down her drawn face.

"Ann, Sweet Jesus, Ann." In three strides he was at the bed, dropping on one knee beside her, grasping her hand, letting his forehead fall onto it. Something he hadn't experienced since he was a small lad escaped him. It was a sob.

"Captain, don't, please."

"Ann, our child. And I never knew. Why, in God's name, didn't you tell me? I would have taken you and Ginny to Halifax, gotten a house where you could have been safe..."

"That's exactly why I didn't tell you." Her voice was soft, reassuring. "Other women have had children at sea. I'm strong. I saw no reason…"

"You're right." He raised his head to look at her. "If anyone could have a child on a privateering vessel, it would be you. And all might have been well if you hadn't come up on deck, if you hadn't taken that God-awful fall…if you'd obeyed your captain and stayed in the cabin."

"You know I've never been especially good at following orders." A small smile raised the corners of her mouth.

"This is my fault." He looked into her eyes. "I should have taken precautions that night after the ball. I should…"

"I could have stopped you, cautioned you. You didn't force yourself on me. There has been one good outcome of this event. I know now that I want other children, your children. You do want children, don't you? Our children?"

The hope mingled with uncertainty he saw in her expression started a warm ache in his heart.

"Of course I do." He kissed the hand he still held. "When we're done privateering, we'll be able to build a fine home for them…an elegant home, where you'll be the mistress and a lady."

He leaned forward and kissed her forehead.

"Time to take your leave, Captain." Ginny stepped into the room and stood, hands on her hips, a small formidable force. "She has to rest."

"Aye." He stood. "Rest." He smiled down at her, feeling tears in his eyes. "We'll be in Halifax soon, where a safe home awaits you."

****

"I tell you, Dunc, this has been an epiphany for me." Caleb sat beside his first mate on the bunk in the latter's small cabin. He lowered his gaze to the whisky in the mug clasped in his hands. "I never realized what she'd come to mean to me until I was in danger of losing her."

"And I reckoned you a smart man." Duncan cast him a sideways glance, a glint of humor in his expression. "Then, for once, I've bested you, Captain Cameron. I've known how I feel about my Ginny for months now. It didn't take a near tragedy to make me realize I love the saucy wench."

"It's not a time for jesting." Caleb jerked to his feet and banged his knee on Duncan's sea chest. "Bloody hell, this is a right rat hole!"

"Perhaps not for jesting, but maybe for giving thanks?" Duncan looked up at him. "Ginny believes Annie will recover fully in time. She simply needs rest and care and good food. She's getting most of that now. Better victuals will soon be available, in Halifax, and I've no doubt my lady wife will cook up some excellent repasts for all of us."

"You're right, Dunc." Caleb sat down again and heaved a deep breath. "Thankful. And wiser. And no more champagne until this war is over."

Chapter Twenty-Five

"January 13, 1813, and still no rulings from the Court of Vice Admiralty on our prizes."

Ginny stood from the rocking chair, laid aside the piece of knitting she'd finished, and went to add another log to the fire blazing on the hearth before them. They'd come to shore and taken up residence in a modest but comfortable house in Halifax for the remainder of the winter. "We'll not be able to purchase supplies for going back to sea, never mind pay our expenses here in this house, if the old buggers don't soon make up their minds."

"I'm quite sure our husbands will not run up any bills they cannot handle." From her chair on the opposite side of the hearth, Annie spoke as she pulled the quilt more snugly about her shoulders.

Although the Halifax doctor Caleb had summoned to attend his wife had assured him she was well on the way to a complete recovery, the captain had insisted on hiring a maidservant to help Ginny with her care. Until the physician could assure him she was entirely well, Ann was not to lift a finger.

"I just wish everyone wouldn't insist on treating me as an invalid," she continued, shifting restlessly. "There's absolutely no need for the captain to carry me upstairs to bed each night and down in the morning."

"I think it gives him a bit of comfort to do what he

can for you, Annie. He feels so responsible for what has befallen you."

"Perhaps. Still…"

"I'm glad that serving girl taught me to knit." Ginny returned to her chair and picked up the red woolen thing she'd fashioned. "Otherwise I'd have gone right off my head with nothing to do. Look." She held up her creation. "Finished just in time. I hear our men arriving."

Annie didn't have an opportunity to reply. The door opened, stopping her words as the captain and his mate burst into the room, coated with snow, both carrying packages, the latter waving a bottle of wine with his free hand.

"Prepare to celebrate, ladies!" he cried. "The *Factor* has been ruled a prize and sold. We're on our way. It's only a matter of a few days before our other conquests will be declared legal seizures and money will come rolling in."

"So I see." Ginny stood and went to peruse his purchases. "And from the smell of your breath, I would believe you've already done a bit of celebrating…at the Crown and Anchor, I'll wager?"

"Ah, now, darlin', don't go denying us a bit of joy on this auspicious day." He dropped his packages and pulled her into his arms to kiss her, the bottle behind her back.

Caleb relieved himself of his packages and began to divest himself of his outerwear. "A bit of restraint, Mr. MacDougal," he advised. "It's only the beginning. Who knows what will become of our other captures? And you must remember the war is not yet over."

"Ah, Cal, don't be a naysayer. Just look at what

I've bought for you, Mrs. MacDougal." The mate ripped away the wrappings on one item and threw wide its contents to display a dark blue, hooded, floor-length cloak lined with fur. "To ward off the winter's chill. I thought it would look well with your brown hair and eyes." The last came out shyly, so shyly Annie glanced up at Duncan to be certain he had voiced the words.

"Oh, Mr. MacDougal, it's beautiful...the most beautiful thing I've ever seen." Eyes sparkling, Ginny stared at the garment.

"Here." He swung it about her shoulders. "Let me see if I've chosen well."

For a moment they stood staring at each other, their joy and happiness palpable in the room.

"And there's something more." Duncan pulled himself back to the moment. "But I'd prefer to share it with you in privacy."

"But it would be rude to leave Annie and the captain..."

"Go along." Annie grinned at her. "I think Captain Cameron and I can be trusted alone for a few minutes."

"Oh, Annie, I wasn't suggesting..." Ginny's consternation showed in her face.

"I know you weren't. Now go along with you." She waved her hand to dismiss the pair, and together they made their way upstairs, Ginny still wearing the cloak and clinging to it.

"I have a gift for you, as well." Caleb opened a package to display a garment similar to Ginny's but forest green in color. "I also chose it because of eye color. Tomorrow when we take you ladies for a sleigh ride, I'll see you bundled into it."

"It's beautiful, Caleb." She resorted to his Christian

name as she often did since they'd come ashore and when they were alone. "But you shouldn't have spent so much..."

"We got a goodly price for the *Factor* and her cargo, Mrs. Cameron." He swept the cloak about her as she sat in the chair. "You should know me well enough by now to know I'll never spend beyond our means. But that's not the most important gift I want to offer you."

He drew a small box from inside his waistcoat, knelt beside her chair, and held it out to her.

"Caleb..."

"Open it, please."

Carefully she raised the lid. A ring with a large emerald at its center surrounded by exquisite diamonds winked in the firelight.

"A wedding ring...if you'll wear it." The words came out faltering, startling from a privateer fearless in battle.

Staring down at it, she hesitated, not quite believing what she saw.

"If you choose not to accept it, I'll understand." He started to rise. "I've been responsible for all that has befallen you since I abducted you last spring. And then the child..."

"Caleb." Feeling tears stinging her eyes, she caught his sleeve and looked up at him. "Tell me you haven't done this out of guilt. If so..."

"Not guilt." He met her gaze squarely. "But partly out of a sense of obligation, of what is right and just. And..."

"And?"

"And out of a feeling that we're a strong team, that

we respect and care for each other, that I see a future for us once this war is over."

She hesitated. No glowing declaration of love, no mention of undying devotion, but still… She held out her hand.

"I shall wear it proudly."

He dropped back on his knee, something she read as relief in his expression. Taking her hand in his, he slid the sparkling ring onto her third finger. He looked up at her, and for a moment their eyes met. Finally he leaned forward to kiss her forehead.

The moment was broken as Ginny dashed down the stairs holding out her left hand.

"Annie, just see what Mr. MacDougal has given me!" She flashed a ring much like the one Annie wore except with a sapphire at its center. "Oh, Annie," she breathed dropping to her knees beside her friend's chair. "He wants it to be a wedding ring."

"That's wonderful, Ginny." Annie smiled at her. "It appears we've both just been made proper wives." She held out her new piece of jewelry.

"Whoever would have thought that such as us—me especially—would ever be wed to a pair like these two." Her brown eyes brightened with tears as she looked up at her friend.

"Now, now, none of that that." Duncan raised his wife to her feet and took her into his arms. "And what do you mean 'wed to a pair like these two'?" He grinned fondly, holding her out from him a moment later. "You might at least have said 'to such a fine pair.' "

"Oh, you are, indeed." Ginny, still overcome by her husband's gesture, smiled up at him and blinked back her tears. "Damnation!" She pulled away to scrub at her eyes with the backs of her hands. "What is happening to me! You, you great lout, with your gifts and marriage ring have made me embarrass myself. The next thing you know, you'll be refusing to take me back to sea with you because I've become too soft for the privateering life!"

"I'd never do that, my love." Duncan chuckled. "I'd be afeard for my manly parts."

"And you'd be right." She struggled into a grin as he took her back into his arms.

"Have a care, Mr. MacDougal," Caleb was quick to caution. "Remember, the war is not yet over."

"I know it all too well." The first mate held his wife out at arm's length. "But as soon as it's finished for us…"

"Oh, wait!" Ginny broke free and darted to the chair where she'd abandoned her knitted creation. "I have something for you, too! I made it myself." She held it up for her husband's inspection.

"It's…a right fine…" He stared and stumbled.

"Why, Mr. MacDougal, anyone can see it's a winter cap with ear covers…and tassels." Annie rushed to help him.

"To keep you warm on deck during storms such as the one we battled coming into Halifax." Ginny's look hovered between expectation and apprehension.

"Why, of course it is." Relief echoed in his words as he took the garment into his hands and examined it carefully. "Just the ticket. My ears have near been freezing off. Thank you, love." He pulled her into his arms, his face bright with emotion. "It's the finest hat I've ever had."

"Put it on." She pulled out from him. "Let me see how it looks."

"Very well." He rolled it over in his hands. "I'll just be figuring which way it will look best."

"Oh, for heaven's sake, let me." Ginny took it and reached up on tiptoe to place it on his head. "There."

Annie gulped in an effort to swallow the laugh that bubbled up her throat. Glancing at her husband she saw he was similarly stifling mirth. Tall, broad-shouldered, handsome First Mate Duncan MacDougal stood before them in the most ridiculous knitted hat they could imagine. Replete with a long tassel at the back and dangling earflaps with knitted ties, the thing destroyed his credibility as a dashing privateer.

"How do I look?" he posed like a swashbuckling sailor, hands on his hips, chest puffed out, making it even more difficult for Annie and Caleb to contain their mirth.

He looks like a medieval court jester. Annie trembled with suppressed laughter.

"Oh, Mr. MacDougal, it's even better than I'd imagined." Ginny, her face bright with joy at the reception of her labored-over gift, clasped her hands and smiled broadly. "I declare you're fair something to clap eyes on. Everyone will notice you."

Chapter Twenty-Six

"Damn, I hate this sitting about, Cal." Duncan MacDougal heaved a great sigh and fingered the handle on his tankard of ale as the two men sat in the Crown and Anchor. "I'm not one for lying around. If I could even find solace in my wife's arms...but we're still under that blasted oath to wait until we're done privateering."

"There's little sense of putting to sea until next month." Caleb understood his mate's frustration, but wisdom prevailed. "With few coasters sneaking past Cape Cod, it wouldn't be worth risking the *Lady Ghost*, not to mention our wives, who would never let us leave shore without them."

"Aye, aye, but come March..."

"Come March, provided we get letters of marque that will allow us to *legally* prey on Americans, we'll be hell on the water."

"Is there a Captain Caleb Cameron in the house?" A red-coated officer stood in the tavern door and bellowed.

"Here, sir." Caleb stood. "What can I do for you?"

"You're to come with me, sir. You and your first mate."

"Bloody hell, what now?" Duncan got to his feet, gathering up his greatcoat and slapping on his hat. "Can't we enjoy a drink without government interference?"

"We'll go along with him quietly," Caleb muttered. "We don't know why we're being summoned, and until we do, we'd best be docile. I wish you wouldn't insist on wearing that ridiculous hat."

"Ginny knitted it for me." He tied the strings under his chin. "I'm determined to wear it and take to task any man who dares make disparaging remarks." He looked ruefully down at bruised knuckles. "Come to think of it, I already have."

Thinking Ginny MacDougal had better stick to privateering, if this was an example of her ability to fashion woolen garments, and that Duncan must indeed be in love to go out into public wearing it, Caleb followed his first mate and the officer out of the tavern.

"Just be sure to take if off before we're ushered into the lieutenant governor's presence," he muttered.

****

"Gentlemen, thank you for coming right smart." Sir John Sherbrooke stuck out a hand as Caleb and Duncan came into his ornate office in Government House. He shook first Caleb's and then Duncan's hand vigorously. "How's that pretty little wife of yours, Mr. MacDougal? Still full of vinegar and pepper?"

"Aye, sir. She often speaks of her evening with you at the ball last year."

"You're a fortunate young man, sir," replied the barrel-chested man, the front of his uniform jacket bright with medals. "If I'd seen her first, well, I can tell you, I'd have given chase with all my might. She's a fine filly, that one. Don't let her far from your sight."

"Aye again, sir."

"Well, well, enough of the pleasantries." The

lieutenant governor rounded a massive mahogany desk, sat down, and waved his hand to indicate they were also to be seated. "The reason I've asked you to come here is because I've managed to secure letters of marque for you and your *Lady Ghost* that are shotproof against the legal batteries of this province. Furthermore, I've been informed all of the prizes you've captured so far are on the cusp of being ruled legal, every blessed one of them. If that's the case, I'd say that would make you tolerably rich men, what?"

"On the cusp? If?" Caleb caught a whiff of qualifying detail that didn't smell pleasant.

"Captain Cameron, I don't believe you're so naive as not to guess that such largess must come at a price." Sir John leaned back in his chair and steepled his fingers over his thick chest.

"And that would be?" *Damn it, I knew it was too good to be true.*

"As you know, these colonies have no official navy. We need privateers, skilled privateers like yourself and your crew, to foil the Americans by intercepting their shipping. The Royal Navy can give us but scant assistance, occupied as they are elsewhere around the world. The price for these letters of marque and clear title to all your prizes past and present is that you continue to do exactly as you have been doing until this ridiculous war ends."

"But that could be months or even years, sir." Duncan spoke up, and Caleb understood. Like himself, he was looking forward to making a home for himself and his wife as soon as their prizes warranted.

"Exactly." Sir John perused them with narrowed eyes.

"Cal?" Duncan looked over at him.

"I don't see what choice we have." He drew a deep breath. "Very well, Sir John. We'll serve as a ragtag navy."

"Good, very good." He stood, and his guests did likewise. "I think we should drink to this agreement. Then there will be papers to sign." He pulled a bell rope near his desk. "Mr. MacDougal…" He rounded the desk and came to stand close beside Duncan to speak confidentially in his ear. "I trust you'll be leaving your charming wife in Halifax when next you sail?"

"Ah, sir, would that I could." Duncan cast him an affable grin, but Caleb knew his mate well enough to guess he was struggling to refrain from punching the rotund man squarely on his bulbous nose. "She barely allows me a scant hour alone in a tavern, never mind leave her ashore."

"You do realize it's highly irregular to have women on a privateering vessel?" The man's words indicated his displeasure. "I'm not entirely sure there isn't some sort of disallowance of the practice in the conditions of letters of marque. Perhaps I should look into the matter."

"Aye, aye, but she's a right vixen when things don't go her way." Duncan feigned an exasperated expression. "She's not always the gentle, refined creature you met at the ball. Do you know, she took a frying pan to my head when I came home too late one night last week from the tavern? Fair rattled my brains, she did. Scraps like a wildcat, biting and scratching, when things don't go her way."

"Good God, man, she must be a rare handful, quite possibly more than a man of my years could begin to cope with."

Behind his back, Duncan winked at Caleb.

Chapter Twenty-Seven

"Hell of a thing, this bloody cold." Duncan addressed Caleb as the captain came on deck to relieve him of his watch. The mate drew his greatcoat more securely about him and pulled his red knitted hat lower on his forehead. Flurries whirled around the *Lady Ghost* as a bitter wind inflated her sails, driving her southward.

"Aye, but this bit of snow gives us good cover. We'll be off Cape Cod by first light tomorrow and not a soul beyond this ship any the wiser. You know the old saying, March comes in like a lion, goes out like a lamb. By the end of this month, I'm thinking we'll have fair sailing and lots of prizes."

"But, Good God, man, sailing out of Halifax in a blizzard—I still can't believe we made it safely to sea."

"You've got a clever captain." Caleb smirked at his companion. "Now stop bellyaching and go below. A bit of warmth and food will mellow your attitude. And you'll get a respite from that hat. Only their respect for you has kept the crew from outright laughing at it."

"Food, maybe, but not much warmth, with the damnable provision you made with our wives." He scowled and turned toward the door leading to their quarters.

"Mr. MacDougal!" Caleb squinted through an interval in the snow squalls. "Bring the glass! Unless

I'm badly mistaken, our first prize of 1813 is not far off to our left."

****

"Four prizes sent back to Halifax in the last nine days, beginning on March 5, 1813, one taken within two miles of the Cape Cod light. So endeth the sea day March 14, 1813."

With a contented sigh, Caleb finished writing up his log, closed the book, and leaned back in his chair to look over at his wife, his mate, and Ginny, who sat awaiting his conclusion although they had scant reason to doubt their success.

"We've done well?" Annie asked.

"We've done very well." He grinned. "But a lot of the credit must go to Doucet. He's done excellent work. His going ashore into enemy territory and ferreting out information has been a definite boon. Since he's French, the Americans assume he's an ally and trust him. When we divide up the spoils, I'll see he's justly rewarded."

"Aye, Captain, Doucet has proven to be worth his weight in gold." Duncan MacDougal concurred.

"But without your and Mrs. MacDougal's efforts I doubt we would have accomplished so much," Caleb continued, turning to his wife. "Men don't work or fight well on empty bellies or, I believe, in dirty surroundings. They've also been inspired by a desire to protect the pair of you...although I can't imagine why, since you've both demonstrated on more than one occasion that you can do a passable job of defending yourselves." Another grin accompanied the last remark.

"Still, it's heartening to feel that *some* men are willing to play the gallants to preserve our honor," she shot back, giving him a sly glance.

"Mrs. Cameron"—he leaned toward her, sobering—"I'd give my life for you, and I believe you know it. And as soon as this war is over…"

"I know." She looked at him, such tenderness in her eyes he had to fight to keep from rounding his desk and taking her into his arms. But they'd made a pact…

"Mr. MacDougal, shouldn't you be on watch?" To break the mood, he turned to his mate.

****

On a beautiful morning in late May 1813, Caleb looked up from his log book. His wife was singing softly as she sat across from him in his cabin, her needle leaving a crooked seam as she attempted to mend one of his shirts.

She may not be able to sew, but, good God, she's wonderful. After this war…

He looked down at the ragged scar on his forearm below his rolled shirtsleeve, a wry grin quirking his lips. She'd made a right mess of mending him, but she'd given it her best effort. He'd carry evidence of that battle wound for the rest of his life in remembrance of the fight but mostly of his wife's courage and undaunted loyalty in the face of adversity.

She glanced up and smiled.

"You appear happy, Captain," she said. "We've been doing well, haven't we?"

"Better than well, Mrs. Cameron. When this war ends—and I'm sure it will be under a year, since neither side shows any sign of winning or seriously continuing a pointless conflict—we'll be able to set up an establishment in Halifax…or wherever we choose, in a style befitting a gentleman and…his lady."

"Lady?" The word was a coy question. "At this time last year, I believe I was far from being any such creature, in your estimation."

"Ah, yes, but then I didn't truly know you." He closed the log book and stood, feeling gratified when she blushed...like a true lady under compliments. "It's a fine morning. Please. Accompany me on deck. A respite from working and planning will do us both good."

"That sounds like a fine idea." She laid aside her work and stood.

On the deck, he took her arm to guide her to the rail. Under a blue sky and light breeze, the *Lady Ghost* rolled gently forward. Off to the port side, in the distance, was a shoreline alive with the bright green vegetation of spring.

"It looks so beautiful." The words were a sigh.

"That's Tarpaulin Cove." He pointed. "On the far side is a lighthouse that I believe has been abandoned these past few years."

"It would be a perfect place for a picnic." She grasped the rail and threw back her head to breathe deeply of the warm spring air. "And it's been so long since we've been ashore."

"What, pray tell, is a picnic?"

"Once Lady Sophia was invited to eat a meal out of doors." She smiled. "It was called a picnic, a custom that has come from France, I believe. It's a meal served outdoors, with blankets spread on the grass, under the trees. With birds singing, and ladies and gentlemen dressed in their finest, and the best food and wine, it's a lovely experience. When the war ends and we've established a residence on dry land, I would dearly love to go on a picnic."

"Then you shall have it." He drew a deep breath and smiled down at her. "And quite possibly before the war ends."

Chapter Twenty-Eight

"Bloody hell!" Caleb handed the spyglass to his mate. "Look!"

"Bollocks! A British naval vessel."

"You're right, Mr. MacDougal." He snatched back the glass and applied it once more to his eye. "Ah-ha! They're coming after us. Hell and damnation! Looking to press merchant sailors such as ours supposedly are into their miserable ranks, I'll wager. We've some of the best fighting seaman aboard this vessel, and I'm not about to lose them. The hell of it is we're at less than half strength in manpower, with a goodly part of our crew gone to take in prizes. You two?" He swung on Annie and Ginny who'd been standing beside them. "Get below...now!"

His tone brooked no refusal. They hurried to the hatch and inside.

The crash of cannon fire had all but drowned out his last words as the ship pulled ahead of the *Lady Ghost* and, although at a good quarter-mile distance, managed to lob a cannonball ahead of her bow. It smashed into the water, throwing up a geyser of spray, mere yards in front of them.

"They mean business, Cal." Duncan looked across at the vessel tacking to run parallel but slightly ahead of them. "I'm counting at least a dozen gun ports on this side alone. They can blow us out of the water in the shake of a lamb's tail. Look at that arse of a captain standing like a peacock on the quarterdeck. The way he's dressed, you'd think he was going on parade, not into battle."

"Fetch my speaking trumpet." Caleb gave the order without taking his eyes from the ship now racing by their side. "Maybe I can talk sense into the bastard."

With the requested instrument in hand, he called out, "This is the privateering vessel *Lady Ghost*. We operate under a letter of marque and reprisal issued by the Court of Vice Admiralty of the province of Nova Scotia. I request that you let us go about our business."

"Then you'll not object to our boarding to examine your documents." The small, stiff figure in the red tunic replied over a similar device. "Slow your progress."

"Bloody hell." Caleb turned to his first mate. "Give the orders, Dunc. We're outgunned, and from what I can see on their deck, outmanned. We'll have to give in to the arrogant little blighter."

Both ships, sails adjusted, slowed their speed until they were all but stopped, parallel in the water. A cutter was lowered from the naval vessel. A snarl rose in the back of Caleb's throat as he watched two sailors row the captain and another officer toward his ship.

"Lower a ladder." He heard Duncan give the order as anger and frustration seethed over him.

Sweet Jesus, we're on the same side. Why can't they leave us alone?

"Captain Henry Blake, sir." The small, imperious man faced Caleb insolently. "Of his majesty's ship *Queen Charlotte*."

"Captain Caleb Cameron, master of the legally licensed privateer *Lady Ghost* out of Halifax." Caleb confronted him, hoping his face mirrored all the contempt he was feeling.

"Ah, well, Captain Cameron, it looks as if you have a fine bunch of men aboard...all Englishmen, I'll wager. I trust you won't mind if Lieutenant Burns looks them over?"

"I do, but I know that will make little difference."

"Lieutenant Burns, inspect this crew. If they're British, they should be serving in the navy, not acting as pirates. Pick the best dozen among them and take them back to the *Queen Charlotte*."

"Dozen...!" The number roared from Caleb's throat. "Twelve?"

"Captain Cameron, what is all this commotion?" His hands were knotting into fists when her voice made him turn. Coming out of the door beneath the quarterdeck was his wife, in the gown she'd been wearing when he'd taken her prisoner. Head held high, she looked every inch a princess. Behind her, Ginny trotted in maid's outfit, the perfect attendant.

"A lady aboard, Captain?" Captain Blake turned to stare in her direction as she came to join the men.

"My wife." The words came out of stunned surprise and sounded hollow.

"Ma'am." The naval officer's weathered face mirrored his astonishment. "We had no idea there were women aboard. Children?"

The reference brought nausea flushing through Caleb's gut. *But for a cruel twist of fate there might have been one...*

"Not as of yet." Apparently able to disguise any emotions the officer's words might have aroused, she held her nose in the air as if the newcomer stank and continued her ruse. "We've been married but a short time. I am Lady Ann Milbank. You may know my brother, the Duke of Haverbrook, a close personal friend of the Prince Regent. My brother and Captain Cameron were at Cambridge together."

Good God, has the woman taken leave of her senses? Willie has no sister.

"Lady Ann." This time the captain snapped to attention and bent in a deeper bow. "I had no idea, your ladyship. Your servant, ma'am."

Caleb almost heaved an audible sigh. Apparently the bloody little twit of an officer didn't know Willie was an only child.

"Well, now you do, and I'd be most grateful if you'd removed yourself and your men from my husband's vessel so that we may proceed." His wife was speaking again. "I would be loath to give my brother a report of your lack of gallantry when next I see him."

"Of course, my lady." Again a bow. "Lieutenant, we'll be returning to the *Queen Charlotte*," he called to his officer. "Safe sailing, my lady." He backed away a few steps before bowing again, turning, and heading for the rope ladder that led down to their waiting boat.

"Safe sailing to you as well, Captain," she called after him. "And I would be most grateful if you'd inform your fellow mariners of the British Navy that the *Lady Ghost* is to be left unmolested to pursue the colonies' enemies."

"Of course." He climbed over the bulwarks and headed down the side of the ship, his lieutenant following.

Once they'd gone and had rowed out of hearing,

Caleb swung on his wife.

"That was a mad escapade," he said. "What if that ridiculous little louse had known the duke has no sister? What if..."

"Oh, do stop sputtering. How many men of his standing will dare to question the existence of Lady Ann Millbrook? Given our present location, he had no one to ask for verification. Furthermore, I doubt he'll be back in England for months. Even then he's hardly likely to be at court or anywhere else of consequence. At the moment, I think you should be telling me how clever I am."

With a swish of her elegant gown, she swung away from him and walked proudly away, Ginny following with equal arrogance, to vanish in the direction of their sleeping quarters.

"All right, lads, get us underway!" Duncan bellowed the order. "The faster we can put a distance between us and those arrogant bastards the better. You might thank God and, when next you encounter her, Mrs. Cameron, that none of you are now members of the British navy."

Glad to be free of the threat of pressed service, the crew rushed to do the mate's bidding as he went to stand close to the captain.

"Hell of a thing, that," Duncan muttered. "If it hadn't been for your wife...and mine, we would have lost some of our best men." A grin broke slowly over Duncan's weather-darkened face. "I think it's time you fittingly thanked your lady."

"I'll speak with her." He headed toward the hatch, then turned back to his first mate. "And what about yours? Surely mine wouldn't have been believable as a lady without a properly arrogant maidservant."

"You know I have to remain on deck until we're well underway." He squinted up at the men climbing the ratlines to unfurl sails. "But never fear, Captain. She'll be fittingly thanked when my watch is over." He lowered his gaze and winked at Caleb.

"Just take care, man, just take care." Caleb continued on his way.

Chapter Twenty-Nine

"Bloody hell, Annie, but I was fair shaking in me boots up there!" Ginny unbuttoned the fastenings on the back of her friend's elegant gown in the captain's cabin. "What if that arrogant little prick of a captain hadn't swallowed your tales? What if…?"

"Calculated risks." Annie stepped free of the garment, and Ginny stooped to gather it up. "Worth it, as it turned out, don't you think?" She went to the captain's bed and began to put on the trousers and shirt she'd been wearing before the encounter.

"I suppose." Ginny removed her maid's outfit and began to don like attire. "Still…"

"I believe our men should shortly be coming to thank us." Annie adjusted the belt on her trousers and smirked over at her friend.

"Perhaps." Ginny finished her redressing and pulled a cap over her curls. A sly smile slowly brightened her countenance. "But this time, Annie, you will take care, won't you?" She frowned.

"Of course," Annie said, going to smooth the covers on the bed. "I won't get so carried away again."

"Good." Ginny headed for the door. "I'll be leaving that maid's outfit here with your finery. There's barely room to move in our cabin, and these dress-up clothes have been getting right crushed. It's probably well that we don't have many garments." She hung the gowns carefully on pegs near the door.

A knocking stopped their conversation.

"Mrs. Cameron, may I come in?" Caleb's voice followed.

"Of course, Captain."

"I'll be going." Ginny slid out past the man as the door opened. "This lot will soon be hungry. You can join me in the galley, Mrs. Cameron, once your meeting with your husband is concluded."

"Definitely, Mrs. MacDougal." They bobbed each other a jesting curtsy that drew a soft scoff from the new arrival.

Once she'd gone, Caleb shut the door and leaned back against the panel, arms crossed on his chest.

He's magnificent. Everything I've ever dreamed of in a husband...except being a gentleman.

With an effort, Annie pulled out of her admiration and managed to drop him an abrupt curtsy. "What may I do for you, sir?"

"Just now on deck. That was a daft thing to attempt."

"Daft perhaps, but the result was worth the risk, I think you'll have to admit."

"Aye, aye." He drew a deep breath and strode across the room to take up a bottle of whisky from a sideboard. "Damned British navy. They can't get men to join up voluntarily because of their miserable treatment of seamen, so they've taken to raiding innocent ships like the *Lady Ghost*."

"Innocent?" She chuckled. "Hardly innocent, Captain."

"No, perhaps that was a misnomer. 'Civilian' might better describe the *Ghost* and her crew."

"At any rate, the present danger is past, and I'm sure the captain of the *Queen Charlotte* will spread the word that the *Lady Ghost*'s master has a lady wife." She shot him a sly smile. "That should insure us safe passage, at least for a time. Now, you must excuse me. I have to join Mrs. MacDougal in the galley. The crew will be looking for food shortly, and as you've said, there's no work or fighting in hungry men."

She started to move past him, but he caught her lightly by the arm. Looking up at him, she felt her breath catch in her throat. Raw longing such as she'd never seen was reflected in his eyes and countenance, making the planes of his weather-bronzed face taut, hard with suppressed desire.

"Ann…" The air hung thick with longing, with a tension so intense it was almost palpable. Her heart burst into a pounding that felt as hard and demanding as a tattoo. *Oh, God, Caleb…*

"No." The word came out in a choke as she forced herself to back away, head swimming. "No, Captain. We made a pact." She swallowed hard and hoped her eyes didn't betray the true desire of her heart.

"Aye." His hand dropped to his side. He reached for the door, pulled it open, and held it for her. "I wish you good day, Mrs. Cameron."

****

"Look there, Cal." Duncan pointed off the leeward bow. "A vessel, but what manner of craft I can't fathom. Only a pair of sails, and not more than twenty feet in length. It seems to be sailing all hell west and crooked."

"Whoever they are, they're in trouble, Dunc. Head us over to see what's wrong."

Shortly the *Lady Ghost* drew abreast of the small sailboat.

"Cal, it's three boys, the oldest not more than sixteen years of age, by the look of him." Duncan glanced back down into the vessel. "God almighty, duck! One of them has a gun aimed at us!"

A musketball flew over their heads.

"Ahoy," Caleb yelled, crouched behind the bulwarks. "We mean you no harm. We only want to help if you're in need of assistance."

"Damned Scotians!" the cry came back, and another musketball flew above them to rip into a sail.

"Now just a cursed minute!" Incensed by the destruction to his ship, Caleb stood and glared down at the three. "We've offered to help. As a result, I don't take kindly to your ripping holes in my sails."

"We'll not be taken captive by damned Scotians!" one, apparently the captain, yelled.

"Then why aren't you shooting at me?" Caleb took a giant gamble. "I'll wager you've spent your ammunition." Looking down at the ragtag trio in a vessel too small to be seaworthy, he saw how gaunt and thin they were. "Come aboard and have a decent meal. Then, if you're still of a mind to return to sea, we'll give you provisions and point you on your way."

The three exchanged looks. The youngest—Caleb guessed he was barely into his teens—glanced hopefully at his companions.

"Come aboard, gentlemen." Annie suddenly appeared at Caleb's side, a smile on her face. "We've got a stew simmering, and lots of bread and tea."

Later, Caleb would think that the appearance of an angel at his side at that moment could not have astonished the trio in the small ship more. They stood staring up at her, mesmerized.

"Well, gentlemen?" Caleb sought to bring them back to the moment. "What's your decision?"

They held a short conference, and then the youthful captain nodded. "We accept your offer, ma'am."

"Good, very good." Caleb turned to Munro. "Lower a ladder for these fine fellows."

Clutching three ancient muskets, they scrambled aboard, casting furtive glances around the deck at the burly sailors watching.

"Nothing to fear, gentlemen." Annie smiled and Caleb spent a brief moment enjoying her beauty. *Small wonder these young lads were struck dumb on seeing her.* "We're all seafarers here, ready to help fellow mariners. Please join us in a meal ready and waiting below. Captain Cameron, will you make certain their ship is securely moored to the *Lady Ghost*?"

"The *Lady Ghost*!" one young lad gasped. "We saw she was painted white, but we couldn't make out her name, coming up as we did. Billy, we're sure and certain done for!" He turned to the one who'd been acting as their captain, his face paling under its freckles. "We're Scotia bound for sure, and prison!"

"What's your cargo?" Caleb looked again over the bulwarks and into the small vessel, which appeared to carry little beyond a pair of sails and oars and an empty box he guessed had once held their provisions. A length of canvas fastened over the bow served as shelter.

"We're carrying naught that would interest the likes of you." The third crewman spoke. Tall and gangly, he faced Caleb defiantly, although his complexion had taken on a grayish tinge at the mention of the ship's name.

"Probably not." Caleb refused to demean them by saying they had nothing at all. He'd been young and poor once, too. "Go with my wife and get yourselves fed. Once you've filled your bellies, you can be off. We've no time to be ferrying three prisoners in to Halifax."

"This way." Annie indicated the way to the crew's eating quarters. "I believe there may even be some fruitcake left."

Behind the three young lads' back, Caleb gave his wife a nod and a wink.

****

"Gentlemen, what may I ask is your profession?" Caleb joined the three at the table as they sat gobbling down stew and bread, cups of steaming tea before them.

The captain paused and hesitated for a moment. "We be privateers, sir."

"American, I take it?" Caleb continued seriously. Over the boys' heads, Ann smiled at him.

"Aye, sir, from the ship *Mistress May*." Encouraged by Caleb's attitude, he continued. "We saw the prizes comin' in and makin' folks rich, so we thought…"

"Much the same as I perceived." Caleb continued. "Makes a man want to see what he can do, right?"

"Aye, sir." The young man wet his lips.

"And we've brothers and sisters at home who…" the youngest started to chime in.

"Daniel, that's enough." Billy, the captain, wasn't about to seek sympathy, Caleb was quick to recognize, and admired him for it.

Desperately poor and probably with a number of

siblings at home in the same way.

"Gentlemen." Caleb stood and headed for the door. "I'll leave you to enjoy your meal. Mrs. Cameron, don't forget that cake you mentioned."

"Aye, Captain." Annie bobbed him a curtsy and favored him with a smile that warmed his innards.

****

A half hour later, Annie followed the three lads back onto the deck. The fog had lifted, and a pale sun was shining on the wind-ruffled water.

"Thank you, sir." Captain Billy paused as the three approached the bulwarks to hold out a hand to Caleb. "We're right grateful."

"No more than one seafarer should do for another." Caleb retained his businesslike countenance. "Perhaps some day you'll be able to return the favor."

"Aye, with pleasure."

"Billy, look!" Daniel was leaning over the bulwarks and staring down toward their small vessel.

Captain Billy came to join him while Duncan looked on, grinning.

"There's three sacks of potatoes and a couple of barrels aboard!" Daniel explained needlessly as the young ship's master stared.

"One sack of potatoes for each of you," Duncan explained. "And one barrel contains beef, the other butter, cheese, and tea. Mind you divide it fair and square among your crew, Captain."

"We can't take it." Although it was apparent Billy was fighting the urge to accept, he stood up proudly and faced Caleb. "You be the enemy, sir."

"Captain." Caleb drew himself up in his not-to-be denied pose. "It's but how I would wish to be treated if ever I'm captured by your people. We may be fighting a war, but that's no need for inhumane conduct, don't you agree?"

The young man paused only a moment longer, then nodded. "Thank ye, sir. You're an officer and a gentleman, certain sure."

"Very well, then, get aboard and head home. You don't want that food to spoil in the damp."

The other two young lads scrambled over the bulwarks and down into the vessel to examine the bounty it held. Their captain held back.

"Well?" Caleb looked at him.

"Sir." He lowered his voice to speak confidentially. "I'm not certain sure how to get home."

"Don't you have a sextant or chronometer?" Caleb couldn't keep incredulity out of his tone.

"No, sir." He hung his head.

"Then how did you hope to navigate?"

"By the sun and stars, sir."

"A risky proposition, at best." *Good God, these children must have been starving to attempt going to sea, never mind on an ocean teeming with privateers and any number of rascals, in a tub that is barely more than a rowboat.*

"Mr. MacDougal." He turned to his mate, who'd been listening. "We've nothing pressing planned for the next few hours. What say we guide these fine lads toward land?"

"I think that's a fine idea, Captain." Duncan didn't hesitate. "I'll tell the men to get us moving."

Caleb swung briskly to the young ship's master. "Captain, if you'll climb aboard your vessel and prepare to sail, we'll head you for shore. What port do you call home?"

"But, sir…" Captain Billy's expression, alive with hope for a moment, shadowed. "You'd be heading into American waters. And knowin' your reputation and how dead set folks are for your capture…"

"You let us worry about that." Caleb held out an arm to indicate the way to the lad's small boat. "Just mind you follow close in our wake. Now again, I ask, what's your home port?"

"Portsmouth, sir. Portsmouth, New Hampshire."

Chapter Thirty

"Listen to this, Cal." Duncan MacDougal read from the newspaper Doucet had brought on board from his last spy mission ashore. "They've dubbed you the evil genius of the coasting trade. Here's what they've written: 'At about five o'clock on Saturday afternoon, Captain Caleb Cameron's *Lady Ghost* took the schooner *Fanny*. Provoked by this, another evidence of the near blockade of our port by a single vessel, the good citizens sent out the brig *New Orleans* on Sunday afternoon, manned with a smart and experienced crew.

" 'The *New Orleans* chased the *Ghost* until she got within a mile and a half of the privateer, when a calm fell. With night coming on, those brazen buccaneers, taking to the sweeps no doubt stolen from the *Fanny*'s cargo, escaped. The following day, the armed vessels *Jefferson* and *Frolic* sailed in pursuit but with no better luck. Like the apparition for which she's named, the *Lady Ghost* appears to have the ability to vanish into thin air.' "

"Thin air." Caleb chuckled. "Vanishing created by clever sailing and good men on the sweeps."

"Aye, but we must be more cautious." Duncan squinted into the fog enveloping the ship as she lay in wait for her next conquest. "We've scotched the Americans, not defeated them. This report confirms their determination to blow us out of the water at all cost."

"I hope you're not losing your nerve, Mr. MacDougal," Caleb narrowed his eyes as he looked at his mate.

"No, but my common sense is kicking in right hard." Duncan faced him squarely. "You're getting too brazen, taking unnecessary risks. We've already captured enough prizes to make us wealthy men. I'm thinking we should head back to Halifax, collect our spoils, and put the *Ghost* in dry dock."

"You're forgetting our deal with the lieutenant governor. You're assuming the Court rules all the vessels we've taken as legitimate prizes." Caleb drew a deep breath. "Without his consent, I'm far from convinced they will. No, we have to continue acting as a naval vessel until this damned war ends."

"Forget that horny old bastard, Cal. If the Court of Vice Admiralty rules even half of them…"

"And who's to say they'd do even that in defiance of Sir John's instructions? No, my friend, we've made a deal with the devil. Now…" He turned to look shoreward. "How do you think our ladies would fancy a picnic ashore? It's some kind of meal eaten outdoors, my wife has informed me. I plan to surprise her with one. Tomorrow is Sunday, supposedly a day of rest. I'm thinking we head into Tarpaulin Cove tonight under cover of fog and darkness. Tomorrow, with clear skies, we'll have that picnic there. She's taken a fancy to the place."

"Are you daft, Cal?" Duncan rounded to stand in front of his captain, his face registering the shock the announcement had given him. "We'd be sailing through the thick of Vineland Sound traffic. Someone would be sure to spot us."

"I think not." Caleb turned and started to walk away. "We'll be sailing at night, no lanterns lit."

"You're getting too damned cocky, Cal!" his companion hissed, grabbing him by the arm. "You'll get us all killed!"

"I'll thank you to take your hand off your commanding officer, Mr. MacDougal." Caleb swung back on him.

"You're doing this as a treat for Annie. Bloody hell, man, you can't keep forever trying to appease the loss of the child! You can't act foolishly in an attempt to…"

"Oh, and you didn't continue to wear that ridiculous hat all winter simply to please your lady?"

"That's different. I wasn't risking life and limb…"

"As I recall, a few of the bar fights it got you into very nearly did just that. Now enough bickering. I know what I'm doing. The men need a respite, and so do you and I…even if you don't realize it. There's no work or fighting in a weary crew. Tonight we sail into Tarpaulin Cove. Doucet!" He summoned the Frenchman. "I'll be sending you back to shore. There are a number of items I want you to purchase."

Chapter Thirty-One

"What a sight!" Ginny burst into the captain's cabin. "Annie, you'll never believe what I saw on deck just now."

"Why were you up there? The captain specifically told us to stay inside today because of the rain and fog."

"Aye, but the slop bucket had to be emptied. Annie, as I live and breathe, most of the crew—well, I didn't linger to count—were up there, stark naked, washing themselves with the water that is showering down off the sails. There's a fair cloudburst underway."

"Ginny, you must have been seeing ghosts in the mist. Perhaps this enforced carnal separation from your husband has made you fancy…"

"Annie Pudden Cameron, I saw what I saw." Ginny's voice rose in exasperation. "Dozens of bare bottoms…and more."

"But why this sudden need for the men to wash?" Annie put a finger to her chin as she pondered. "God knows most of them could stand it, but why now? And why are the sails up when we're becalmed in this rain?"

"I'm thinking the sails were put up for the purpose they're now serving."

"Something is afoot, Ginny." Annie sat down on the bed, frowning. "It's been some time since our husbands have sought to keep us unapprised of a situation. This must be unique, indeed."

****

"I'm getting right tired of staying cooped up down here." Scowling, Ginny MacDougal plunked her bottom down into a chair in the captain's cabin. "From what I can see, it's a lovely day, sunny and warm. We should be up on deck enjoying it before we once more head into combat and are forced to hide out."

"Captain Cameron has been most mysterious." Annie adjusted her muslin gown. "He had a cat-in-the-cream expression on his face when he asked us both to don the dresses and sunbonnets we purchased in Saint John that first day in port there. Perhaps we're to have tea on deck and pretend we're in an English drawing room or parlor."

"Hardly." Ginny guffawed. "The men would laugh the captain out of his master's ticket for such foolishness."

"I think his men have far too much respect for him to scoff at anything he did."

"All the same, something daft must be afoot."

"Ladies, are you decently attired?" Captain Cameron's words accompanied his knock on the door.

"Aye, Captain." Ann smiled and headed for the door.

Opening it, she suppressed a gasp. Her husband stood before her dressed in a white shirt, neckcloth, black coat, and tan breeches. Below, ebony-colored boots gleamed with polish.

His mate stood behind him, similarly attired, grinning.

"Your chariot awaits, ladies." The captain and his mate bowed to the ladies and offered their arms.

On deck, Annie was astounded to find several of

the sailors as clean and well dressed as she'd ever seen them. They stood like a guard of honor all the way to one area in the bulwarks.

"Where are we?" Annie glanced around to see that the *Lady Ghost* was anchored in a wide cove.

"Tarpaulin Cove, my lady." Her husband adjusted her hand on his arm and led her past the men to the ship's side. There he caught her up in his arms and hoisted her to the rail. "Make your way down carefully," he said. Looking below, Annie saw Higgins and Munro at the sweeps of the ship's cutter, several covered baskets in the bow.

"Captain, what is all this?" Seated on the bulwark, she stared at him in astonishment.

"You said you'd enjoy a picnic, so we're having one...on the shore, beneath the trees yonder in that cove you found so inviting." He was grinning. "I had Munro scout an appropriate place. Some of the crew are already ashore setting out all of the fine foods Doucet purchased on one of his forays ashore."

She stared at him, astonished. "But can this be safe? We must still be in American waters."

"Look around. Do you think any passing vessel will notice the *Lady Ghost*? They'd never expect to find her so close to shore. And I've been given to understand that lighthouse on the far shore is no longer manned."

"So we *are* in American territory." She turned to get back aboard the ship. "We have to leave at once."

"No." He stopped her with a hand on her arm. "My lady wife expressed a desire to have a picnic, and so she shall. Furthermore, these hard-working, hard-fighting men of our crew have gotten themselves all cleaned up for it. To disappoint them would be shameful."

She looked back at the expectant faces of the men, at their attempts to make themselves presentable, and could refuse no longer.

"Very well, Captain Cameron. Let us have our picnic."

****

"Caleb, this is like a dream…a beautiful dream." Annie sat on a blanket on the grass with Caleb, supported on one forearm, lying beside her. He grinned up at her enjoyment.

From farther back in the trees came the raucous shouts of the men. Involved in rough games, they, too, were enjoying themselves.

"The crew seems to be happy with the day," he said. "They needed a bit of time off."

"And is that the only reason for this lovely picnic?" She smiled down at him, aware it had been for her, because of her wish.

"I think you know the answer to that, Mrs. Cameron. And were we not held in check by our privateering agreement, I'd sweep you up in my arms and carry you into the trees, back beyond where the men could find us, and…"

"Annie!" Ginny, with Duncan following, burst in on what for Annie had fast been becoming a most seductive moment. "We've found wild strawberries! Imagine! Strawberries this early in the year."

"Aye, we've been berry picking." Eyes twinkling, Duncan gazed at his wife.

"Dunc…" The captain began.

"Ah, not to worry, Captain, sir. Only a couple of chaste kisses. You can't go denying that to a married man."

"I suppose not, but it can lead to…"

"But it didn't." As Ginny dropped beside Annie on the blanket, Duncan eased down to join them, his back against a tree trunk and grimaced.

"Nevertheless, Mr. MacDougal, you have the look of a man whose back is bothering him." Caleb stared suspiciously at his mate. "A few innocent kisses wouldn't…"

"Bloody hell, Cal! I hurt my back swinging all the bits and pieces necessary for this party over the bulwarks. Ginny and I made the same pact as you and Miss Annie. We're not about to break it until this blessed war ends. But…" He turned his gaze on his wife, a gaze so filled with lustful passion Annie felt a blush climbing her own cheeks. "The minute peace is declared, I don't care where we are…"

"Mr. MacDougal!" Ginny admonished, but her eyes were gleaming with similar desire.

A blast of musket fire broke the silence. Caleb and Duncan bolted to their feet as the cries and roars of their men told them something had gone dreadfully wrong.

"Captain, sir!" Munro burst in upon them. "We've been sighted! Three young men were in that old lighthouse! One shot Higgins before they fled into the bush! I reckon it will only be a half hour before they get to the nearest village. We must sail at once!"

Chapter Thirty-Two

"I told you this was a daft idea!" Duncan paused amid the frantic preparations to get the *Lady Ghost* out of Tarpaulin Cove. "By now those lads will have told their tale to the nearest militia men and a dozen armed vessels will be getting ready to give chase. Never mind the cost to Higgins."

He turned to where their wives were ministering to a shoulder wound on the giant who sat with his back against the mainmast.

"He'll live. Now, enough bellyaching and guilt laying! Get men on the sweeps. There's not enough of a breeze to give us speed until we're well out on the water. With luck, it will take any pursuers a fair length of time to get after us."

****

"We've outrun them!" Duncan MacDougal lowered his glass and heaved a relieved sigh. "I never thought we would make it to open water, with three of them hot on our arse. I have to give it to you, Captain Cameron. You can make this lady fly like a witch and vanish like a ghost."

"Were you doubting my ability, Mr. MacDougal?" He curled a corner of his lip as he looked over at his mate.

"Never your ability, Captain Cameron, but at times your devil-may-care attitude fair gives me pause."

"You must be getting old. Once upon a time you would have reveled in a squeaking close escape like today."

"Not old, just wiser. I have a young wife to think of now."

"And may I hazard a guess that you think of her far too often?"

"Come on, Cal. Don't tell me the beautiful Annie Cameron doesn't haunt your dreams."

"This is not the time to be discussing our personal lives. Because we've outrun our enemies this time doesn't mean they won't come after us again."

****

On June 11, 1813, Caleb stood beside the mainmast and surveyed the horizon. The *Lady Ghost* lay with sails close furled, waiting to see what the day would bring. He'd have to be careful what ships he challenged, he knew. He had only twenty men aboard, the rest away with prizes.

"Sail, Captain, sail!" A man high in the rigging yelled down to him. "To port, standing out to sea."

Caleb followed the direction of the man's outstretched arm and saw it, a sail just where his man had indicated.

"Hold her steady! Best not to make a move until we know what's coming at us. Mr. MacDougal, make ready."

"Aye, Captain."

The crew held the *Lady Ghost* nearly motionless until the course of the stranger brought her into clear view.

"Good God, Cal!" Duncan came to stand by his captain's side. "They're heading dead at us! What in hell…!"

"She's a large schooner with square topsails." Caleb squinted through the glass Duncan handed him. "Damn, but there's something strange about the way she cuts down the distance. This is no merchantman bound for Havannah, Mr. MacDougal. She's altogether too eager to make our acquaintance."

Duncan took back the glass and raised it to his eye.

"Sweet Jesus! An American privateer! Captain, orders!" He turned to Caleb.

"All sheets to the wind!" Caleb made a quick decision. "We'll give him a race if we can't give him a fight. Mr. MacDougal, order all hands on deck!"

With a thunder of thrashing canvas, banging of blocks, and whine and purr of travelling gear, the *Lady Ghost* was off and running.

The stranger took up the chase. As she came near enough for a clear view, Caleb saw the Stars and Stripes blowing out from her topmast head and gaff end.

"It's the *Thomas* out of Portsmouth, sir," Doucet yelled to Caleb, his eyes wide. "I saw her on one of my trips ashore. She's double the size of the *Ghost* and armed to the teeth. Ten big guns, five to a side, and four more swivels on the rail. May the good God have mercy on us!"

"I never thought to see you show fear, Doucet." He turned to the man.

"And I don't now, Monsieur le Captaine, but…the *Tom*!"

The first of the carriage-guns spoke. A cannonball ricocheted over the waves like a skipping stone to drop into the water within a quarter mile of the *Lady Ghost*'s bow.

"A twenty-four-pounder, sure," Duncan yelled.

"Only a twelve," Doucet estimated. "And if that's the *Tom* of Portsmouth, that's the heaviest she's got."

"Certain sure, it's the *Tom*! Big and heavy, and no match for the *Ghost* in a good run," Munro yelled, and Caleb knew the sailor's optimistic tone was to hearten the crew after Doucet's dire pronouncement. "Heave to it, men! We'll leave those buggers a mile behind in our wake in no time. Let the old cat come, and we'll trim his whiskers, lads!"

Caleb appreciated his crewman's rallying cry. Munro was too experienced a seaman not to know their vessel was ill matched against such a mighty vessel, especially at one-third crew, but he wasn't about to show apprehension.

"Aye!"

Good men. Not a single coward among this crew. I've got to do my best for them.

"Our short-range twelve-pounders are useless against this big bastard." He turned to Duncan. "We can't afford ballast in a race. Throw them overboard."

"But Captain…"

"Just do as I say, Mr. MacDougal. And order every inch of canvas up."

"Aye." Forcing the doubtful frown from his face, the first mate turned away and began bellowing orders.

"Oh, and Mr. MacDougal." Caleb followed him.

"Aye, what now?" Exasperation colored his words as he turned back to his captain

"Those two four-pounders… Throw them overboard, as well. Have the men drag Shiny Sam to the stern and prepare the old devil to fire. He's a long ranger, and he might just save us."

"One six-pounder against the Tom's big guns? We'll have to pray we can outsail the buggers. You, there, lads!" Duncan swung back to yell at the crew. "Get to work! The captain says we're to make a race of it!"

****

As the ship, racing before the gale, canted precariously, water surging over her bulwarks on the starboard side, Ginny and Annie scrambled onto deck.

"What's happening?" Annie slipped and skidded to join Duncan where he stood amidships yelling orders to the crew. "Are we after another prize?"

"Get below, woman!" he barked. "We're in a run for our lives, don't you see?" He swung his arm to indicate the pursuing ship. "You women will only be a hindrance on deck."

"Do you think they'll catch us?"

"Not with any luck and smart sailing. Now get below!"

Annie turned back to where Ginny stood at the hatch, drenched by the spray.

"Well?" she asked.

"We'd best do as your man says," Annie surprised her by responding. "We'll be of little use on deck."

"We're to obey…without question?"

"Yes."

Once below in the companionway, she whirled on Ginny.

"We've little chance of escape, I can tell from the expression on your man's face, but I have a plan…a plan that may save this ship and its crew. Come on. We've no time to lose."

****

"Sweet Jesus, Cal," Duncan joined the captain, who'd taken over the helm himself in the last of seven weary hours of racing before the *Tom*. "We can't keep this up. Unless the breeze freshens something fierce, we're in for it. Doucet says the *Tom* is Baltimore built, just out of port, her copper bottom smooth as an eel. We're furry and foul from months at sea. I respect your ability, but still…"

"I'm not ready to give up yet, Mr. MacDougal." He looked at his mate, hoping his expression showed bright challenge, not the apprehension of possible defeat. "Every time that stern chaser fires a shot, the force of the ball hitting the water behind us drives us ahead and them back. If the breeze doesn't freshen within the hour, we'll put the men to the sweeps. Make certain every man is armed to the teeth."

"You're expecting hand-to-hand combat." Duncan indicated the pistol stuck in Caleb's belt and the sword hanging from a belt in a sheath at his side.

"Aren't you?" Caleb returned his attention to the helm.

****

Throwing up a geyser of water, a cannonball splashed down only a few yards in front of the *Lady Ghost*.

"Bloody hell, will you look at that!" Caleb followed his mate's upward gaze and saw a great hole ripped through the fore topsail. "It went right over our heads."

The *Lady Ghost* jolted as a second cannonball hit the water yards from her stern.

"Good God, Cal! They're going to blow us out of

the water!"

"Stop sounding like a nervous old woman and get back to your station!" he bellowed. "Order the men to fire when she gets within a quarter mile."

"Load her with six-pound shot!" Duncan yelled to the men manning their last cannon thrust through the break in the stern bulwarks.

"We've none left, Mr. MacDougal." Higgins, his broad face red and wet, turned to him.

"Then wrap four-pound balls in canvas and fire!" Caleb bellowed the command. He'd left his post at the helm to Munro and come to stand beside his mate.

The men hesitated.

"Well, get to it!" he roared.

"Captain, sir, beggin' your pardon but…" Higgins tried to protest.

"Just do as I say."

Shortly the weapon was loaded as Caleb had described.

"Light the fuse and stand back!" he yelled.

There was the acrid smell of burning as his command was carried out. The gun struggled with its unusual load, choked, shuddered, and exploded.

The men ducked as pieces of gun and its unorthodox load flew through the air.

"Mother of God, there goes our last hope!" he heard a sailor mutter.

Looking out from beside the ruined gun, Caleb saw the pursuing schooner so near he could distinguish the carving of a tomcat's snarling countenance on her bow. His men were crouched, muskets ready. They knew what was coming. Good men, brave men. The *Tom* was fast drawing abreast of them.

If they'd been officially in the king's service, it would have been their duty to fight to the death. Supposing he followed this tradition, fought while there was a cartridge to fire and not a man left standing and then blew the *Lady Ghost* out of the water? Brave but inhumane. He couldn't do that to his men, Duncan, and the two women below deck.

A volley of musket fire ripped across his deck as the *Tom* came fully abreast. One of his men screamed as he was hit, another staggered and cursed, holding his shoulder. Captain Caleb Cameron made a decision. Surrender. Give them what they really only wanted…Captain Caleb Cameron, the evil genius of the coasting trade. His men would be imprisoned for a short time until they were traded for American prisoners in Nova Scotia. The women, he had to hope and pray, would be treated honorably. What happened to him wasn't important. He couldn't allow Ann, her friend, and his men to be slaughtered.

"Haul down the colors!" With excruciating inward pain, the order ripped from his throat. He seized the ensign halyards himself as another shower of shot flew across his deck.

Shortening sail as both vessels slowed, the enemy's cry of, "No quarter, no quarter. Kill the pirates!" rang loud and clear across the water.

Within minutes the *Lady Ghost* was overrun with American sailors leaping aboard under cover of blazing muskets.

Sweet Jesus, they're not accepting surrender!

A grunt and a dull thud made him turn. Duncan MacDougal lay flat on the deck behind him, blood flowing from a wound in his chest.

"Dunc!" He made to kneel beside him, but another volley of gunfire ripped between him and the first mate. Whirling, incensed, he faced the invaders. He yanked the pistol from his belt and fired point blank at the marine. The man roared and jerked backward.

"No surrender! Give them hell, men!" he roared pulling his sword from its sheath. "For Mr. MacDougal!"

Out to avenge their officer and fellow crew members although outnumbered three to one, the men of the *Lady Ghost* returned musket blasts, then, as the enemy flooded aboard, attacked with gun butts, boarding pikes, swords, and belaying pins. Roaring like savages, they charged, their captain leading them.

Chapter Thirty-Three

"Bloody hell, Annie, how much longer must we stifle ourselves in this miserable hole?" Ginny MacDougal tried to move cramped limbs in the secret closet in the captain's cabin.

"Hush! Listen. I think Captain Cameron and his crew have been captured and secured in the hold forward. From the sounds above deck, those privateers, firm in the belief that the entire crew is in custody, are having a celebration...at least the small group left aboard to sail the *Lady Ghost* into the nearest American port. Remember that door at the bottom of the ladder, the one that opens from the companionway into the hold? As soon as we deem it safe, we'll slip forward and free the captain and his crew."

"Annie Pudden, you're a blinking genius. And here I thought you had us hidden away in fear of losing our virtue."

"I'm not entirely without brains." Annie smirked in the darkness. "And I had a fine tutor in the art of handling wild adventures." Her voice faltered over the last.

"Lady Sophia is in heaven now, Annie, love." She felt Ginny's hand on her arm. "Where her many deeds of kindness will be rewarded."

"Hush. Listen. Time to put our plan into action."

Easing their way out of the closet and across the

cabin, they paused at the closed door and listened. Annie slowly opened the door, and they tiptoed down the companionway to the barred entrance to the hold.

Together they shoved away the thick plank holding the door shut and pushed inward. Duncan MacDougal and the rest of the crew sat on the floor of the hold.

"Mr. MacDougal!" Ginny stumbled over men and debris to get to her husband, who lay against the ship's side, naked to the waist, his shirt wrapped around his chest and wet with blood. A large blue bruise had raised a lump over his left eye.

"Oh, love, what have they done to you?"

"Just knocked the wind out of me and tore off a bit of meat, darlin'." He forced a grin on a face blanched and wet with sweat. "I banged my head on a capstan on the way down. Once you stitch me up, I'll be right as rain."

"Quiet!" Annie hissed. "Do you want to send out an alarm?" She peered around the darkened hold. "Mr. MacDougal, where is Captain Cameron?"

Looking down at his bloody hands, Duncan MacDougal hesitated.

"Mr. MacDougal, where is my husband?" Her heart suddenly pounding like a sledge hammer against her ribs, Annie repeated, her tone demanding an answer.

"They've taken him." He grimaced as he tried to pull himself upright, distress mirrored in his eyes.

"Taken him? Where? Why?" Dumbfounded, she stammered out the words.

"They reckoned him too dangerous to be left aboard, even with a ship raided of its ammunition. They took him onto the *Tom*, with the *Lady Ghost* forced ahead of her as a prize. We're headed for Portsmouth, New Hampshire, from what I overheard."

"To parade him about the streets as the best prize of all!" Anger and fear exploded over her. The thought of her husband being made sport of by a jeering crowd sickened her.

"The Americans don't know Ginny and I are aboard," she said slowly, an idea taking shape in her thoughts.

"Mrs. Cameron, what wild scheme are you hatching?" Duncan looked over at her, eyes narrowing. "I swear to God, you and the captain are well matched in the boldness of your plans."

"When we get to Portsmouth, they'll take you and the crew to a place of confinement..." She spoke slowly but was thinking fast.

"Prison." The mate replaced her euphemism with a harsher term, to be answered by disgruntled mutters from the crew.

"If you will." She avoided the downcast expressions the words brought their faces.

"As soon as they get you on deck, Ginny and I will march ourselves into view, once more as Lady Ann Millbank and her faithful maid." Annie drew a deep breath as more and more of the plan formed in her busy brain. "That impersonation got us out of a tight place once before, you'll recall. As you'll also remember, as privateers, we were forbidden to molest any ship carrying women and/or children. I'm sure American privateers are bound by similar chivalrous rules. Therefore, we must be ruled an illegal capture and released."

"Bloody hell, Annie, it sounds so daft it just might

work." Ginny's expression brightened. "But first we have to get this lot patched up. We'll need them fit, to get the *Lady Ghost* out of Portsmouth under full sail and back to Halifax if you can manage to finesse those damned Americans. Stay still, Mr. MacDougal, darlin'. I'm off to fetch bandages and my sewing kit before this rabble decide to take possession of our cabin."

Chapter Thirty-Four

Shackled, his back to the mainmast of the *Thomas*, Captain Caleb Cameron watched the *Lady Ghost* moving into the harbor of Portsmouth, New Hampshire, her mainsail in tatters but still moving proudly. Not even capture would bow his gallant lady. But what of his flesh-and-blood lady? And her companion? And his best friend? And his crew? As they moved in from sea, past Fort Constitution and its lighthouse, his innards knotted in fear for them. Pray God these Americans would see fit to give Duncan MacDougal a decent burial.

The prize crew from the *Thomas* drew the *Lady Ghost* up to Shaw's Wharf, and even from the distance the *Tom* was behind her Caleb could hear the shouts of victory going up from the crowd assembled on the pier.

As the men of the *Thomas* dropped anchor off shore to await the unloading of the prisoners from the bowels of the *Lady Ghost*, Captain Caleb Cameron let his chin drop to his bare chest. His shirt was in tatters from the fighting, and he was filthy from blood and gunsmoke. It didn't matter. Nothing mattered any more. His best friend was dead. His crew would be marched through the streets, flaunted and mocked. God only knew what would become of his wife and her friend. And it was all his fault. That brazen foray into Tarpaulin Cove had been his undoing.

****

The bodies of the three members of Caleb's crew who had been killed were brought to shore. The others, several wounded among them, led by Duncan MacDougal with his hands shackled behind him, were brought up from the hold and marched down the gangplank. Roars of derision went up from the waiting crowd. Clods of earth and rotten fruit flew through the air. Too busy reviling the captives, no one seemed to notice the neat bandages the wounded, including the first mate, wore.

Peering out from behind the door of their quarters, Annie and Ginny watched, awaiting the appropriate moment to make an entrance.

"Rotten bastards!" As a piece of earth struck Duncan on the side of his head, Ginny's words muttered in Annie's ear made her place a restraining hand on her friend's arm.

"Hush! We must stay hidden until there's a person in authority present who will listen to us. Look. Someone is coming now."

"Hie, there!" A carriage had driven onto the dock and a heavyset man in a military uniform swung to the ground. "That will be enough of that! You'll treat these prisoners with the same respect we hope our captured men will receive in Nova Scotia. You don't want to imagine them being pelted with dirt and rotten food."

As the big man, followed by several officers, proceeded toward the *Lady Ghost*'s crew, the crowd silenced to a few mutters.

"Liberty Braymore, United States Marshal," he introduced himself when he confronted Duncan. "Are you the commanding officer of these men?"

"At the moment, since you've taken our captain, I am." Duncan drew himself up. "First Mate Duncan MacDougal."

Annie saw him flinch as, she guessed, the stitches Ginny had put in his side pulled. Beside her Ginny muttered an expletive best suited to a drunken sailor.

"Hush!" she admonished.

"So you're first officer to that elusive bugger Caleb Cameron." The man put his hands on his hips and pursed his lips as he looked over Duncan and the men behind him. In spite of injuries and present position, each stood up proudly. "Well, I must say it appears he's picked a hearty bunch. Not a single one licking his wounds or begging for mercy."

"We expect to be treated fairly, sir, as prisoners as war." Duncan, ragged and filthy, faced him squarely. "We also expect that our three fallen crewmen will be given decent burials. I further request that such among my men as require a surgeon will be granted one."

In the deckhouse, Ginny drew herself up and stuck out her chin. "That's my man. You tell him," she hissed.

"You're a cocky one, I'll grant you that, Mr. MacDougal, but it appears to me, from the state of your bandages, that you and your men have already had treatment. Perhaps you had a sawbones of some skill aboard. At any rate, we'll get you into quarters at the prison on Islington Street. Then I'll let the local powers decide your fate."

"Perhaps it is we who will be deciding *your* fate, Mr. Liberty Braymore." Annie, dressed in her princess gown and with Ginny attired as her maid, swept out onto the deck. Haughty as the aristocrat she was impersonating, head held high, she proceeded to the top of the gangplank to glower down at the marshal.

"Sweet Jesus—excuse me, mistress. Who might you be?" The man stared up at the pair as if he'd been confronted by a mystical event.

"Lady Ann Millbank, sir, wife of Captain Caleb Cameron, master of the ship your forces have so ignominiously attacked and illegally captured."

"Good God!" The words were a mutter as he continued to stare up at the two women. He sucked in a deep breath before continuing. "I had no idea the man was married, certainly not that he had his lady wife aboard his vessel."

"As I'm sure you're aware, sir, it's a gentleman's agreement on both sides of this ridiculous war that ships with women and/or children aboard must not be attacked." Having no idea if she was correct in supposing a similar pact on the part of the Americans, or if indeed that condition extended to privateers other than her own ship, she could only hope to bluff her way forward. "To do so and then declare that vessel and its contents captive would be a most grievous offense. My brother, the Duke of Haverbrook, will be most unhappy when he learns what has transpired. He and his good friend the Prince Regent might feel compelled to send a convoy of British ships to bombard your lovely little township when he hears with what contempt and disrespect his brother-in-law, with his family and crew, has been treated."

"Hell and damnation!" the marshal muttered. "This is turning out to be one fine mess." He turned to his officers. "Men, escort this bunch to the jail. I'll need time to sort out this affair." Looking back up at the pair on the deck of the ragged, battle weary ship, he continued, "Ladies, come with me. Fortunately the governor and his wife are here in Portsmouth at the moment. I'll let him decide what's to be done."

Chapter Thirty-Five

"Lady Ann Millbank, sir." The pompous butler stood aside to allow Annie and Ginny to enter the governor's high-ceilinged office. Its wide windows looking out over Portsmouth Harbor let in hot rays of summer sunshine.

"Sir." Annie favored the governor with a slight nod of recognition as the rotund official rose from behind his desk.

"Lady Ann." He returned her greeting with a deep bow. "My pleasure, ma'am. Marshal Braymore sent a message concerning you and your lady's maid before he had to rush off to attend to prisoners. A rather confusing message, I must admit. Something about the pair of you having been brought ashore from the *Lady Ghost* and that you are the wife of that plague of our coastal trade, Captain Caleb Cameron. I believe Liberty Braymore is quite at the end of his tether to know what to do about the situation. Please be seated while we discuss the matter."

Ann gratefully sank into the seat indicated. She'd been walking and standing about for hours.

"Please, Ginny, be seated." She turned to her friend, guessing she was equally fatigued after a long day of awaiting transport to the governor's lodgings. She ignored the official's scowl at what she guessed he'd interpret as an unacceptable invitation to a servant.

"Now, Lady Ann." Governor John Taylor Gilman sat down and looked across at her, his stern weathered face giving her no indication in her favor. "I understand you've threatened to have our little township blown to smithereens if we don't adhere to some unwritten agreement between our countries to the effect that ships carrying women are automatically ruled illegal prizes."

"That is correct, sir."

"Ah, yes." John Gilman leaned back in his chair and hooked his thumbs into his waistcoat, a smug smile warming his face. "But you must understand the capture of your husband and his ship is not a regular prize. The man has fair been driving us mad with his pilfering of our supply vessels. His craft is well named the *Lady Ghost*. She's been almost impossible to sight and, I'm told, under his command can fly like a witch before the slightest breath of wind. The blighter slides in and out around Cape Cod as slippery as an eel. But no more. Now he rests in irons in the town jail."

"But you see, there is a problem with that very condition." Annie forced a sad little half smile and lowered her gaze to her clasped hands. The image of Caleb imprisoned in irons made her stomach knot. "Captain Caleb Cameron is not only my husband but also the father of my four sons, the Duke of Haverbrook's nephews."

"What...what's that you say?" The big man bolted forward on his chair. "Brother-in-law to a duke, a royal duke?"

"Yes, a man very well connected at court." She looked up at him, eyes suddenly narrowing and turning hard and cold. "Thus you can appreciate my threat of Royal Navy involvement isn't a hollow one."

"Good God! I may as well have the Prince Regent in chains!"

"Very nearly." She stuck out her chin and faced him boldly. "So you see, you'd best release my husband. Otherwise, I've no doubt my brother will have his friend muster all the resources of the Royal Navy to sail against the good people of Portsmouth. I'm sure you don't want to suffer a bombardment."

"Damn and blast!" The governor stood and began to pace the room. "I can't let the man go. They've labeled him the Sea Wolf, and that's exactly what he is, preying on American shipping. If released, I've no doubt he'd be back at it in short order. On the other hand…" He stopped pacing and swung on her, his face bright.

"As the brother-in-law to a duke, he could fetch a fine ransom. Aye, that's the ticket. I'll hold him for ransom."

"You don't seriously believe my brother will pay." Alarmed by this turn of events, Annie struggled to change the course of the discussion. "The British have a long history of never paying for the release of prisoners, and I doubt they have anyone of equal importance to exchange for Captain Cameron." Although she had no idea if that were a fact, she was grasping at straws. "Therefore, with no one to dicker for and refusing to pay ransom, they'd have no choice but to raze your township in retribution."

"We'll have to wait and see, won't we, my lady?" He stood to glower down at her, his face still bright with his decision.

She looked up at him, hoping she looked haughty and arrogant in the face of his veiled threat.

"John, I heard voices." A tall, slender, elegantly dressed woman stepped into the room. "Do we have visitors?"

"May I present Lady Ann Millbank." The big man turned to her. "Lady Ann, my wife."

"Mrs. Gilman." Ann inclined her head.

"Lady Ann." The woman's astonishment was registered in her expression for a moment before she recovered her poise and dropped into a curtsy. "I am delighted. You'll stay to dinner, of course."

"Thank you. That is most kind of you, Mrs. Gilman." Annie gave a small gasp and put a hand to her forehead. "Oh, dear."

"John!" Mrs. Gilman was instantly at her side, putting a supporting arm about her waist. "Help me."

The governor's lady knelt beside her, her face so knotted with concern Annie felt a pang of guilt. But it was all in a good cause. She brushed aside her apprehensions.

"Are you unwell, my dear?" the woman asked softly.

"Our fifth child is on the way." Annie prayed she looked fittingly ill. "If you'll just allow my maid to fetch me a glass of water…"

"Through there and down the hall." Mrs. Gilman indicated the way, and after a furtively admonishing glance at Annie, Ginny scuttled off.

"Now, my dear, you must let me help you to a bed. Where are you staying in Portsmouth?"

"I've only arrived today…as a captive."

"What?" Deborah Gilman swung on her husband. "Surely not! No women are to be taken prisoners of war. You've said so yourself, John." She turned back to

Annie. "You'll be our guest, you and your little maid servant, until my husband gets this deplorable situation straightened out."

"But…" The governor made to protest, but his lady's glare stopped him.

"Come, my dear." She helped Annie to her feet. "Let me take you up to a guest room. Mr. Gilman, send Daisy to us immediately. I'll need her to bring fresh linen."

Chapter Thirty-Six

Captain Caleb Cameron sat propped against the cold stone wall of the dungeon-like cell in the long jail on Islington Street. A manacle about one ankle held him leashed to the wall. Every bone in his body ached from the long, mad race to elude the *Tom* and the ensuing battle. Hungry and cold, he nevertheless had no thoughts of himself and his position. He put out of his mind the long march in irons, from the wharf through the town, forgot the dirt and rotten food thrown at him and the cries of "Dam'd Scotia" from those who believed him a native of Nova Scotia. His thoughts were filled with the memory of Duncan MacDougal, his best friend, lying dead on the deck, and—what had become of his wife and her companion?

What would they do with them, women prisoners of war? Would they adhere to the unwritten code that no women were to be taken captive, and return them to Halifax? Or would they keep them, thrusting them into prison or demeaning servitude? Surely not. They must recognize his record for fairness throughout his privateering career. In his many months at sea, he'd never been guilty of a single act of cruelty or outrage. He may not have been gentle, but he was always just. Would that record be of any use to the woman he loved and her companion?

He drank some of the tepid water left for him, and

exhaustion forced him into an uneasy sleep…a sleep where he imagined the worst atrocities happening to Ann. When he awoke in pitch darkness, he was drenched with sweat.

If he ever got the women and his crew out of this mess, he'd never privateer again.

"Hssst! Captain Cameron!" A freckled face appeared at the high window above him.

"Daniel…Daniel the privateer." He recognized the lad. "What are you doing here?"

"We was in the crowd along the street when they brought you here, sir." He saw that the boy's face was pale and realized the lad was taking a dangerous risk coming to see him. "We couldn't help you, not then, but—until we can do more for you, here." He thrust a metal flask through between the bars and dropped it down to Caleb.

Caleb pulled the cork and sniffed. "Brandy. Where did the likes of you get brandy?"

"From him as his wife will be glad we did." A grin quirked out from among the freckles. "And here." He disappeared for an instant, then reappeared to toss a small package wrapped in a cloth down to him. "A bit of bread from my ma's oven. When I told her it was for you, she wanted to send more, but…"

"But she has a family," Caleb finished as the lad's words faltered. "She's quite right. I thank you and her most heartily, lad, but now you must be off before someone sees you and you land in here with me." A thought struck him. "How have you managed to reach this window? I reckon as it's fair high off the ground."

"I'm standing on the backs of the crew of the *Mistress May*."

****

"That was a fine dinner, Mrs. Gilman." Annie sat down opposite the woman in the drawing room, where long windows had been thrown open to let in the air of a fine summer's evening. "I am sorry to have put you to inconvenience, especially since Mr. Gilman wasn't able to join us. I'm sure, left on your own, you would have had a much less elegant repast."

"Perhaps I should have, but I must say I enjoyed your company immensely. What adventures you've had at sea! Your bravery in accompanying your husband does you much credit, Lady Ann, especially in one so apparently raised in luxury and safety."

"Luxury and safety can become boring, Mrs. Gilman." She smiled, recalling the tales she'd so carefully spun. "And I am very much in love with my husband."

"Ah, yes." Deborah Gilman stood and went to gaze out the window into the burgeoning gardens beyond. "Definitely." She paused in what Annie interpreted as thought before swinging back to her guest. "Lady Ann, what would you say to you and me, accompanied by your lady's maid, embarking on a small adventure this very night?"

"Adventure?" Annie looked up her with what she hoped was wide-eyed innocence, but her heartbeat had upped.

"My husband is gone to Maine to meet with that colony's governor. It appears the good citizens of that area have chosen to ignore the fact that we Americans are at war with the British province of New Brunswick and have continued to trade and nurture friendships with its residents. Mr. Gilman has been called upon to offer his suggestions on how to end this troublesome situation. He was a Minute Man in the Revolution and remains staunchly loyal to the United States. We ladies are on our own tonight." Brown eyes bright, she looked over at her guest. "Therefore…"

"Therefore…?" Annie tried not to visibly hold her breath as the governor's lady once again paused.

"Therefore there is nothing to stop us paying a visit to your husband this midnight." The words came out in a whisper, harsh with excitement.

"Oh, Mrs. Gilman…" Annie could barely believe her good fortune. "You're not suggesting…"

"Hush, child. Of course I'm not." Deborah smirked and winked, and Annie knew exactly what she was not just suggesting but proposing.

"But why?" Annie was too astute to take this apparent help at face value.

"This is a foolish war." Deborah Gilman paced the room. "It should never have taken place. And it wouldn't have, except for a few warmongers in Washington. The desire to annex the British colonies to the north has needlessly cost many lives…my brother and uncle among them. I want it stopped. Furthermore," she continued after a slight pause, "stories have circulated in Portsmouth and around the area of how three young American lads were saved from a terrible death at sea by the crew of the *Lady Ghost*. At great risk to themselves, these men guided the boys safely to shore and provided them with victuals. While many are ready to dismiss the story as mere tale spinning by young boys, I am not. My brother was but a lad when he joined the fight. I pray he met with such kindness and altruism along the way."

She stared out the window, and Annie allowed her time for her thoughts.

"My assistance comes with only one clause." Mrs. Gilman finally turned back to face her guest.

"And that is?" Annie found she could barely breathe. Was this going to prove too good to be true?

"That you will promise to have your husband sign a document to the effect that he will give up privateering and leave American commerce along our coasts in peace from this day forth."

"He's a strong-minded, willful man." Annie could be nothing but honest. "But he is also a fair and just one. I believe, in return for the freedom of himself *and* his crew, he will agree to your condition."

"And his crew? A rather large order, but I think it can be done. Your ship, the *Lady Ghost*, is tied up at Shaw's Wharf, I believe?" She seated herself at a small desk in a corner and took from a drawer a paper with an official-looking crest on its top. Using a quill, she began to write.

"After all these years of marriage, I can imitate my husband's script rather well," she said casting a sly look at Annie.

****

At midnight three figures in dark cloaks, their heads covered by hoods, left the governor's lodgings by a rear entrance and glided into the shadows beyond. Shortly they presented themselves at the jail on Islington Street.

"Ye cannot come in here!" The jailer, roused from his doze, confronted the trio of figures. "I've a most dangerous prisoner to guard. I've..."

"My good man, you'll keep your voice down and

do exactly as I say." From the folds of her robe, one pulled a pistol and pointed it at the man's chest. "Now take us to Captain Cameron's cell, and do not forget to bring along your keys."

"You'd not dare use that thing!" In the dim light his eyes glistened with drink and cunning. "It would bring the sentries, it would…"

"Ah, the sentries. The two gentlemen we left firmly trussed up against the outer wall. You'll be getting no assistance from them, my good fellow, so I'd advise you to move along." The figure stepped forward to nudge him with her gun barrel. "Otherwise I'll be forced to blow your foot off."

She nodded to her companions, who immediately produced pistols.

"All right, all right!" The man stumbled to grab a ring of keys from the wall as the speaker pointed her weapon at his left boot. "You'll not be making a cripple of me, not for all the privateering captains this side of the Atlantic. I didn't think this night could get any worse after I received that letter from the governor to release the bunch of buggers what crewed that pirate ship."

****

"Captain Cameron!" Annie's words were a hissed whisper as she swung open the door of his cell and peered into the darkness.

"Ann?" His voice came out of the shadows under the high, barred window. Incredulity permeated his tone.

"Aye, Captain." She advanced across the dank, foul-smelling room and knelt beside him where he sat shackled to the wall. Pulling the ring of keys from inside her robe, she used the one the jailer had indicated would fit his bonds, and set to removing his restraints.

"Sweet Jesus!" He rubbed his wrists once she had removed the manacles. Then, looking up at her, he breathed, "Ann," the word holding all the reverence of a prayer. "How…?"

"Never mind." She took his arm and pulled him to his feet. "We have to get out of here. Time is of the essence."

Stumbling, Caleb staggered through the open doorway, to be confronted by two other dark robed figures.

"Ginny…Mrs. MacDougal…but who…"

"Never mind who. I'll explain later. Right now," she turned to the unknown figure who withdrew a rolled-up paper from her sleeve. "You must sign this document. To secure your freedom, I pledged that you would."

On a stone slab that served as a table, Deborah Gilman flattened out the document and held out a pencil. "Sign," she ordered.

"What…does it say?" He squinted in the darkness. "What will I be signing?"

"It states that, given your freedom and that of your wife and crew, you will swear never again to privateer against Americans." Annie took the writing instrument and pressed it into his hand.

Without hesitation, he bent forward and scrawled his name. Deborah Gilman gathered up and rerolled the sheet of paper.

"Now you must hurry." She turned to Annie. "Your crew has been released and is on your ship at the dock. You must get away before anyone such as

Marshal Liberty Braymore has time to question my husband's orders."

"Thank you—most sincerely, thank you." Annie paused to breathe.

"No need. It's been the best fun I've had in years. Now, be off with you." Deborah shoved another paper into Ann's hand. "This will get you past the sentries. Issued by my husband, no one will dare question. When this ridiculous war is over, I'm hoping we'll meet again."

Chapter Thirty-Seven

"It's about time you showed up." The familiar voice coming out of the dark silhouette at the top of the *Lady Ghost*'s gangplank made him stop short.

"Dunc?" Frozen with disbelief, he stared.

"Aye, Captain. Now, are you going to get aboard and start spouting orders? We need to get away from this blasted town."

"Dunc!" He was up the plank in long strides to grasp his first mate's hand in his right and clamp him on the shoulder with his left. "Sweet Jesus, I thought you dead! When I saw you lying on the deck..."

"Musketball knocked me on my backside. I banged my head on a capstan on the way down. It'll take more than a bit of a scrap to put an end to me. Now stop yanking my arm. You're pulling on the stitches my guid wife put in my side. We have to get underway before someone in this place decides they made a mistake in letting us go."

"Aye." Ignoring his need for rest, food, and washing away the signs of battle and wounds, he turned to his crew standing ready. "Get to it, men. Cast off the lines. Up with what sails we have left, and head us for open water."

"Aye, Captain." The reply was soft, every man among them knowing the need to make their escape as noiseless as possible. Like black ghosts they scuttled off to do his bidding.

"Damn, but we're a ragged pair." Duncan's voice held a grin as the two men stood for a moment looking at each other.

"But free and alive. Now to work, Mr. MacDougal. I won't be easy until Portsmouth disappears behind our wake."

****

"Well, Captain, the *Lady Ghost* is once more under your command." Annie joined her husband as he stood at the bulwarks, watching Portsmouth vanish into darkness. The moon was down, and only a few stars shone in a black sky.

"Aye." He turned to face her, standing proud in spite of the filth of battle and prison still clinging to him. "Thanks to you in no small way."

"I'll wager when we were first attacked by the *Tom* you thought we were hiding away, afraid of the amorous attentions of those picaroons." She favored him with a saucy grin.

He turned his attention back to the sea.

"Tell me, is that what you thought?" She moved to look up into his face.

"If you must know…" He rounded on her, his expression so dark and angry she fell back a step. "*I* was afraid. Those bastards swarmed over the ship in such numbers I lost track of you and your friend. When I realized you were missing, I thought they'd abducted you. Men who'd been at sea for months would have no hesitation to enjoying you both as part of their booty."

"We disappeared below before we were noticed and hid in your secret compartment."

"How did you know…?" He stared at her.

"I saw you taking out your log book one night when you thought I was asleep. I tucked the information safely away in my head in case I someday needed it. And I did. Clever, wasn't I?"

"Sly would be a more appropriate description." She saw one corner of his mouth curl in what could be a repressed grin.

"Call it what you will. My knowledge of your secret compartment came in handy." She hesitated. "But are you truly willing to abide by the conditions of that document you signed. .that you'll give up privateering against the Americans? Because if you're not…"

"My signature is my bond…as you well know." He looked down at her. "Furthermore, you somehow managed to get my crew and me released by promising my adherence to the condition. I'm not about to negate your work." He turned back to look out to sea. "Best of all, it will release me from that blasted agreement with Sir John that my ship and crew serve as surrogate navy until the end of the war. No matter how he's been lusting after Mrs. MacDougal, I believe he's a man of honor and will abide by any agreement I was forced to sign with the Americans."

He paused before continuing, "And why not give up this life of marine banditry. It's time to consider settling down. I believe the lieutenant governor will allow us our fair share of the prizes we've taken. We've done more than our part for the war effort." He rotated his shoulders. "I'm also getting weary of being struck by belaying pins and choking on the stench of gunpowder. I'm ready to build a house, maybe start a farm, become a country squire. How does that sound to you, Mrs. Cameron? Are you ready to put aside weapons and bandages and a rolling deck for a nice home amid green pastures?"

"You're including me in your plans?" She looked up at him, astonished.

"You *are* my wife." He returned his attention to the sea, a slight tick in his jaw betraying his tension. "And I owe you more than my life is worth."

"Is that all?" She struggled to keep intonations of hurt and regret from her words.

"What more do you want?" He swung on her, his face dark with a scowl. "I'm offering to share my life with you."

"I want you to say you love me." The words came out in a way she hated to think sounded squeaky.

"Good God, woman!" He grasped her by the shoulders. "Doesn't that go without speaking? Of course I love you. You've saved my life and ship on more than one occasion, you're brave and bold and…"

"And?" She gazed up at him, hoping the trembling he'd started deep within her wasn't palpable.

"And beautiful, and I admire and respect you with every ounce of body and soul." He lowered his head and kissed her with a passion that could leave no doubt as to the truth of his words.

When he finally allowed her to surface from the ethereal realm into which his kisses always thrust her, he narrowed those wonderful blue eyes and asked, "What about you, Mrs. Cameron? I've not gotten your response."

"Response to what?" She cast him a coy glance and backed out of his arms.

"As to whether you return my feelings?"

"Are you asking if I love you, Captain Cameron?"

"Sweet Jesus, woman, don't tease! Of course I'm asking."

"Very well. Certainly I do…even though you took me away with you by mistake, even though you thought you were getting a princess, not a serving girl."

"You're wrong." He watched her return to the bulwarks, her hair rippling in the wind. "I may have made a mistake in the woman I abducted, but I did get a princess… a privateer's princess."

"Then in that case I would love a home in the country…with you." She turned her gaze out to sea, afraid that he might see the utter joy his thoughts had aroused.

"Good, then, very good. Duncan will be asking your friend the same question. We've a mind to establish ourselves near each other…if that pleases you."

"Yes, oh, yes, Captain!" This time she didn't try to hide her happiness. To have a home, the man she loved, and her best friend nearby…never in her wildest dream had she imagined such a situation. She flung her arms about his neck. And when he lowered his head to kiss her again, she responded with an ardor produced by the intense happiness she was feeling.

"Mrs. Cameron," he breathed softly in her ear. "You realize the war is over for us."

"Oh, aye, Captain." She looked up at him coyly. "And that would mean that we might once again share a cabin, unbound by wartime restrictions?"

"Aye, my princess." Blue eyes hot with desire seared into her soul, and she knew what the term "being all a-tremble" meant.

"Then I will await you below when your watch is finished, sir." She backed out of his arms, a smile curling her lips.

"Aye, you do that…my love." The last two words came out so sensuously that, as she turned away, Annie Cameron realized waiting for this sea watch to end would be among the longest minutes of her life.

****

Caleb entered his cabin and stopped as abruptly as if struck by lightning. In the room lighted by two low-burning lanterns, beside that long unused tub now filled with water, stood his wife wearing—*Good God, what is she wearing? Some kind of flimsy thing through which I can see her entire body shape. And her hair…cascading about her shoulders and down her back…*

"Good evening, Captain." She smiled. "Or perhaps I should say good morning, since I believe dawn is about to break not only on the new day but also on the new status of our relationship."

He watched her come to him, the most beautifully sensuous creature he could have imagined. When she began to unlace his dirty, ragged shirt, he felt he could restrain himself no longer. But as he reached to take in his arms, she shook her head and stepped back.

"Remove your shirt, Captain, and the rest of your filthy clothing." She swung her arm to indicate the tub. "You'll be needing a bath before we…can proceed." The smile curling her lips made him wrench the filthy, torn shirt over his head. But when his hand went to the buckle at his waist, he paused, looking at her.

"Oh, for heaven's sake!" She turned her back and swaggered across the room to where a bottle of wine sat beside two tankards. "I won't invade your modesty. Get into the water."

He smirked. Modesty. Bloody hell, why was he suddenly shy in front of this woman? It wasn't as if she was his first. Nor was it even his first time with her. But something in his head told him this time would be different. *This time will bind us together forever. I don't want to make any mistakes that might leave her with reservations or distaste.*

"Where did you get that...thing?" he asked. He couldn't think of a name for the diaphanous garment she was wearing.

"Ginny and I each bought clothing we believed appropriate if and when our husbands took a carnal interest in us."

"Brazen hussies." He chuckled.

"Oh, aye? Would you be preferring shrinking violets?"

"Good God, no. Shrinking violets wouldn't have lasted an hour on this warship."

He stripped and lowered himself into the tub. A sigh escaped his lips. It felt so good to relax battle-weary muscles, cuts, and bruises in warm, soothing water.

"Are you decent?" He caught the humor in her voice as she poured wine.

"As decent as I will be getting this night." He matched her tone.

"Guid, then, verrae guid." She mocked Duncan's Scottish inflection as she came to kneel beside the tub and extend a tankard to him. "A wee drop from a bottle, one of several Ginny and I managed to hide away when those American privateers were about to overtake us."

"God bless your initiative." He accepted it from her

and took a drink. "Not as good as whisky, but I assume you didn't manage to save any of my best?"

"We did, but I fancy wine this night." She took a sip, placed her tankard on the floor, and took up a washcloth and soap.

"Now, Captain, let me see to that dirt and blood." She wet the cloth and began to carefully wash his chest. He stood it until her cleaning fell below his waist. With a muttered expletive, he dropped his drink and pulled her, laughing, into the tub with him.

Chapter Thirty-Eight

"I still can't believe His Grace the Duke of Haverbrook hasn't sought retaliation for your mistake." Duncan MacDougal leaned back in the comfortable chair on the veranda of the mansion they'd rented in Halifax and frowned over at his friend.

"Willie hasn't got the courage to come after me. He's done his worst by attempting to get our request for letters of marque denied. He'd never dare confront me in person."

"Still, I can't rest easy…"

"Now who's behaving like a nervous old woman? I've told you, Willie's a dyed-in-the-wool coward."

"Very well, if you say so. Nevertheless, I'm thinking we'll be getting fat and lazy, Captain, if we don't soon bestir ourselves and do some work that doesn't involve pushing a quill and doing up sums in ledgers to check if we've received the right share of those hard-won prizes."

"Right, well, I've an idea." Caleb squinted over at his friend in the July sunshine.

"Aye, and that would be?" Suspicion tinged both Duncan's expression and words. "It seems every time you have an idea, we find ourselves arse deep in trouble."

"Come on, Dunc." Caleb grinned over at him. "Where's your sense of adventure? Don't tell me it vanished with your marriage. If anyone was up for the excitement of new experiences, it's your wife, so don't let that be your excuse."

"Sadly, I know it. Very well. Let's have it. Let me hear your next daft plan."

"The timber trade is booming in New Brunswick. I'm thinking you and I might haul our sorry behinds up there and start a business. I've already told Ann our idea about establishing farms as our future homes, with maybe a timber harvesting business and a sawmill in an auxiliary position. She thinks it's a fine idea. She understands I don't fancy spending the rest of my life rocking on a verandah."

"I thought once you were wealthy and had a fine lady as a wife, you'd be satisfied."

"Aye, that was the plan, but now I find all this ease is lying heavy on me. We can build houses in New Brunswick and do a thriving business that will have us working again, not just sitting on a porch. Ann's enthusiasm even increased once I told her you and Ginny would be taking up land next to ours." The corner of his mouth quirked.

"Give me time to think this over…and an opportunity to talk to my guid wife." Duncan drew himself up in his chair. "It sounds like a fine idea, but I'm getting older and wiser and more inclined to proceed with a bit of caution before joining with any of your plots or plans."

"What can possibly go wrong with anything as tame as the timber business?" Caleb looked over at him, surprised at his reluctance.

"I don't know. I didn't think much could go wrong with your last venture of taking two women to a convent here in the colonies, but look how that turned out. I've got a big, ugly scar on my side and nearly ended up in an American prison for God only knows how long."

"Ah, but think of the positive side." Caleb grinned. "You got a wonderful wife and had enough adventures to keep your grandchildren amused on winter nights for years."

"So perhaps this farming and lumbering business in New Brunswick isn't such a bad idea." Duncan leaned back, looking smug. "Since we're both now serious family men, we'll be needing proper homes."

"I thought you'd feel that way." Caleb paused and looked off across the lawn to where their wives, dressed in delicate gowns, bonnets hanging on strings about their necks, were having tea beneath a spreading tree. "I've secured a generous land grant along the Miramichi River in New Brunswick. Several acres already cleared, with prime timber on the back acreage, I'm told, and a stream running through it, just right for damming and setting up a sawmill."

"I trust you have all this on good authority from…?"

"The best. Lieutenant Governor George Stacey Smyth himself. I met with him on the day I turned in our letters of marque and reprisal and explained the reason to Sir John. He said his province needs men such as us and that his chief surveyor had told him this parcel of land was prime, and he described it to me as I have to you."

"And how much will all this prime territory be costing us?" Duncan narrowed his eyes as he looked suspiciously over at Caleb.

"Knowing how you and our wives view me as a skinflint, can you seriously think I'd be snookered into paying an outrageous sum?" He drew a deep breath and stood to saunter over to the edge of the veranda and grasp one of its posts.

"Stop your posturing and give me the cost, man!"

Grinning broadly, Caleb turned back to him. "Not a penny. It's to be a grant, payment for our service in the war."

"Good God, Cal!" Duncan was on his feet and beside him in a single stride. His facial expression reflected astonished joy. "That means we can build fine houses, buy good stock…"

"Aye." Caleb grinned at his friend. "It comes with only one condition."

"I knew it! Some nasty codicil that will render all the good bits moot. Well, let me have it."

"That I become magistrate for the district. It appears the man who formerly held the position, Harry Wallace, has fallen from grace by letting a fugitive escape his custody."

Duncan stared at him, then burst out laughing as he pointed at his friend.

"You…an officer of the law! Captain Caleb Cameron, privateer and all-around outlaw! This is the most ridiculous thing I've ever heard."

"So funny you'd have me refuse the position and let those land grants go? So funny you'd rather not have a fine estate for your wife and, most probably, children?"

Duncan got his mirth under control at those statements.

"No, not that amusing. If your becoming an officer

of the law confirms our grants, I'll stand behind you all the way, as I always have. And pray to God you're a better magistrate than that drunken old lout Jacob Lock." He finished with a chuckle.

"About that, Dunc. I'm thinking we should find a minister or priest or whomever the ladies wish and get married again...for sure and certain." He looked out at the pair playing ladies in the shade.

"Aye, aye, I couldn't agree more, Captain. But we'd best get to it soon...before the Reverend or Father thinks it's because of necessity." He looked back at his wife demurely serving tea to her friend and chuckled.

"What's so amusing?"

"I just had an image of my darlin' sewing up Higgins's arse on the deck of the *Lady Ghost*. You wouldn't believe it, looking at her now, would you, Captain?"

"She surely looks the fine lady." Caleb let a grin curl his lips, then sobered. "I'm sorry some of the crew didn't see fit to take work ashore with us, but then they're seafaring men. Working on dry land wouldn't appeal to them. But maybe someday when they're getting too old and stiff to climb the ratlines they'll come back to us."

Chapter Thirty-Nine

Singing a ribald chantey, Caleb rode out of the village of Riverhaven, New Brunswick, toward his holdings, further up along the Miramichi River, that abutted Duncan's land. With the retired *Lady Ghost* tied up at a dock in front of his farm, he'd put his outlaw days behind him. The work of building a house, barn, and outbuildings, of purchasing stock, of damming the stream between the properties and building a sawmill had him and his former first mate busy from sunrise to sunset. Happily, contentedly busy.

What more could he and Duncan MacDougal want? Large tracts of land, a bright future, but most of all two remarkable women as wives. And soon, children. He clucked to the spirited bay stallion he rode and let him go forward at a smooth canter. He was eager to get home…home to Ann.

****

"Ann, where are you?" Caleb entered the nearly completed house and called up the stairway. The workers had gone for the day, but he knew his wife would be somewhere inside, planning where furniture should go, what window hangings would be best, choosing carpet colors, and the like. They were already using the master bedroom and the kitchen. Ann had been so eager to move in he couldn't say no even though tripping over planks and avoiding unfinished sections of floor had taken getting used to.

When he received no answer, he bounded up the stairs, taking two at a time. Now that their privateering days were officially over, there'd been no impediments to their having marital relations, and he was enjoying the condition to the fullest.

"Ann!" This time her name was a bellow. "Ann, where are you?"

Something cold began to slide about in his gut. She should have been here.

Bursting into the master bedroom, he saw it. A note on a pillow.

Snatching it up, he read, "I have your wife. If you wish to see her alive one last time, you'll come to the wharf at midnight...alone."

"Jesus!" He dropped to sit on the edge of the elegant bed, the paper in his hand. For a moment he stayed frozen in place, the horror of it making him sick.

"Argh!" With a roar, he jumped to his feet, crumpling the paper into a ball in his fist before slamming it into the unlit fireplace. "Good God! That bastard Willie! Dunc was right. He is seeking retaliation!"

****

Except for a single lantern on a post, the dock was enveloped in darkness, but he could see the *Lady Ghost* was missing from her mooring. Looking out across the river, under an ominous sky that rumbled the threat of a major storm, he saw his ship floating on the deadly calm, an ebony silhouette in the weird night.

"Sweet Jesus!" He strode to the edge of the dock and stared. *What...?*

"Surprised, Captain Cameron?" Her voice, syrupy

sweet, made him whirl.

Behind him, three figures emerged out of the night. In the light of the lantern carried by the one at the rear, Caleb could see one was smaller than the other two and held what he assumed was a pistol, aimed at his chest.

"Lizzie!" Recognizing her voice, shock engulfed him. "What in hell…?"

"Elizabeth to you, you miserable bastard!" she snapped.

"What…why…?"

"You ruined my chance to become a duchess when you kidnapped the wrong woman, you stupid cur," she snarled, advancing to stand close in front of him, pistol at the ready, aimed at his heart. "It was my one chance to become rich and respectable. It was all that mattered to me. Now you'll pay. I'm going to take everything that is important from you."

"Lizzie…"

"Do you know who is on your precious ship? Your beloved wife. You're about to lose them both. Burt, give the signal!"

One of the two men behind her raised a pistol in the air and fired. At the same instant, a bolt of lightning lighted the surroundings. In its illumination he saw Ann tied to the mainmast of the *Lady Ghost*.

"Torch the bitch!" Lizzie Harrison's cry rang out over the water, and the next moment, flames sprang from the *Lady Ghost*'s bow. In the light of a following bolt of lightning, Caleb could see a small boat with two men aboard rowing out from behind the ship and heading for the opposite shore.

"No!" His bellow mingled with the crash of thunder as he dropped to the wharf to wrench off his boots. "No!"

Out of the tail of his eye, he saw Lizzie raising her pistol to strike him a blow. He ducked, and she stumbled and fell headlong into the water. In the same instant, a great gust of wind swept down the river. Screaming, Elizabeth Harrison was carried away.

For a split second Caleb hesitated. The woman was crying out that she couldn't swim, but there was his wife, tied to a flaming ship, his wife who the other woman had planned to murder.

He leaped into the roiling water and began to swim against wind and current with long, desperate strokes toward the burning ship. Alone in the wild, mad night, Captain Caleb Cameron employed every ounce of his strength.

Ahead of him, tall flames shot up from the *Lady Ghost*, engulfing her front quarter as the ship bucked in the suddenly wild river.

His gut ached with knots so severe he thought he couldn't go on, but he did. Desperation powered each stroke through the murky waters. *Ann! Ann!* Her name pounded through his brain, giving him strength he wouldn't have believed he possessed.

Once at the vessel, he had to swim down its length, searching for a way to climb up a side. A rope dangling near the stern from where it had been slashed to set the vessel free caught his attention. Grasping it, he fought his way to the deck.

"Ann!" he yelled as he gained footing at the rear of the vessel. Smoke and fumes choked him, and he couldn't call out again. Staggering, he made his way to the woman bound to the mast.

"Caleb!" She stared at him, eyes round in the

firelight. "Go back! There's no time!"

"Not without you." He worked frantically at her bonds, willing his fingers to stop trembling. When the ropes finally gave way, the fire was mere feet from them. Grasping her hand, he pulled her with him to the rear of the ship. He paused and looked at her, hoping his eyes told her all that was in his heart. She smiled, and he knew she had seen.

"Jump!" he yelled, and together, hands united, they leaped into the black waters.

Chapter Forty

"Dunc!" With what seemed the last of his strength, Caleb pulled himself up the side of the dock until his head was over it. An incredible sense of relief gushed over him as he recognized his friend. "Help...us."

"Sweet Jesus!" Duncan MacDougal leaped up from where he'd been hunched on the wharf, holding his wife in his arms as rain bucketed over the pair. "Cal?"

"Aye, still in the flesh. Give us a hand up."

"Annie?" Ginny appeared, a black silhouette beside her husband in the dim light of a single lantern that hadn't yet been extinguished by the storm. "Annie? Oh, God, Duncan, get her up here!"

With Caleb steadying her and Duncan's hand about her wrist, Ann Cameron, drenched and bedraggled, was pulled up onto the wharf. She sank to her knees as Ginny dropped with her to wrap her arms around her.

"Duncan, we must get her up to the house at once," she yelled to her husband above the wind and rain of the storm. The lightning was moving off, leaving in its wake gales and a deluge.

"Aye, aye. Cal, can you make it on your own?"

"Aye." Caleb climbed up onto the wharf and staggered to his feet. "Go ahead. Get her safe and dry. I'll follow."

He bent forward, hands on his knees, and fought to catch his breath as his friend headed off, running with his wife in his arms, Ginny close behind him. Finally, straightening, he looked back out over the river where his ship bucked in the waves, a writhing ball of flame. A pain shot through his heart. He and the *Lady Ghost* had been through so much together.

He watched as she burned, watched until she vanished beneath the waves leaving only a hissing cloud of steam to mark her passing. Then he turned to follow his friends and his wife. It was but a ship, he told himself. Wood and canvas and spars. What was important had been saved.

****

He stumbled into his house to find Duncan alone in the kitchen, adding logs to the fire on the hearth.

"Where…?" He looked about.

"I took her to your bedroom." Duncan turned to him. "Ginny is caring for her. Now, man, out of those wet clothes. You must be near frozen. I brought these from your upstairs." He indicated a shirt and breeches hanging over the back of a chair. "I helped myself to some of your finery." He swept out an arm to indicate his attire. "I fair couldn't wait to get dry." He indicated the sodden heap of his clothing lying by the hearth.

"Good, good." Caleb stripped. For a moment he stood before the leaping flames on the hearth. The warmth seeped into his flesh, warming and reassuring. "I pray God Ann will be all right. After what happened last time…"

"Good God, laddie, are you telling me Ann is with child…again?"

"I am." In spite of the recent near-death experience he and his wife had just been through, Caleb couldn't keep a smile from his face.

"Congratulations!" Duncan slapped him on the back, all but knocking Caleb, in his exhausted state, off his feet.

"Thank you, Dunc," he managed. "I wish the same good fortune for you and Ginny."

"No need." Duncan grinned. "The deed has already been done. This calls for a celebration, laddie." He went to a dresser near the door and took down a flask from the top shelf. "A wee dram of your best brandy?"

"Aye, aye. And more than a wee dram, Mr. MacDougal." Caleb began to pull on the dry clothing. "I'm chilled to the bone."

Duncan poured generous amounts into a pair of tankards he took from a lower shelf and handed one to his friend.

"To us and our astonishing wives." He raised his drink, and Caleb touched his to it in salute. He took a swallow, bared his teeth, and continued, "Now some questions must be answered. What became of Lizzie's two accomplices? Did you see them when you came to the wharf? And why did you and Ginny come to the dock at midnight?"

"Let's put things in proper order." Duncan sat down, indicating a chair across the table from him to Caleb. "Annie invited us to supper this past evening. When we arrived, we found no one at home. Suspicious, we began to search the house. It was Ginny who found that note in the unlighted fireplace in your bedroom. We decided to pay a visit to the dock ourselves...in hiding. But Ginny took a spill, passing through the trees in the dark, and that slowed us down. We arrived just as that woman tumbled into the water and you dove in to save Annie."

"And the two men?"

"Trounced them right well, with the assistance of my darlin' wife." Duncan grinned. "They won't be coming around to cause you grief any time soon. Now a question for you. Where did you go between the time you found the note and when you showed up as ordered on the dock at midnight?"

"I rode everywhere I could think of where kidnappers might be holding Ann. I even made a furtive visit to the *Lady Ghost* on the off chance they were already there. Finally I gave up and decided I'd do as ordered. I didn't want to put Ann's life at any further peril than it already was."

"And I'm grateful." Turning Caleb saw his wife in a white nightgown, a shawl pulled about her shoulders, standing in the kitchen doorway. Ginny stood behind her, similarly garbed.

"Ann." He was on his feet in an instant, going to take her into his arms. "You shouldn't be up."

"Nonsense." She brushed him lightly aside. "We've invited guests to dinner, and dinner we shall have. The soup was already made when I was…interrupted. I will heat it and get out bread and cheese. I'm sure we can all do with a small repast." She moved toward a sideboard and began to prepare food. "I'm not about to let a small adventure postpone our soiree with Mr. and Mrs. MacDougal. It will not be the fine meal I'd planned, but still we'll extend our hospitality to them. They've earned it, don't you agree?" Over her shoulder, she smiled at him.

"Very well." Caleb made way for her. He knew better than to argue with his wife.

"If we're staying for a meal, we'd best get

ourselves comfortable, Mrs. MacDougal." Duncan caught his wife and pulled her onto his lap.

"Ah, you're a randy bugger." Ginny slipped her arms about his neck and gave him a quick kiss. "And I wouldn't have it any other way."

Caleb grinned. Duncan MacDougal might not have gotten a lady in manners but he definitely had the wife that was perfect for him in every way.

As for himself, while he'd lost his beloved ship, what he cared for most in the world was moving about his kitchen in a nightgown and preparing dinner for their guests with all the grace of a true lady. But she was much more than just a lady.

She was his privateer's princess.

A word about the author...

Gail is an award-winning author of 26 published books.

macgail@nbnet.nb.ca

Other books by Gail MacMillan
Available from The Wild Rose Press, Inc.

Thank you for purchasing
this publication of The Wild Rose Press, Inc.

If you enjoyed the story, we would appreciate your
letting others know by leaving a review.

For other wonderful stories,
please visit our on-line bookstore at
www.thewildrosepress.com.

For questions or more information
contact us at
info@thewildrosepress.com.

The Wild Rose Press, Inc.
www.thewildrosepress.com

Stay current with The Wild Rose Press, Inc.

Like us on Facebook

https://www.facebook.com/TheWildRosePress

And Follow us on Twitter
https://twitter.com/WildRosePress